NIGHT WITCHES

LJ Adlington

Hodder
Children's
Books

A division of Hachette Children's Books

First published in Great Britain in 2013
by Hodder Children's Books

1

A Catalogue record for this book is available from the British Library

ISBN: 978 1 444 90431 4

Typeset by Berkeley by Avon DataSet Ltd, Bidford-on-Avon, Warwickshire

Printed and bound by CPI Group (UK) Ltd, Croydon, CR0 4YY

The paper and board used in this paperback by
Hodder Children's Books are natural recyclable products
made from wood grown in sustainable forests. The manufacturing
processes conform to the environmental regulations of
the country of origin.

Hodder Children's Books
a division of Hachette Children's Books
338 Euston Road, London NW1 3BH
An Hachette UK company

www.hachette.co.uk

NIGHT WITCHES

In memory of the original Russian Night Witches
who fought with great courage and loyalty.

1

FLIGHT

I never wanted to fly. That was Cousin Zoya's bright idea.

'Everybody's doing it,' she said. 'I've been up five times already.'

'You're not going,' Mama told me straight off. 'You're too young. What if something happens to you?'

'Nothing's going to happen to me, Mama,' I said. 'Nothing ever does.'

Mama looked at Papi.

'It's far too dangerous,' he agreed quickly. 'You can't even tell left from right, let alone up from down or sky from ground.'

'What did I miss? What's dangerous?' Our neighbour Pedla Rue is always scuttling over from her apartment to ours to spread gloom and gossip. Alert to an argument, she said, 'Are you talking about the lift being broken again? I've reported it to Aura a dozen times today already.'

Mama folded her arms and explained about my plan to sign up for the Air Cadets.

'Flying!' snorted Pedla. 'Don't let her try anything like that. It's not normal. My husband always used to say, if

1

we'd been meant to fly we'd have wings, and then we'd be no different from wi—'

'Hush!' we all said in one voice. You never know who's listening.

Papi and Mama quickly backtracked. 'If Zoya looks after you and Aura agrees, you can fly,' they said. Anything not to go along with Pedla or her stupid, superstitious husband.

Which is why I'm here, trapped in the sleek, white shell of a People's Number Fifty-nine Tutor Plane. I've got a parachute strapped to my rear, a control stick between my legs and an instructor yawning at my side. I've also got Zoya breathing enthusiasm down the back of my neck.

'Told you you'd love it. It's easy, isn't it, Pip?'

'Focus on the flying, Pip,' says the instructor.

I want to say *My name's not Pip, it's Rain*, but Cousin Zoya calls me Pipsqueak – Pip for short – and I don't like to make a fuss.

The instructor doesn't care what my name is. He's clearly bored out of his skull doing cadet flights in the empty skies above flat foodlands and featureless towns. I'm not that excited myself. Aura streams calm instructions into my head from the keypad at my side and everything's so smooth we might as well be in a simulator. I can't feel the air or the sun.

'This is my sixth time,' Zoya tells the instructor. 'Everybody says I'm a natural. I'm not normally in the back seat. As soon as we're old enough me and Pip are going to

2

join the Air Force and fly with Marina Furey.'

The instructor rolls his eyes. Marina Furey is Rodina's greatest and most glamorous pilot – the first person to fly solo round the world. We're just kids in drab blue overalls.

I interrupt. 'I'm getting course corrections from Aura to keep clear of the cloud that's building up ahead. Should I try a turn?'

The instructor nods. 'You have control.'

I tell the plane to bank left. There's hardly any sensation of movement. I find my mind wandering. School again tomorrow. More tests. Project work's finished at least – a *Survey of Biofood Yields in the Lim Lands of West Rodina* – boring, but a big percentage of this term's grade. My bedroom's already tidy so that's one less thing to worry about, and . . .

'Keep her steady,' the instructor warns as the plane dips suddenly.

I blush. 'That wasn't me . . .'

'Just a bit of turbulence. Perfectly normal. Aura says wind speed is increasing.'

The plane jolts some more. The instructor stays calm. 'All right, that's enough for your first trip, Pip. I have control now.'

'You have control,' I echo, as I've been taught.

Behind us, Zoya's just started chewing on a snack bar, but her mouth drops open as she picks up a new message.

'Er, is this right? I've got reports of other planes in our sector.'

The instructor frowns. 'There are no scheduled flights in . . . *Na!*' The plane lurches badly as something large and dark passes over. Everything shudders. Is this normal? A hole appears in the tinted windscreen. Sunlight pokes through.

'What *was* that?' shouts Zoya.

The instructor is silent.

I start to panic. 'I can't get action-requirements from Aura – there's nothing . . .'

The instructor leans forward. The plane begins to dive. Why's he letting it do that? I flick a glance at him. He's got a small red spot in the centre of his forehead. The headrest of his seat is dark with blood and worse.

Dead. Shot. How?

'Go up!' Zoya screams as the ground rises to meet us. She's yanking at the instructor, trying to get at his controls, but he's too lumpy to move. I abandon the keypad and seize my control stick with both hands. Somehow we stagger into open sky. Bullets spit into the fuselage behind us.

Zoya shakes me instead of the instructor. 'Someone's shooting at us! Do something, Pip! Shoot back!'

'With what?'

'I don't know, just get away from it!'

'*How?*'

I can't even blink. As I try to heave the plane away from the bullets all I can think is, *Flying's easy after all . . . Wonder what landing's like?*

2
CRASH

A voice whispers – *Wake up.*

Why move? I'm toasty warm in bed, wrapped in heavy covers, wondering whether to bother brushing snow off my face.

Snow? No snow in bed.

I open my eyes. No bed, just the broken bioweave of a wrecked wing. No covers, just heavy fluff tickling my nose. Not fluff – what's the word? *Fur.* This fur is stretched over sharp bones. It has a strange face with bright silver-black eyes, clouds of bad breath and teeth strung with half-chewed meat. *What . . . ?*

Then it comes. A memory so old it's worn almost to pieces. In the memory I'm nestled in my mother's arms staring at a picture being streamed on the screen at the end of the bed. *'Look, Rain, look what sort of monsters are waiting to eat girls who go wandering off into the woods. Be good, and they won't get you.'*

Wolf!

I go utterly rigid with shock. The wolf gives a low growl.

'Get away!' I shout, though my voice is more of a croak, deep in my throat.

Amazingly, the wolf shakes itself and walks off into the big white, leaving me lighter, colder and covered in fine silver hairs. That's when I realise it's been curled up with me, keeping me warm.

I struggle upright and look around. Say '*Lights*' but no lights come on. This is not Sea-Ways City. This is bad. I've never been in a place without lights – big, bold, lovely lamps, so warm all snow melts before it can settle. Here there are no lights, no walls, no windows with a cityscape view. Just snow, trees and mist, all monochrome. I reach up and feel a flying visor on my head. Smell charred bioweave, corroded circuits and burned feathers.

Feathers?

Hundreds of glossy black feathers still fall all around, mingling with snow, some landing on the plane wing, some nestling in the pawprints the wolf made. My eyes are suddenly so sharp I can count every snowflake, every needle on every spindly, silver-bark tree. This isn't normal!

Quickly I fumble for my keypad to ask Aura what's going on. Nothing. No familiar comfort of connection. No *welcome rain aranoza*. Not a whisper.

Come on, come on, tell me what to do next!

Not being able to connect is like finding your body's suddenly disappeared, or that the world's been whisked away and replaced with grey.

Like this place.

A sound cracks the silence – a rough bird-croak from high above.

I start to flounder in the snow, scattering feathers and flakes. What should I do? Trust my instincts. *What instincts?* How can I have instincts when there's almost always been Aura to tell me what to do, or Mama, or Papi, or Cousin Zoya . . .

Zoya! *Where's Zoya?*

No sign of her in the snow. Which way should I go? Bone-white branches block all ways but one – a tunnel of trees that seem to part to let me pass. The trees thin. I fall into open air and find myself standing, barely breathing, on a shore of frosted stones. The sky is sunless and grey. Still, grey water stretches to a hazy, grey horizon.

It's a dead place. No, a place that seems to be waiting for death.

Bits of aircraft are scattered in and out of the water – pieces of our People's Number Fifty-nine Tutor Plane. There's a body at the edge of the lake, boots submerged.

'Zoya?'

Even as I run towards her I swear the water rises without rippling, swallowing her legs . . .

'Zoya!'

I grab her overalls and heave her out of the clinging water. Is she dead? A hole opens in my heart. She can't be! Sweet relief – she gasps and coughs.

'Zoya – wake up, please!'

Her eyes open. They go so wide I swear I can see my

face reflected in them – my thin, frightened face, black hair hanging all round it. She shrinks back.

'Where am I? What are you?'

'Ssh, idiot, it's me. You know me.'

'Pip?' She frowns and sags a bit. 'Back then, I thought, I mean, I saw . . . That plane came after us, then there were birds. Black ones. Hundreds of them.' Straight away she's reaching for her keypad. '*Yash!* I can't connect.'

'Me neither. There's no Aura here.'

'Don't be stupid, how can there not be Aura?' She keeps pressing and pressing the keypad, then she squints at the grey all around. 'Where is *here*? Where's Sea-Ways? This isn't normal. It's not Rodina.'

I barely dare say what I'm thinking out loud. 'Do you remember Pedla Rue used to tell us about a place beyond the edge of Lim lands? A forest called the Morass?'

Zoya shakes her head violently. 'Don't be stupid! We can't have landed in a place that's just from stories to scare kids.'

'Actually, I think it was more of a crash than a landing. We're lucky to be alive.'

'If we don't freeze to death. Aren't there any heaters? Haven't you got a coat?'

I almost laugh – it's as if she expects me to produce warmth from thin air. Then I see the pad of her parachute.

'Unclip yourself.' I fumble with straps and buckles, tearing the parachute pack open to let the fine biofabric spill out. Quickly Zoya bundles it around herself, still shivering. That's when I wonder how I wasn't wearing a parachute when we crashed. Shouldn't I be a mess of broken bones and bruises? I feel . . . I feel . . . strange. I'm wondering if a bed of black feathers broke my fall, or if that was all part of a dream.

Zoya blows on her hands and squints past me. 'Shift out of the way a bit. What are those lights on the water?'

'Don't look at the lights!' My words tumble out too quickly to stop. 'I mean, in the stories there were *things* in the forest that hung lights in the air – not proper, real, technology lights, but witch-lamps made of fire-flowers – to trick victims into coming closer.'

These lights are glowing where the mist is thickest – pretty little bobbing things, like toys above a baby's cradle. A whisper glides over the grey water of the lake.

Welcome, Rain . . .

'Honestly, Pip, are you sure you didn't bang your head in the crash? They'll be lights from a rescue squad, obviously. Can't you see them? *Hey – over here! Help!*' Her voice falls dead to the ground.

'Ssh! We don't know who's listening. We should move. Are you OK to walk? Hold on, let me help you up . . .'

'Ow! Careful! I think I've sprained something.'

'You're probably stiff from the cold. Lean on me; I can take your weight.'

Zoya snorts. 'That's a laugh – you'd snap! I'm staying right here till Aura sends someone.'

This is not good! Can't she feel the ground trembling?

9

Can't she hear the whisper of wolf fur snagging on twigs? The faint scrape of feathers high up in shadowy branches? The sound of someone stepping oh-so-carefully through the snow?

'There are three rules,' Pedla Rue used to tell me, when I had to go and wait in her apartment after school, before Mama and Papi got home from Glissom's Gun Factory. Pedla scared me with all sorts of Old Nation tales until Papi found out and told her to keep her tongue behind her teeth. 'Three rules,' Pedla said, 'if you want to stay safe in the woods.'

I like rules. I want rules. What were the rules? I'm sure I can remember them. *Be very careful* something something, *be very careful* something else and . . . Got it!

Rule Number One – *Be very careful who you meet . . .*

I swallow fear down. 'I can hear footsteps . . .'

'Those lights have got to be the rescue squad,' says Zoya. 'If the water's shallow enough we could wade out to them . . .'

She squelches in sodden boots back to the water's edge. The lake laps greedily at her toe caps.

Cautiously I step further along the shore to a scattering of debris too strange to be from our crash. I make out the skeleton of a plane, still nailed with bits of . . . what – fabric? Not a shred of bioweave anywhere. One piece shows two slashes of white in a diagonal cross – a Crux emblem. What are Crux doing anywhere near our Nation? Filthy, god-rotten Crux should stay behind their own borders, where they belong, not come corrupting Rodina!

'Over here!' I call to Zoya.

Reluctantly she tears her eyes from the lights. She's waded into the water up to her boot-tops. 'What is it?'

'A plane – maybe the one that attacked us. Looks like it's Crux. Why are you paddling?'

Puzzled, she looks down, then quickly splashes on to dry land and limps over to me. 'There aren't any Crux in Rodina,' she says, but she's still craning her neck to look at the lights.

'There *shouldn't* be.' I kick against a broken section of plane with dials showing needles that point at numbers. I pick up harsh smells – fire and crude fuel. 'It's not bioweave; it must be wood.'

'What's wood?'

'You know, like the trees. I did a project on it once. People used to build houses out of wood and stone.'

'Shows how backward things were before Aura. How can a plane made of wood even fly?'

'Unsuccessfully, judging by this.' Splinters of memory are pricking my mind. A Crux plane. A sky-wide chase. A storm-cloud collision. Black feathers.

Zoya yelps. 'Ugh – look in the lake!'

I look. If there are any fish, they're lurking far out from the shore in deeper waters. I see only strange distorted shapes beneath the surface – sodden leaves, lumps, spikes, spines, bones and wrecks. Nothing alive – all dead. A white-grey hand rises up, one finger beckoning. We both scream and stagger back. A body floats. It's wearing a Crux uniform with navigator's wings stitched to the collar.

The footsteps crunch closer.

'Please, Zoya, we really should get away from here. I can hear someone. It's not . . . not how a rescue squad should sound.' I hear engines too. Weird ones, not smooth like bioweave at work. This is a rough racket of tracks turning. I'm itchy to move move *move* but Zoya rolls her eyes.

'I told you the rescue squad would come. Aura knows we were out on a flight.'

'But Aura doesn't know where we've crashed. That we're . . . here.'

'You're not scared of the forest, are you?' she mocks, coming all older-cousin on me. 'If this *is* the Morass, it's just empty wilderness, everyone knows that. All that story-trash about witches and wolves – it's only kids' stuff, Pip. Things people made up before Aura got them educated.'

She's right. Stories are kids' stuff, for kids like me – little Pip. Little Pipsqueak – the tiddler. Smallest girl in school. '*Delicate*,' Papi always said, although I've never been ill in my life. '*Keep an eye on Rain*,' he told Zoya when we left for Air Cadet camp. Zoya nodded. '*Sure. She's only little.*'

Right now I'm wishing I was small enough to creep under a frosty pebble to hide until everything goes back to normal again.

'We could at least get away from the lakeshore, so we're not so exposed.'

'I guess. Away from that disgusting dead body at least.' Zoya hobbles to the tree line, half an eye on the lights I refuse to look at. '*Na* – my ankle really hurts. Maybe I should rest first.'

No time to rest. The air brings scents of gunmetal, sweat and dirt.

Thunk, thunk, click.

I know that sound from shooting lessons on the school firing range.

A People's Number Five Glissom Gun is being loaded.

Time stretches. I twist round to try and block Zoya with my body – a crazy idea, when she's so tall and I'm so slight. We freeze.

There's a boy in the trees. The most beautiful boy I've ever seen. Bright eyes, dark hair.

Friend or enemy?

No question from his expression he'll shoot to kill. No question he'll hit me.

Our eyes lock. He lowers the gun a fraction. His voice, when he speaks, is the clearest sound I've heard since coming out of unconsciousness.

'You?' he asks. 'You again?'

I've never seen him before in my life.

3
TRAPTION

I stare at him as if he's the only thing that exists in the world. Light snow falls, hair strands drift across my face, but nothing distracts, not even the fast, shallow beat of my heart.

I notice every detail about him, even the flecks of ice on his scarf where his breath has frozen. He's tall but not towering. His white camouflage jacket and trousers are uncreased and clean, as if ready for inspection. The slick polish of his boots is frosted over – the boot straps fused solid with ice. Is he real? Real enough to touch?

I remember to breathe.

He blinks, showing lids that are inked with black eye designs, so that even when closed he seems to be watching us.

Zoya gasps. 'He's a Scrutiner!'

Eyes in the Dark, we call them. Aura's eyes – trained to make sure that everything in Rodina Nation is normal and nice.

His voice is cold. 'Haze? I told you to stay in the camp.

It's not safe to come back here now the wolves know your scent.'

I shake my head. 'Sorry, I don't know any Haze. It's not me.'

Recognition fades from his eyes. 'Who are you? What are you doing here?'

'We're normal,' Zoya answers quickly. 'Just Air Cadets on a training flight. I'm Zoya Mentira, this is my cousin Pip . . . Rain Aranoza. We were attacked. We can't connect.'

'We crashed,' I add pointlessly.

The boy's eyes flick through the trees to debris at the lakeside. His fingers tighten on the gun. I think, please god, don't let him shoot us, except what's the point of asking god for anything? God doesn't exist any more, except for the twisted cranks of the Crux nation, pressing up against our borders, just waiting to try and convert us. God isn't normal. Everybody knows that.

The boy's lips move. Is he about to speak? Too late. I get the strangest sensation, as if time has stopped. No – more like time is stretching. The air pauses. I could dance between the pieces of falling snow as they glisten, poised, in the stillness. Only my heartbeat stays the same. Something cuts between the trees. Parts a snowflake. Melts it.

A bullet.

I see it clearly before I hear the sound of gunshot. It spins in a graceful trajectory, with near-invisible grooves from a gun barrel. Against all laws of science it slows. I step out of its path. I breathe in, breathe out. The bullet moves on. I watch it pass and time speeds up, super-fast, it seems. Normal fast. *Crack!* The bullet smacks into a tree trunk just behind me. Wood splinters. A cloud of spores billows from the bark. More bullets follow, real time now, puffing up the snow when they hit the ground then making Zoya scream as they tear through her skin.

The boy dives towards us. To kill us with his bare hands? No – to push us to the ground.

'Crux creepers!' he shouts.

'What are creepers?' I yell out, my voice muffled by a mouthful of snow.

I don't know why I'm surprised at how cold the snow is when my face ploughs into it. Creepers sound bad – are they snipers? Sent to kill us, or just shooting for the fun of it? I ask Aura on the keypad. Aura doesn't answer.

'Traptions!' the boy shouts next. 'Dodge side to side and run!'

Traptions?

They must be the clumsy, clanking machines I hear, tearing down trees, their engines blowing out billows of black fug. Already I retch at the stench as the tracks trample towards us. The nozzle of a long gun gouges through a tree trunk. It's nothing like the sleek sweep of Rodina's war machines that we see in People's Army parades around Sea-Ways City. This gun looks lo-tech but lethal. The ground quakes.

The boy flips on his front in the snow, shooting creepers.

Me, I'm dragging Zoya away, shouting, 'Get up get up get up and move!'

'I'm hit! I can't run – my leg!'

'I'll carry you!'

'Pip, no!'

She's weeping with pain as I try and hoist her over my shoulder. My boots sink in the snow and blood drops red on the white. Yash! Those Crux monsters really have hit her.

The clamour of a traption closing in is excruciating. Any moment now it'll burst upon us.

'P-put me down!' Zoya's juddering with each step I take. 'You can't do this.'

'I can!'

'What's happening? Is it an earthquake?'

'Traption,' I gasp.

'W-what? W-why?'

All I can think is, which way now? I remember back to Pedla Rue's ramblings – *Three rules to stay safe in the forest* . . . What was the third? I know it! The Third Rule: *Don't step off the path.*

What path?

There is no path, just deranged twists of silver-white trees in every direction.

The traption fires a shell from that grey gun nozzle. Splinters of wood spray the air and birds caw in outrage. A second shell spews out. More trees explode. Bark and snow scatter. This is nothing like the war games we play at home on stream-screens. This is loud, confusing and can kill us!

I shudder. Duck. Stumble. Run a few steps, bent double under Zoya's weight, but the shell blast shoves us over. Zoya slides from my back and falls, pulling me with her. My bare skin touches the ground. For a second I have the sensation of looking right down into the frozen earth, deep into the planet, seeing ancient tree roots tangling round ancient rock, feeling the force at the heart of the forest, all shrunk and old and dying . . .

A third shell fires, right where our heads would have been if we hadn't collapsed. The traption makes my bones shake. It makes all the bones in the forest soil shake too – skeletons of wolves, birds, rablets, mice and people even, all dead-white like my face must be as I twist and look up to see grey metal looming over us and brace for the agony of being crushed.

Forget that!

I'm not ready to die.

I stagger upright.

'Hey! Hey, you! Crux!'

The traption gun turret swivels. It's hung with red metal bells that jangle and shake as the engine vibrates. Strung between the bells are banners of scrawl that I suppose must be prayers. We used to have prayers and things in Rodina, before Aura was introduced so science could triumph over superstition, and all Crux were kicked back behind the borders of their own nation. When I was a kid there used to be bells ringing in the old god-houses and people leaving bee-sweet cakes for the saynts.

Cakes won't appease this machine. Inside the ugly metal carapace there are Crux soldiers loading new shells.

'Yes – over here!' I shout.

'Are you mad? Are you completely *disconnected*?' Zoya gasps.

Probably.

I yell at her to stay down, stay low, don't move. No time for anything else. I'm already running, backwards at first, waving my arms at the traption . . . *Look at me, look at me, follow me, fire on me, not her – me, not her . . .*

'Don't leave me, Pip! Don't leave me alone!'

Zoya's screams are just one more noise in the chaos. I turn, expecting my back to be blistered with shell-fire at any moment.

The traption follows. Good. I speed up, just enough to stay ahead of those clanking, crunching tracks, but not so fast it'll lose me. I dodge a fourth shell. Dodge trees. Dodge the snow that still trickles through the dense canopy of branches above. Fumes belch black in the white forest. The traption's going flat out . . . flat over anything that gets in its way. *Na* – it's fast! So I go faster. I'm surging forward, sprinting hard, legs pumping, heart racing, skin glowing, mind singing . . . *Catch me, catch me, catch me if you can . . .*

There are birds zooming alongside me, black to the last feather.

You can't run like this in the city, in Sea-Ways. Not on

the spongy-safe biofloors sprayed with caution notices and light strips to show the way. Not with people turning to look at you if you do a single thing different from anyone else. Not with Aura guiding and Scrutiners gliding by, soundlessly watching.

This is glorious! I almost love it – the speed, the danger, the . . .

. . . dare I say it?

The freedom.

Yes! If I could I'd run right out of my skin and jump free, leaping, yelling . . .

. . . tripping . . .

. . . falling . . .

. . . going headlong over a block of stone, over the edge of a cliff. This time when I fall there's absolutely nothing, no snow, no ground to catch me.

4
RIFT

I crash through a crazy criss-cross of knotted bushes. They're thatched over nothing thicker than air. I grab what I can. Roots rip one heartbeat at a time.

The traption heaves up over the same stone block that tripped me and, for a few mind-grinding moments, hovers above me on the edge of the cliff, tracks turning, bells jingling, prayers flapping, gears grinding, engine raging . . . then it tips and falls, gun first, down into the mist of a rift. For long moments I hear nothing. Then comes a dull, whumping sound, as if the traption has been swallowed by cloud.

I hang.

A few hours ago my biggest headache was a total inability to find two clean socks that matched, or to work out which way my new blue cadet uniform fastened. Now I'm dangling in a rift filled with black-barked trees that reach down to invisible ground and up to a pale grey sky. Instead of the factory-crafted plant sculptures back home, these trees are wild and wicked-looking. They have black-sheened leaves like a million mirrored eyes spinning on stalks to look at me. Mist licks my boots, tugs on my legs, strokes my body, breathes on my hair . . .

Rain . . .

There's a whisper. My name – touching my ears as soft as snow. A connection? No, it's nothing like Aura. This is an old voice, creased and worn, with an edge of death.

'Who's there?' I call.

Hurry, Rain, comes the voice again. *There isn't much time* . . .

I brace my arms to try and haul myself up. Roots rip. I scream. Drop. Stop. Breathe. Close my eyes. Open them. Slowly I twist in the air. I won't look down. I won't see shapes or hear voices in the mist. Absolutely not. I look up instead.

Above, all wrapped in roots, are more blocks of stone, cut into straight lines and right angles. There was once a wall here. A building. Set into a stone frame is a window of cracked, coloured glass. There's a pattern in the glass, perhaps a picture, but it's covered in snow that's scrunched into shapes like petals – snow flowers. From where I'm hanging, it looks like a picture of someone with sun for hair.

People must have been here once. Did they fall and die too? I don't want to die, but I can't hold on any longer, I just can't! Where's Zoya when I need her? She's always been there for me, from my first day of being bullied at school, to this last day of my life when I got shoved out of my place in the canteen queue for breakfast.

'Somebody – *please* – somebody help me!'

A face looks over the rift edge and I nearly drop from the shock of it. *Be careful what you wish for . . .* A wolf is there, eyes bright, tongue out, panting. Its muzzle reaches low – to eat my hand or pull on my sleeve? Gunshot cracks the silence. The air mists with blood and the wolf slumps, completely eyes-dark dead.

'Hey! Hello? Rain Aranoza, are you there?'

A voice I know! Like a silver net it scoops me up. There's the dark-haired Scrutiner leaning over the edge of the rift to spy me out, sending snow specked with wolf-blood spattering down.

'I'm here – down here!'

'Hold tight, I'll pull you up! Don't let go!'

He grips my sleeve. He's strong but still out of breath by the time I'm up out of the emptiness and sprawling on the snow at his side. Close by, the wolf corpse is slowly cooling, and beyond it are the stone blocks with the glass picture.

The boy studies me closely. That's Scrutiner training – always watching for what's not supposed to be there. I laugh, a little too loudly.

'The ground disappeared.'

'It's the trees,' he says without a flicker of emotion. 'They eat it. They grow down instead of up.'

I roll on my stomach, away from the rift edge and hungry trees. The boy rolls over too and that sort of makes him closer to me. The wide world shrinks to this patch of now. Time doesn't bother slowing. It doesn't even exist. The snow between us seems to clump into delicate crystal flowers – tiny snow roses that grow then melt from our body heat.

I hear the boy's heart quicken. His cheeks take on a warmer tinge. I feel like I'm in one of Pedla's stories, all that Old Nation nonsense about gods, monsters and enchantment. I shiver at the intimacy.

'You're cold,' he says abruptly. He stands and brushes snow from his uniform so it's as smart as new again.

'I'm fine.' I get up too, suddenly wishing I was older, taller and dazzlingly beautiful.

Nothing story-like about his reply. He's all common sense and science.

'You don't feel chilled now because you're fired with adrenaline. Without more layers your core body temperature will drop so quickly you'll hardly notice you're dying. Take this thermal wrap and these gloves, they're spare. Are you injured?'

'I'm OK.'

'Are you sure?'

Yes. Incredibly, against the odds, I am OK, though I feel strange, like the time Cousin Zoya said cherry brandy was completely harmless, so we sneaked some at Pedla Rue's and it made me see shapes in my head, and Zoya sicked up her lunch all the way down the stairwell as she tried to stagger home.

My mind widens. The spell breaks. Real life rushes in.

How could I forget Zoya? You don't ever, ever put yourself first, before others. Individuals don't count as much as community – we learn that from the cradle. *One of Many* – that's the motto we live and die by in Rodina. Loyalty, that's what binds our friendships, our families, our Nation together.

This time when I run the forest flashes past – snow, bare branches, black birds – scant seconds only before I'm at the patch of ground where I left her. Is it the right place? I see a bright-red pool of blood in the snow, and bootprints all around.

Zoya's not there.

I'm so mad at myself I could rip trees up by the roots. I shouldn't have left her like that! Why do I always get things wrong? No wonder Papi gets that quiet, *disappointed* look whenever I speak. No wonder Mama reckons I'm not fit to be left alone ever. *Be a good girl*, she always says, even though I've never been anything *but* good all my life.

'Zoya's gone!' I shout the moment the boy catches up with me. 'The Crux have got her!'

He examines the bootprints and shakes his head. 'Don't worry, she's safe. My men will be helping her to our camp at the edge of the forest where we have medics. We need to get there as quickly as possible too. We do not want to be in the woods when night comes. Keep close behind me. Tread where I tread. Whatever you do, don't step off the path.'

Don't step off the path. Pedla Rue knew what she was talking about there. What about her First Rule? *Be very careful who you meet . . .*

The boy sets off. I don't move.

'Sorry, but there's no Aura and I don't know . . . what's your name?'

'I'm Reef. Reef Starzak. Now let's go. Try to keep up.' He gives a half-smile. 'Judging by how fast you can run, that shouldn't be a problem.'

'Sorry. I was worried about Zoya.'

'You should be.'

'Because of the Crux? What are they even doing in the forest? Why did they attack us? Why can't we connect to Aura and find out what's going on?'

He stops and looks back. 'You ask a lot of questions.'

I freeze. There's a saying in Rodina – *The weed that sprouts up gets yanked out.* The best thing I can do now is keep quiet and be good.

'Sorry. It's not normal here.'

Reef's laughing at me now, I'm sure of it, behind that mask of a face. 'You've noticed that?'

I notice everything. Every strand of colour in his eyes, every shade of blood under the soft skin of his lips.

A bird lands on a nearby branch. Reef grips his gun, making me think of the wolf on the rift edge, with life trickling out of bullet-holed fur.

'I got more than I expected on this hunting trip,' he

says, staring down at me.

'You mean, finding Crux as well as wolves?'

'No. I came here hunting witches. Instead I found you.'

5

THE PATH

'There's no such thing as witches,' I say straight off.

'Of course not,' Reef replies. 'Stories and fey-tales were the Old Nation way of making sense of things they didn't have the proper education to explain scientifically. We know better now. My job is to prove these things don't exist. It's the only way to stamp out superstitions from Old Nation days.'

'Like people believing in witches?' It feels bad just saying such a word to a Scrutiner. I remember the night they came for Pedla Rue's husband, all because he kept going on and on about smelling witch-sweat in the stairwell.

Reef's eyes darken. 'Exactly. Civilisation can't survive if imagination is allowed to run riot. Science can prove that wolves are just wild meat-eaters, for example, not fey-tale monsters. The trouble is, stories don't die easily. Despite all the education Aura's given us, people still insist on believing in things that can't possibly be true.'

Some emotion roughens his voice, but he's walking too fast for me to see his face. His legs are longer than mine and I have to leap to keep within his bootprints in the snow. My fingers twitch to access Aura for answers to all my questions. How do people even *know* things if they can't connect? I try to keep quiet by concentrating on counting the birds flying alongside the path.

'They're called corvils.' I jump as Reef speaks, answering a question I haven't even asked out loud. 'They're carnivorous – meat-eaters. They like their meals fresh.'

'The forest must be hungry.'

'What?'

'Sorry. Nothing.'

I just had this impression of a starving land, with birds, wolves, trees and water even, all greedy to eat, to lap up, to swallow and stay alive. Fortunately, Reef doesn't seem to have heard me properly. He pulls a food bar from a pocket and throws it back to me.

'This will take the edge off your hunger. It isn't safe to stop to make something hot. Wolves won't be far behind us. I've already come up against one pack who were tracking a Lim girl lost in the forest.'

'The one you called Haze?'

He pauses to bend a branch out of my way. 'Are you sure you don't know her?'

I shake my head.

'You don't have any family in the foodlands? No Lim relatives out in villages near the forest?'

'No, it's just me and my parents.'

'And your friend? Zoya Mentira?'

'She's my cousin. Her father's a famous scientist, Cramer Mentira. He works—'

'. . . for Aura. I know. But you don't have any siblings? No sisters?'

'Mama said one kid was enough. She's kind of protective. Something about when I was a baby I nearly died.'

Reef glances at me. 'You're obviously used to escaping death.'

Is that good? Bad? Normal? I just say, 'Mm.'

'When I saw you back at the lake edge I thought you were Haze, come back to the forest despite the wolves. The likeness is uncanny at first.'

I bite my lip nervously. *Uncanny* is not a word you want Scrutiners to use about you. 'I guess I look pretty average.'

He stops and examines me properly, and that's enough to make me burn inside. When do people ever notice me? Never. I'm just Pip. Just *One of Many*.

'Not average,' Reef says eventually. 'No, not that.'

Our breaths blow out and mingle. Even though we're not moving, we seem to circle each other. We set off again. The interrogation isn't over.

'Do you live somewhere in the Lim lands?' he asks next. 'Sorrowdale, perhaps, or Rimm?'

'No – we live in Sea-Ways.'

'You've always lived there?'

'Y-es.' Why the pause? Of course we've always lived in the city. Always in the same apartment. Always with the same neighbours, except when someone gets arrested, like Pedla Rue's husband.

'Do you like it there?' Reef asks.

I hate it. I hate the busy rush of the river that divides the city, the shadows cast by the vast factories, and I absolutely loathe the salty noise of the sea. 'Yes, it's nice.'

'And you've been in the Air Cadets long?'

'No, I just joined. It was my first time flying.'

I am so grateful he doesn't turn round at that point to see me blush. He must think I'm an utter ineffectual to crash on my first flight.

There's a long pause while he steps lightly across some moss-covered boulders and I scramble after him, refusing help in case he thinks I'm just some kid who can't cope. He stands on the highest rock to get his bearings. We've been climbing steadily so we're above the tree-tops of the valleys. There's not much to see even from this height. A few stark branches poke up through a dense mist, and there are mountains further west, near the Crux border. These mountains are high, but the greatest defence against invasion from the Crux has always been the measureless Morass.

Apparently, not any more.

If the Crux have dared to invade the forest, what else might we find once we're back in civilisation again? A sense of urgency drives us both on. There can't be a lot of daylight left. Night in the forest would be unbearable.

The path gets wider, so Reef and I walk side by side. I

can see more of his face now. Sometimes our arms touch and our gloved hands knock together. He starts asking about the crash, especially about the Crux plane wreckage, and the Crux body in the lake.

'And you're sure you lost contact with Aura before you reached the Morass?'

'We were nowhere near the Morass. It was just a regular Air Cadet training thing. I lost track of how many klicks we flew off course while I was chasing the Crux plane.'

Reef stops dead. 'You *chased* it?'

'I'm sorry, was that bad? There was no Aura. We didn't have guns to defend ourselves, and I was mad that it shot our instructor, and scared it would kill us too . . .'

My explanation trails off. Reef's got a funny look on his face. Surely not admiration? No one's ever admired me – why would they? I've never done anything or been anywhere.

What about Reef? Where's he from? How old is he? Why did he train for Scrutiny when he could be in school? He's not really a boy; not quite a man. Zoya's age? Young enough to have night-vision still? Children and teenagers have enough to make out shapes and movement in the dark. Or is Reef too old for that? Reaching adulthood means losing even minimal night-sight, although no one can predict exactly when this will happen. Grown-ups go blind in the dark. Utterly. Completely.

When will it be dark in this winter wilderness? I daren't ask. I really, truly hope we won't still be in the forest when the sun sets and Planet Umbra rises to cross the sky. I've never known a time when rooms and roads weren't as bright as day from dusk to dawn. It's one of the first things you learn as a child – love the light and leave it lit. The last Long Night – the last total solar eclipse – was when I was born. As for the next, it's due in a few short months.

How many hours do we hike? Impossible to tell without Aura. There's no sign of sun or stars, only shadows gathering under the trees.

'We're not lost,' Reef says eventually. 'We just can't get straight to where we're going.'

It's true. Every time he says we need to bear right or head to lower ground, the way is blocked by thorny thickets, or rocks bulging in the snow, or trees clustering so closely they look like they're squeezing themselves to death.

It's as if the forest doesn't want us to leave.

Reef picks up the trail only to stop dead at the edge of a pool that's frozen chill-blue solid.

'Can you make it over?' Reef asks.

Automatically I connect to ask Aura, but of course there's no reply. Who knows what I can do without Papi around to tell me I'm to be careful; without Mama here to flutter and flap. I quite like the idea of a challenge and it hardly seems dangerous, the ice is so utterly still.

'Are there rivers in the Morass?' I ask.

Reef shakes his head. 'If there are, our surveys haven't found them. Water wells up to make pools and lakes. In spring the snow-melt just soaks into the ground.'

What was it Pedla Rue once said about water? It was during a really bad rain-storm when the streets of Sea-Ways were flooded and the harbour walls were broken by giant waves. I remember her pointing from the window of her apartment.

'*One thing witches hate,*' she lectured, '*is running water. Streams, rills, rivers – they won't cross them willingly. So if a witch comes for you, ring your bells and run to a river. Or to the sea – they hate salt almost as much as bane-metal. Do you understand?*'

Of course I didn't understand. I still don't. It's just stories.

I don't ask Reef where we'll run to if witches come for us, because witches don't exist. I step down on to the ice, arms out, like a dancer. I didn't know it would be so slippery. We never get ice in Sea-Ways. Is it safe? Will it hold? I grab Reef's sleeve and we skid together halfway across the pool, then I stop. I sense movement. Smell blood. Hear a strange creaking, twisting noise . . . metal rubbing, fabric stretching, someone breathing. There – beyond the stretch of ice – something wrong is bleeding.

Two black corvils fly in that direction, swift and low. I stop to hear better. Reef stretches back to grab my jacket but I'm already gliding towards the sounds.

'*Don't step off the path!*'

'Listen, can't you hear that?'

Instantly he slips his gun from its holster, slides off the ice and scans the trees. 'What? Where? Traptions? Creepers?'

'Something over there – high up.'

We walk softly, softly in the snow, leaving two tracks of bootprints side by side. Ahead, something is swinging from a tree. A parachute is caught in the branches. Under it an airman is swinging like a toy to tease a baby. His face, his uniform, his *smell,* they're so strange he's got to be Crux. Disgusting! A corvil flies down to perch on his head. Reef wasn't wrong when he said the birds like their meat fresh . . .

'Hold this.'

Reef passes me the gun, then he's off, climbing the tree like . . . like some sort of animal I can't think of a name for because we don't have real animals back in Sea-Ways, except for the great sea elephants that sometimes swim in the harbour, and they would flatten a tree if they ever tried going up it. Startled, the corvil hops away, with an indignant *caa-caa* cry.

I clutch the gun and wonder if I can remember my lessons on the school firing range. I also wonder if this is one of the weapons Mama and Papi make at Glissom's, back home – the People's Number Forty-two Gun Factory. I never really thought about people using them. Shooting them.

Reef unsheathes a knife – the first one I've ever seen for real. In the communal kitchen at home the meal packets all have seals you can tear open by hand once they're heated, and it's all food you can just fork up. Cold metal cuts a parachute strap. The pilot lurches lower. Reef sets the blade to the next strap. The pilot's head lolls to and fro with the motion. When he eventually falls he's a dead weight. I don't so much catch him as cushion him. His face knocks against my face. Skin against skin. My mind flashes. A vision dazzles me, brighter than snow.

I see this Crux pilot, absolutely *see* him, his grey eyes open, his mouth open, his hands reaching out to fend off death – to fend *me* off. What's the place we're in? Some kind of massive, stone building. A god-house? A fire is burning but that's not what kills him. In the vision I am the one who rips the life out of his eyes. I am his death.

6

THE PRISONER

Reef leaps down to my side and hauls the pilot off me.

'Are you OK?'

OK? How can I be OK? Shot at, crash-landed, wolf-warmed, traption-hunted, rift-hung and hallucinating – what's *OK* about that? I want to be home with my mama, curled up eating cake and watching streams without wolves or weird visions. I want to be normal, normal, *normal*.

Nothing normal in the Morass.

'Rain?'

'I'm fine. He was heavy, that's all.'

Reef yanks the pilot's head back so we can see his face clearly. I don't need to look long. My vision was enough. I know every feature. Now I can't believe there's a real, live Crux, sprawled at my feet of all places! Someone who believes in a god and worships the sun. Aura's always telling us what backward people they are. How they're stunted intellectually. Hardly fit to be called the same species.

I didn't think he'd look so . . . normal. Almost like a person.

He's young, like Reef, maybe a few years older, tops. Perhaps still young enough to have sight at night. The Crux are the same as us in one way – they lose their night-vision in young adulthood too. His hair is close-shaved with a white diagonal cross dyed on to the stubble. His face is angular, with a sharp nose and high cheekbones. His neck is thick, or is that just his silky white scarf bulking it out? The rest of his clothes are good quality as far as I can tell – a slim-fitting tunic and trousers with white braces looped over his shoulders and heavy, metal-reinforced boots. Nothing he's wearing is made of bioweave.

He's deathly pale from the cold. His eyes open when Reef shakes him hard. Yes, they're concrete-grey, just like the ones I hallucinated.

'Who are you?' Reef demands. 'What are you doing in the Morass?'

No answer.

Then, before Reef can speak again, the Crux explodes into life with such a stunning burst of energy I can't tell where to point the gun. There's a crack of bone on bone from a head butt, the thump of a fist in Reef's gut, the crunch of another fist on Reef's jaw. Reef staggers back. Red blood sprays the snow. The Crux has his fists up to fight again. He makes a savage swing with his right arm. Block, grip, twist, shove, throw . . . in five smooth moves Reef has the Crux face down in the snow with both arms trapped. The Crux rages and kicks for long moments until the last of his strength seeps away.

Reef ties his arms and hobbles his legs tight enough to allow only walking, not kicking.

'Not my eyes!' the Crux snarls as Reef unwinds that white scarf to blindfold him. His accent is distorted, rougher than the proper Rodina way of speaking.

Blinding someone is a form of torture. It's what they do to traitors. They seal their eyelids permanently shut so they'll never see light again. For a god-of-light worshipper this would be a nightmare torment.

'You deserve far worse than blinding and you'll get it.'

Next, Reef takes the gun from me. I'm surprised he doesn't say anything about how useless I was with it. He searches the pilot and finds nothing but a silver god-book, which he tosses into the snow. I nudge it with my boot.

'I don't understand. It doesn't switch on, and there's no keypad to connect to it. What's it made of?'

'Paper. There are sheets of it, called pages.'

Reef's right. The book has leaves inside that darken with damp as they touch snow. I vaguely remember this sort of thing from early days in infant school, before Aura was fully operational. I bend down for a closer look. The brainless god-follower has written his name on the first open page.

'It says *Property of Steen Verdessica. Praise the Light Bringer!*'

Underneath there's a picture that doesn't even move, of saynts praying beneath an image of the Crux god, with hair like white sunbeams and eyes that burn. It reminds me of . . . of nothing, because that's all Old Nation lies. Idiot Crux – worshipping light. In Rodina we just say *lights* and let technology do the rest.

'Leave that alone if you can't respect it,' Steen Verdessica snaps.

'What are you doing in the Morass?' Reef asks.

Steen scowls. 'Looking for God.'

Reef is all cold scorn. 'In the forest?'

'There were god-houses here once.'

'But no god to live in them! Everybody knows science is the only way to achieve civilisation.'

Steen dares to laugh. 'Oh yes, just as cannibalism is one way to get a high-protein diet. The whole of Rodina has crept into spiritual darkness. Be glad we've made the sacrifice of coming to your rescue.'

'With war planes and traptions?' Reef snaps back at him. 'That reeks of invasion.'

'Was it you?' Steen turns to me abruptly.

Alarmed, I step backwards and almost fall over.

'Me?'

'Were you the one who chased me out of the sky in your little training plane – your People's Number Fifty-nine Tutor? You put up a good fight, I'll give you that. They're like midges, the rest of the Rodina Air Force, buzzing around waiting to get slapped. But you, cadet girl, you're good. Don't look so surprised at the compliment. You'd have to be good to best me.'

I flick a glance at Reef. Has *he* got any idea what the Crux is talking about? I certainly don't!

Steen just keeps on talking. 'Look, on my wrist, there's a bracelet. I suppose Captain Normal here won't let me offer it myself, but it's yours. It's valuable in ways you're both too blind and godless to understand. Take it.'

I see a glint of metal between cuff and glove. I don't want it. More than that, the very sight of it makes me feel sick. The metal is the colour of dried blood and it smells like blood too. Who does he think he is to offer me something so nasty?

'Keep your trash, Crux!'

He flinches. 'So you won't take it?'

'We do not accept gifts from the enemy!'

Reef breaks the bracelet from Steen's wrist. It's got tiny bells and white crosses twisted into a cluster of metal strands. It rings with a nasty chime, like the bells hung on the Crux traption that chased me.

Reef takes one look at it and says, 'A bane-metal god-token. These trinkets are banned in Rodina. They're all Old Nation. Worthless junk.'

'If you say so.' For a moment Steen's voice loses its arrogance. 'I'll have it back if *she* won't take it for protection. There are things in these woods that can't be stopped by guns . . .'

'I'll be sure to let them feast on you first,' Reef promises. 'Now, get to your feet and *move*.'

* * *

41

A dreamy purple-orange light begins to seep through sky-grazing branches. It's nearly dark but not quite. I keep flicking looks at Reef. Does he really think we'd survive a night out here without lights, or could he make a fire – that flickering, air-licking, light-living thing I've seen on news-streams but never for real? And I hope I never do. I'd rather be cold than go near flames. Fire looks dangerous. Just pictures of it make my scalp prickle. I'd rather wrap myself in a wolf to keep me warm.

With Steen stumbling along in front we follow a road of sorts. It winds through the trees with deep ruts where wheels once rolled. Signs of civilisation!

Don't go . . . whisper frost-crisp leaves in a light winter breeze.

Don't go . . . caw the corvils, swooping low to the snow.

Don't go . . . howl wolves deep in the darker wilds.

Do I imagine the sorrowful sigh of someone unbearably old? Someone who murmurs my name before surrendering to silence?

I can't wait to get back to normal again, to see Zoya and know she's all right. Mama and Papi will be going crazy, not knowing what's happened to me. Pedla Rue will be camped out at our apartment waiting for news, the worse the better . . .

We speed up, all three of us scrunching closer together as shadows deepen. Soon I hear the welcome hum of technology – heat machines that burn off ice and snow, lamps that defy the darkness, saws that slice through silence and wood. There's something else – a spray, a spatter, a rain of black – ugh! I hide my face as a foul stickiness spurts towards us all.

'It's all right,' shouts Reef, neatly stepping away from the spray. 'It's Slick, a new normalisation compound. Your uncle had a part in creating the formula.'

Through red-watery eyes I watch as sexless, faceless figures in hooded white move past us, spraying great swathes of thick, dripping chemicals that leave Morass plants wilting into a bad-smelling mush.

'Is it poisonous?'

'Only for the forest,' Reef replies, and just for a moment I can't tell if it's the smell that's making his lip curl or the sight of so much destruction. 'Once perfected, Slick will kill anything abnormal, leaving room for new towns and foodlands . . .'

I miss the rest of what he's saying. To my utter, total embarrassment I'm on my knees being sick.

'Go away,' are the first words I manage, though I accept a flask of something hot.

Reef takes to his keypad instead. Eventually he halts and gets that faraway look on his face that shows he's connected. I've never told anyone, but I sometimes wonder if that expression is what sex looks like. Or would he keep his eyes open and gaze into mine as we . . .

Enough!

I shut my eyes. When I open them Reef is looking straight at me. Into me. A Scrutiner.

'Better now? Did you get your updates OK?'

Na – I didn't even think of connecting myself! Where's the keypad gone? Here it is . . . Connection again! Hello, Aura . . . where were you when I needed you?

welcome rain aranoza – updating – location: sorrowdale district, lim lands grid ref. 23:4072 – you have 15 messages – keep alert for action-requirements – please wait for action-requirements – updating – please wait please wait please wait please wait

'Don't worry,' says Reef. 'Connection strength improves the further we go from the forest.'

I glance back at the wasteland of Slick-ridden trees. No wonder Aura's ordered normalisation. The forest swallows the safe rules of science.

Steen doesn't have a keypad to get connected. I wonder who he'd message if he could? He hasn't said a word through all our march, though his lips are moving – some kind of prayer, I suppose. Is there a kind of Slick that would cure him of faith? He catches me looking at him.

'Gloating?' he asks.

I want to ask – why did you attack us? I can't believe it was only this morning that I flew with Zoya and we got shot. We took off at dawn, as Planet Umbra sank and the sun rose. Now I'm escaping from a story-like land with the guy who shot me as prisoner.

We burst out into open sky and gulp in great lungfuls of fresh air. It's so good to see the red circle of Umbra again, rising to begin its night-long journey across the sky. Light blinds us – the gorgeous, glorious glow of proper lamps strung round real, bioweave buildings. If I was a Crux I'd thank god for civilisation.

I turn to Reef.

'You're safe now,' he says. 'While you're waiting for updates go and find your friend, she'll be worried about you. Aura can guide you to the medical centre.'

That's it then. Back to normal. I'll just go and never see him again. He'll probably forget about me anyway, the moment I disappear from view . . .

'Wait! Rain . . .'

Heart leaps to mouth, making me too mute to ask, *Yes?*

Reef bites his lower lip; not a very Scrutiner thing to do. 'Back there in the forest you were . . .'

Disobedient, crazy, abnormal?

'. . . very brave. The way you handled the traptions, the Crux, everything. I'll mention it all in my report to Aura.'

I suddenly find my boot-caps unutterably interesting. Mustn't get excited at compliments. Mustn't take his praise too seriously. Remember what Papi always says – *The weed that sprouts up gets yanked out.* I want to stay nice and average. Normal.

I also want to reach out and touch Reef's face.

I shove my hands in my pockets instead.

'I'll connect soon,' he continues. 'No, don't tell me your Aura code now. I'll find you.'

He leans in, and I guess he's going to do that Lim thing I've heard about, where they kiss cheeks to say *goodbye-*

and-go-well, but I've still not shaken off the sensation of seeing that Crux's death and I *do not* want a repeat with Reef. I flinch and step back, leaving his lips to brush air, not skin. We both say sorry together. I swallow my heart down. His eyes shadow a little.

'Pip, Pip, Pip!' Zoya's voice cuts through the muddle of other noises. There she is, waving from a brightly lit building. 'Over here!'

I trot over and we hug, which is awkward, because I'm anxious not to touch her skin either.

'Aura said you were back. I was worried sick about you until the guys told me you were probably with the Scrutiner. That's him, isn't it, over there? The one who was shooting the Crux creepers. He was amazing.'

'Did they heal all your wounds?' I ask.

She grins. 'Sprayed, sealed and sound again, with my ankle all strapped up. I had this Lim girl looking after me. Weirdest thing – she's like your twin, but taller and stronger. I told her and she said she doesn't have a sister but she asked what you were like. Hey, look at you – you're not even scratched or bruised.'

She's right. When I do a quick inventory for aches and injuries, despite all I've been through I'm absolutely fine.

Zoya's tone changes. 'You shouldn't've run off and left me like that.'

'I was trying to—'

'It's OK. I know you were scared. We both were.'

'That's not why I—'

'Oh, who cares now? You should message Aunty Aranoza to let her know you're safe. Your papi told me to keep an eye on you, you know. It's good we're out of the forest, isn't it? The medics are keen on feeding us up after the ordeal and the food's not bad. Doesn't Rodina look lovely from up here? The lights from the towns are pretty bright over there. They must be having some kind of evening festival.'

We're on a gentle slope with West Rodina spreading out like a panoramic stream-screen image. I spot towns I only know as names from maps in school projects, but my eyes are sharper than Zoya's. I can see these are not happy festival lights. In fact, the horizon is a blood-scarlet backdrop to a devastating view. There's Hardhills, heart of the foodlands, lit by fierce fires; Blackmoss, home to half a dozen tractor factories, with no lights at all; Noonsun, the summer resort, no more than a pit in the ground. I'm so glad Sea-Ways is safe, away behind me to the east. Of course it is! Nothing could happen to *my* family and my house – right? My hands tremble as I reach to connect to Mama and Papi, only to get the same *please wait please wait please wait* message.

The sky crumples with the sound of distant explosions. This is what I've been afraid of ever since seeing Crux face to face.

'It's *war*,' I whisper.

'What is? Really? Aura's not said so.'

I can see for myself without Aura's information. It's a

real war in real places, not just on the stream-screens. For now it's hundreds of klicks away. Nearer to us, towns like Sorrowdale and Rimm are blazing with normal lights. The Crux will never get this far. Aura won't allow it.

Zoya's forgotten the wider landscape. She's noticed the Crux pilot.

'Ugh! What's *that* you've dragged out of the forest? Why's he looking at you like that?'

As if he's got something to say to me . . .

More explosions crackle faintly away west.

Zoya pulls on my arm. 'Come on, let's get inside where there's more light. Night is coming.'

Steen sneers at her, like she's cack on his boots. 'Sooner than you think,' he calls out. 'And darker than you dare believe.'

7
HOME

'Wake up, Pip,' says Zoya. 'This is Sea-Ways Station.'

'I wasn't sleeping.'

'Me neither.'

Zoya's been asleep and snoring. Me, I've been awake with my eyes closed the whole train journey, as if this will somehow make me invisible. Most of the other passengers are hunched over their keypads, flicking glances up from time to time but not daring to discuss whatever messages they're getting.

A woman nearby starts to ask, 'Has anyone heard from folk in Hardhills . . . ?' but she's quickly told to hush, so she sits and fidgets instead.

Our carriage is so packed that once it pulls into the city centre station we're squeezed out of it like toothpaste from a tube. There seem to be more Scrutiners in position than usual.

'What are you waiting for?' Zoya asks as I shrink from the lights and noise. 'Stick with me – the platform's jammed. Aren't you boiling with those gloves on? There's heat machines everywhere. Hey – look at the big screen!

That's her! Marina Furey!'

We push through the press of people to get a better view of the roof-high screen in the station hall. News banners scroll down the sides of the main picture – industrial production targets fulfilled, a hundred jobs created at Glissom's Gun Factory, three more criminals convicted of superstition . . . Nothing about traptions in the forest, or Air Cadet crashes. Who cares about that, when Marina Furey's face is smiling down at us all?

She looks amazing, with hair all suntan brown, leaning against the fuselage of a People's Number Forty-eight Fighter Jet. The HRN medal is the biggest and brightest of all in the row on her immaculate uniform – Hero of Rodina Nation, the highest award a person can win. I bet she could single-handedly wipe out the entire Crux Air Force, Steen Verdessica included.

As she looks out of the screen her eyes seem to rest on each and every one of us. First she talks about pride, hard work and loyalty. Everyone stops dead to listen. Then she drops the bomb.

'It saddens me to say a threat has risen up against Rodina. Without warning, provocation, logic or reason, Crux forces have attacked innocent civilian towns along our western border. This despicable act of aggression has been met with a quick and crushing response by brave Rodinan soldiers.'

Over the rising waves of shock and outrage Furey reassures us all. 'Victory will be certain and soon! If we stand together as a Nation we will defeat all our enemies. Together we are normal, innumerable, invincible! You are not one, but *One of Many!*'

'*One of Many!*' we chant in reply.

There are crowds but no chaos. Aura's orders give pattern and purpose. We are just tiny dots in a massive city, full of life. Street lamps shine on sweaty workers just finishing afternoon factory shifts. Shop windows are all lit with adverts for new, exciting products designed by Rodina's brilliant engineers. Screens update viewers on scientific advances occurring every day in the hub of laboratories at Corona City. *Progress and Pride* is streamed above the doors of all the city schools, now spilling out students at the end of the day's lessons.

This is the real world, where trees don't grow, no birds fly and there's never more than one, normal path to follow.

Messages from school friends pour in and we drink them up – *you're back, was flying good? did you see that stream with marina furey? can you believe crux would dare set foot on our land? you missed the test today, lucky you – aura says you were allowed an extra day's training at the air cadet base . . . jealous!*

This is when I first realise Aura can lie.

We plough through the crowds and follow braids of light that trace our route back home.

'Want me to come up with you?' Zoya asks when we reach People's Number 2032 Housing Block – my front door. 'I can check with Aura, hang on . . . oh, sorry, my father's home early. Gotta go . . .'

She only lives a few blocks away, where the streets are wider and the buildings newer. Uncle Mentira is a chemical scientist so he can afford a bigger apartment with a view right out over the city centre to the industrial estates in the suburbs. As soon as we've said *goodbye-and-go-well* we wave. Zoya walks on a bit then messages.

you going to be all right? she asks.

fine. you?

depends what's for dinner i'm starving

it's been strange

i know but everything's normal now

The lift is still broken so I run up the ten flights of stairs to our floor, not even out of breath when I make it to the landing. Before I can key the code to our apartment, the door opposite cracks open. Pedla Rue is twisted round it, beckoning.

'Tsst, *Rain* – over here!'

'Hi, Pedla, how are you?'

'Ssh! Listen – your mama isn't home yet.'

'I know, she messaged she'd be at Glissom's till late. I can get my own food packets sorted, don't worry.'

Pedla shakes her head. Her grey hair is so short and sparse I can see the blotchy skin of her scalp underneath. She's always on at me to cut my hair. I'm glad I've got it stuffed under an Air Cadet cap right now so she can't start on with the same complaint.

'Watch yourself,' she hisses. 'Trouble's coming . . .'

'Aura says we're not to panic about the Crux. They're practically beaten already.'

'Not them! There's someone waiting for you. One of those *Eyes in the Dark*!'

A Scrutiner! My heart leaps. It jumps, it soars, it flies without wings! *I'll find you*, Reef says, and here he is already! Quick quick quick, I must try and smarten up, if that's at all possible in these lumpy blue overalls. I'm so excited I practically fall through the door. There he is.

It's not Reef.

A stranger in a white uniform stands in our apartment. He's a bone-thin older man with lightless eyes, nothing like Reef at all.

'Rain Aranoza.' Statement, not question.

I nod, shut the front door and lean against it. Why does it seem as though the room has shrunk? It's suddenly so hot, so bright.

'My name is Clint Roke,' the Scrutiner says. 'We'll start with a normalcy test.'

'I . . . I already messaged Aura about what happened.'

'I know.'

Roke sets a keypad on the table and points to a chair. I sit. First he shines a light right into my eyes and I just have to hold still and let him do it. Then he takes a needle and signs for me to remove my gloves.

It's not the needle that makes me yelp, it's the vision that bludgeons my mind the moment Roke's skin touches mine. I see him, absolutely *see* this Scrutiner, as a massive block of darkness slams down on him, breaking every piece of his skeleton except one of those tiny, delicate bones in his right eardrum. What's *wrong* with me, imagining people's deaths when our skins connect?

Roke's eyes narrow.

'Low p-pain threshold,' I stutter, unable to stop the trembling.

He gives nothing away. Why would he? He's a Scrutiner. He stores the bead of blood from my finger then shoots questions at me so quickly I barely have time to answer them all.

No, I don't remember why or when our plane crashed. *Yes*, there were abnormal life-forms in the Morass. *Yes*, I was under observation by a Scrutiner most of the time. (What has Reef reported about me?)

Am I, or have I ever been, a believer in god? *No*.

Do I own, or have I ever owned, any bells or bane-metal for protection against abnormal creatures? *Never*.

Did I interact with the Crux pilot? *Yes*.

No need to mention I'm still plagued by after-images of Steen Verdessica's face as I kill him. I wonder where Steen is and what they're doing to him. Whatever it is, I hope it hurts, especially if he fights back, which he's bound to do, he's so arrogant and defiant.

Finally the Scrutiner makes a steeple of his fingers, like the bell tower of an Old Nation god-house. He simply observes me. I notice that, for all his smart uniform, the skin round his nails is ragged and scabbed. He's an anxious man. What does a Scrutiner have to be worried about?

Without another word he stands, packs away his equipment and turns to leave. I remember how, as children, me and Zoya always said Scrutiners had eyes in the back of their heads.

He's gone. I'm left shaking and scared. I turn the lights down – they're too bright – peel off my Slick-streaked overalls, stuff them down the recycling chute and do a quick message check. There's a *hello pip good to be back hurrah for hot water and proper lights* from Zoya. Nothing about undergoing Scrutiny.

Now here's Mama back from work, squashing me in a hug, but that's OK because I've got sleeves pulled low over my hands and a high-neck top on.

'Horrible about the Crux attack, isn't it? What an outrage! No warning and no provocation! I'm so glad you're all right,' she says. 'You *are* all right, aren't you? You look all right.' All my life she's been peering at me like this.

Here's Papi too, escaping the clutches of Pedla Rue.

'That woman! They should take her to the border to *talk* the Crux to death. Rain! Glad you're safe and sound.' He stares at me anxiously. 'At least we won't be hearing any more about flying lessons, will we? Yes, Aura's updated me all about your failure to impress the instructors at Air Cadets, even after an extra day's tuition . . . Rain! Don't connect when I'm talking to you!'

55

'Sorry . . .' I put my keypad away. I hadn't even realised I was still wondering if Reef would be in touch.

'Why've you meddled with the light settings? It's dim in here.' Papi tells the lights to brighten.

'Sorry, I thought you'd put them up or something, they were really strong when I got home.'

He frowns. I frown too, but only on the inside.

'Well,' says Mama. 'Here we all are again, nice and normal.'

The invasion isn't crushed overnight.

The Crux are defeated, we all know that, it's just that they don't seem to realise it. Purely as a precaution, afternoon school classes are cut so students can do war work around the city. Me and Zoya get put on shifts at Glissom's. Every day Aura predicts imminent final Victory. A month after the crash in the Morass I'm nesting assault rifles in boxes to be transported to the borders when Zoya comes pushing through all the conveyors and cases. She could've talked her uncle into getting a nicer job at his lab, but she said she wanted to get stuck in with everyone else.

'I've been messaging you!' she shouts over the noise on the factory floor. 'Aren't you even checking?'

Not so much. I dread connecting these days in case there's news about the blood sample Roke the Scrutiner took, though there can't really be anything wrong with it, can there, or I'd've known by now? I haven't heard from Reef either. I got my nerve up to try messaging him once.

No connection. Is he blocking me, or is he deep in forest snows again?

I step away from the packing line and try my keypad.

'Well?' asks Zoya. 'Are you getting the same alert as me?'

I blink. 'I've got to report to People's Number One Airbase at Loren in three days' time.'

'Me too! Everybody will die of envy when they hear! Loren's *the* main Air Force base, Pip. The centre of the flying world! The absolute home of Rodina's best fighters and bombers.' She stops dead. 'Wonder what they want *us* to do?'

8
SQUADRON

'You're not going,' says Mama for the hundredth time, the morning I'm meant to leave. 'I lost you once, I won't lose you again.'

'I wasn't lost, I was just at Air Cadets for training, like Aura said.'

'I don't mean that! I mean *before*, back when you were just a baby. You were too young to remember . . .'

'Never mind all that,' says Papi quickly. 'I just don't understand why Rain would be any use for Victory work at an airbase. Still, we have to let her go if that's what Aura says is best.'

Mama wails, 'Why can't she stay safe in Sea-Ways, making guns?'

'We'll be safe in Loren,' I interrupt timidly. 'It's hundreds of klicks from the front line.'

'And how long will it stay safe when those Crux barbarians just keep on coming whatever we do to try and stop them? It'll be over before it's begun, that's what everyone said – and now we're told it'll be Victory by Long Night, but—'

There's a knock at the door.

Mama goes grey. For a moment we all think, *Is it a Scrutiner, listening in on Mama's negative talk?*

It's only Pedla Rue, with a sweetly sour smile.

'Heard you're leaving today,' she says. 'You should be careful. Loren's a long way off, near strange parts – Lim lands and worse. Take this with you. It was my husband's. I hid it when he had to go away. You never know when you might need it.'

She holds out a small bracelet with bells like the one that Steen tried to give me.

Mama practically explodes. 'What are you doing with *bane-metal* in the building? You know charms are illegal. Destroy it, quickly!'

'Shan't!' says Pedla, with her chin jutting out. 'It keeps witches away.'

Papi snatches the thing from Pedla and tells her to shut up before he sicks a Scrutiner on her.

'You wouldn't! Not after what they did to my poor husband, and me just an old lady, no harm to anyone, and your neighbour all these years . . .'

Papi pushes past her. 'Come on, Rain. We'll go and collect Cousin Zoya and head to the station.'

I get away without Mama kissing me and pretend it doesn't cut me up to see her crying. She's working extra shifts at the factory and can't see me off. Her last words to me are *'Be a good girl, Rain.'*

When am I not?

Pedla won't keep her distance. She reaches out to tweak my cheek just as we get to the stairwell and I have to pretend I'm stumbling on the stairs when I get *slammed* with a vision of her, flat in a street with a gunshot wound right where her babbling mouth used to be. These visions have got to *stop*. I dip my face into my coat collar and hide my hands in Reef's gloves.

It's crazy at the station, with bundles of refugees staggering off the trains and ranks of soldiers marching on to them. We've got two seats booked on the big double-deck Transnation service that used to go right to the border and beyond. Now we don't even know where the border is any more, because maps are no longer accessible to anyone outside the military.

While Zoya says *goodbye-and-go-well* to Uncle Mentira, Papi pulls me away for a moment, down the side wall of a snack bar. I'm not really paying attention to him because I'm listening to Zoya saying she'll be homesick, while Uncle Mentira lectures, 'Loyalty to the Nation comes first. Aura will tell you that any time of the day or night, any time . . .'

'Before you leave . . .' Papi begins.

'Papi, the train's already here.'

'I know, but listen. Your mother, she's worried about you. That's why she gets so . . . emotional.'

'She shouldn't worry. It's just some Victory work. I'll be fine.'

'Your eyes – how are your eyes? Still sensitive to strong light?'

I look down quickly. 'They're totally normal, Papi.'

'Good. Good. But . . .' I've never noticed how many more grey hairs Papi has these days. He's always been old, of course, but now he really looks it. It must be the war. He waits while a random Scrutiner goes past. 'Here,' he whispers. 'Take this.'

'That's Pedla's charm! It's illegal. Why . . . ?'

'Just take it. Don't tell your mama I gave it to you. Don't tell anyone. Listen, Rain, we all know there's no such thing as witches – no, don't roll your eyes at me, you're too young to remember things – but if you do see any, *stay away from them*.'

'Papi!'

His words tumble out, bashing against each other in more bad logic. 'Long Night isn't so far off, and they like the dark, these monsters, so stay out of the shadows. Another thing, Rain – are you listening? – whatever you do, *don't look at the lights!*'

How can he be talking like this? It's worse than Pedla's ramblings. And *what* am I too young to remember? As soon as he's gone I drop the bane-metal charm on to the tracks so the train will crush it. Nasty Old Nation nonsense.

He stands on the platform as we pull away, messaging *be good, be safe . . .*

* * *

Loren is a long journey north-west of Sea-Ways. The Transnation train route would be more direct if it weren't for the Morass, which swallows up uncounted klicks of land. Is that why we saw Crux traptions and troops after we crashed? Have they braved the forest to come sneaking past Rodina's front-line defences? I shouldn't worry about military tactics, that's Aura's job, but I can't help it. I'm thinking of Steen Verdessica saying he was hunting god in the forest. Then I think of Reef Starzak, hunting witches.

The train rushes through Lim foodlands, one vast field after another. At Loren Station an Air Force truck picks us up and speeds us through a light snowfall to the airbase, a few klicks away from the actual city. It's painfully exciting to arrive.

Monumental bomber planes roar off the runways while super-slick fighter planes tear through the sky, all off to crush Crux forces. Hundreds of men and women march in neat formation on parade squares surrounded by block after block of bioweave buildings.

'It's like we're actually in one of the Victory reports that everyone sees, isn't it?' Zoya says.

It takes ages to drive round the airfield, where hangars big enough to hold whole streets of houses are set in rows. We go past the end of a runway marked with strips of different-coloured lights. Snow begins to cover our tracks. Just when it seems we'll drive so far out we'll hit the perimeter fence, the truck stops. We've reached a long, low hut squatting at the side of a shabby-looking hangar, well away from the main action. The driver jerks her head towards it. We clamber down with our kit bags. The truck can't quit us quickly enough.

'Want me to help you with that, Pipsqueak?' Zoya asks. As soon as she opens her mouth snowflakes fly in.

I hoist my bag higher over one shoulder. 'I can manage, thanks.'

'My father said I should look after you. Keep an eye on you. It was nice of him to see me off at the station, don't you think? He doesn't normally get the chance to do stuff like that. Too busy with work, I guess. He's been pretty nice since I got back from – from you know where.' She sniffs a couple of times.

'Are you crying?'

'No! My eyes are cold. Shall we go inside, instead of standing here freezing to death? I hope they feed us; I'm starving. Don't look so scared. Whatever we're here for, it's for the Nation. For Victory!'

I nod vigorously, but I've just noticed one stark feature of the hangar – there's a large black bird standing sentinel on the roof. Surely that can't be a corvil, this far from the Morass?

Zoya pushes through the double doors of the hut and I follow.

It's barely warmer inside than out. The bioweave of the building is a drab browny-grey, long past its proper regeneration date. A rather flickery screen is streaming the latest Victory updates on one wall. Patchy blinds cover all windows. The lights are harsh and unshaded.

A roomful of people turn to look at us. A round-faced girl with a cloud of white-blonde hair uncurls from a battered armchair.

'More new recruits!' she calls out. 'Hi, I'm Mossalka – Mossie to my friends. Welcome to the crew-room. Dump your bags with ours and make yourselves comfy.'

'On *these* chairs?' mocks an older, browner girl, fiddling with an unsmoked choke. 'Fat chance of that – they were probably ancient in Old Nation days.'

'Don't mind her, it's choke withdrawal symptoms,' says Mossie. 'She's Lida. Her family are big in aviation engineering.'

'There's no smoking in the crew-room,' cuts in a strong, loud voice. It's a bulky girl with dark eyes and spot-speckled cheeks. Her boldness makes me smile inside. I've never been like that. 'And by the way, my brother *owns* a plane.'

'That's Ang,' explains Mossie. 'She tells us she's won the Glissom Gunner's Firing Range Trophy.'

'*Twice*, remember?'

'Er, twice.'

Ang looks us over. 'It's sweet you're both wearing your Air Cadet uniforms. I was in the Cadets, ages ago.'

Lida yawns and mimes flicking choke ash on the floor. 'I'm way too old for that yash Cadet stuff.'

'No older than me!' objects Ang.

'I probably taught you how to fly.'

64

'How forgettable that would have been!'

'Because your head was so far stuffed up your—'

'I found cookies!' shouts someone with a muffled voice, halfway inside a cupboard.

Lida forgets her quarrel. 'Chuck them over.'

'I'll have a couple,' says Ang.

The person in the cupboard bangs her head and slowly unfolds to stand taller than anyone else in the room.

'Hi,' says Zoya. 'What sort of cookies are they? I'm Zoya Mentira. This is Pip.'

'My name's not Pip, it's—'

'Help yourself, Zoya.' The packet of cookies comes flying our way. 'I'm Petra. I got here first, so that makes me an expert on where everything is and how to work the kettle. Want a brew?'

A chorus of voices calls out for drinks.

Zoya messages me *is petra a boy or a girl?*

don't know – girl? does it matter? I like her hair, short and spiky

it'd suit you, instead of those old-fashioned plaits you won't ever cut

I look around the crew-room and realise I'm the only person with really long hair. I guess I don't look like I fit in. If I ever do trim my hair, I find myself gathering all the clippings up carefully so none of them are left lying around. Mama says my hair's a disgrace but she's given up trying to get scissors to it.

'After the journey we've had, I'll drink anything hot,'

65

Zoya tells Petra. 'Is there **anything** else to eat? I'm starving!'

'I'll see what we can rustle up,' says Petra.

Before I can draw back, Mossie links her arm through mine and points around the room. I flinch, thinking *Please, please don't let her touch my skin.* She doesn't. She introduces a ton of older kids I can hardly remember then ends with a couple who look different from the others. Sadder.

'Those two over there are brother and sister, called Henke and Rill, from Hardhills.'

Henke is humming a popular balika song, and his fingers faintly move, as if plucking imaginary balika strings. Rill is obviously lost in connection.

Mossie lowers her voice to a whisper. 'You heard what happened to Hardhills when the Crux bombed it? Both their parents were killed – bodies never found. Henke and Rill are lucky to be alive.'

Ang barges in. 'I've been to Hardhills *loads* of times before the war. It was a bit of a dead-end town.'

'What about the guy doing pull-ups?' Zoya is mesmerised by a lad with a chest-hugging tunic who's got his fingers cramped on a door frame at the far end of the room, heaving himself up to a sweaty count – *forty-one, forty-two, forty-three, forty-four . . .*

He drops down, wipes his hands on his trousers and grins at her. 'I'm Yeldon.'

Zoya pulls a face. 'You obviously live in a gym.'

'That's not strictly true,' says a girl with a thin face, who is lining up mugs by the kettle so their handles all point the same way. 'Hello, Zoya. Hello, Pip – is that your real name? I'm Dee. Mossie forgot to mention me. For your information, Zoya, people don't actually live in gyms. They just exercise there a lot.'

'That's me, kid,' brags Yeldon. 'See these?' He pulls his tunic neck open to show a sculptured shoulder. 'I've got triple-heads on my deltoids.'

Zoya winces but has a good look anyway. 'Sounds painful.'

'It's a muscle thing,' Mossie explains. 'Yeldon here is a perfect specimen. Of what, I don't like to speculate.'

'If I ever worked out I'd be pretty fit,' says Ang.

Yeldon is asking, 'Is there a mirror round here, do you think?' when suddenly Rill, the quiet girl from Hardhills, pipes up.

'Did you hear about the man who invented the rear-view mirror? He never looked back . . .'

Her brother Henke punches her, but he's got a little smile twisting the corner of his mouth. Everyone else laughs – it's such a bad joke – except the straight-faced girl, Dee, who says, 'Actually, it was a woman who invented the rear-view mirror and she didn't even earn a lot of money for it, so . . .'

Now we all groan and Ang scornfully tries to explain to Dee how Rill's joke was supposed to be funny.

Zoya grabs a few extra cookies and messages me again – *is that dee girl for real? and what about ang? her nickname has got to be ang two-times – you know the sort – anything you've done, she's done twice – you get cold, she's got flu – you bruise your knee, she has hers amputated*

I nudge her gently. Now is *not* a good time to start giggling, not while the older girl, Lida, is still sneering at our overalls.

'What's with you two *Cadets* being here?' Lida asks suddenly. 'Shouldn't you be in *school* or something? I mean, how much flying has anyone here actually done, apart from me? I know *I'm* experienced.'

There's a jumble of answers ranging from months to years.

'I've flown five times,' says Zoya, with her chin up. 'Actually, six, including last time.'

Lida's gaze comes to rest on me. 'And you?'

The room goes quiet except for the bubbling of water in the kettle. Even Zoya would have trouble blustering out of this one.

'Just one flight,' I admit.

Lida bursts out laughing and drops her choke. '*One* yash flight? Are you totally *disconnected*? It must've been a good one – did you beat Furey's round-the-world-record?'

My face flames red. 'We crashed.'

'I know someone who crashed,' interrupts Ang.

Zoya squares up. 'Well, *we* crashed and got shot. Medics took three bullets out of me.'

shut up about that I message quickly, but Zoya's not connected any more and Ang's revving up for a bigger boast.

'Oh, yeah? The guy *I* knew killed three civilian passengers *and* ploughed up a school playground.'

'You win, Ang, you win!' cries Mossie, laughing. Little does she know that the full story of our crash would wipe the floor with Ang's anecdote.

Zoya glowers and mutters, '*Two-Times.*'

'Kettle's boiled,' calls Petra.

At that point Dee raises a hand, like a kid at the back of class. 'Sorry, I know this is all nice and I hope I can remember everyone's names eventually – only, does anyone have the slightest idea *what we're doing here*?'

'Kid's got a point,' drawls Lida. 'It can't just be training for some half-assed Victory effort. Mossie's never flown before, Yeldon neither.'

'I'm a techie,' objects Yeldon. 'I could probably build you a People's Number Nine Glissom Bomber with my eyes shut – doesn't mean you'd catch me going up in one.'

'I'm a techie too!' cries Mossie.

Petra winks at her. 'Bet you're good,' she mouths. Mossie actually blushes.

'Right,' says Lida, and we all turn to listen because she's got this authority thing about her. 'So we've all got something to do with aircraft, *fine*. That doesn't explain why Aura's picked *us* in particular to be here.'

Zoya says, 'Everybody should just wait till we're told why.'

I'm too conscious of the *weed-that-sprouts-up-gets-yanked-out* danger to say what's leaping out at me, because we've definitely got at least one thing in common. We're all young.

'It's obvious what's going on,' grunts Yeldon, cracking his knuckles. 'We're actually some super-skilled squad, headhunted for ultra-special duties.'

That makes us all laugh, it sounds so disconnected.

Petra passes mugs around. Lida leaps out of her chair and shouts at me when my mug drops to the floor, spilling hot liquid all over her arm on the way.

'Hey – watch what you're doing, Cadet girl!'

'Sorry, I . . . I'm a bit clumsy.'

'Great. That blows my theory of a super-skilled squad,' says Yeldon sarcastically.

Zoya looks at me. She knows I'm not usually clumsy. She'll probably put the spill down to nerves. In fact, I dropped the mug from shock. I looked down at the drink for a moment and inside the circle of the tea I saw a round vision of black birds flying across a red night sky, then thick, slick black rain falling like funeral tears.

Just an illusion. A trick of the light.

I tense. There are voices outside, mingling with the sound of the cold wind. The hut doors bang open. A man and a woman are blown inside. We automatically jump and stand in ranks, as we've been taught right from day one of infant school.

The man tries to brush snow from the woman's uniform. She swats him away. Snowflakes are melting on her medals.

I am just about die and bury myself. I know this woman!

I recognise that face! Who hasn't seen her streamed on every screen in the Nation? Who's not heard about the glory she's reaped for Rodina? At my side Zoya is practically hyperventilating. Dee is the only one who manages to get words out.

'That,' she informs us starkly, 'is none other than Marina Furey, the greatest pilot in the Nation. Ever.'

Marina Furey stamps her boots, shakes her hair and rips her gloves off. Finally she notices us all, united in awe.

Her face goes grey.

'You have got to be kidding me. *This* is our next, best hope against the Crux?' She scans our faces and stops at mine. 'Is this some kind of joke? Aren't you that refugee Lim girl who works in the canteen? Please – someone tell me I haven't got a *cook* to train up!'

THE PLANE

The man with Marina Furey checks his keyboard then squints at me. He's dressed in brown engineer overalls with a natty scarf knotted round his neck.

'It's not the cook,' he says. 'Looks a lot like her, but Haze, the Lim girl, is bigger. This one's Rain Aranoza, a school student from Sea-Ways. Who knows, in another couple of years she might even grow tall enough to reach the plane controls.'

A couple of people snigger, I'm guessing Ang and Yeldon. If there was a tree-eaten rift handy I would gladly leap into it right at this moment. Fortunately, Marina Furey's already forgotten I exist. She's connecting, and she's clearly one of those people who talks back to her messages even though no one else can hear what's being streamed into her head.

'*How* many? By *when*? Impossible!' She disconnects and speaks to the engineer. 'Test results are back from normalisation crews. Morass effects are spreading more quickly than previously estimated. Aura's scheduled our first mission for twenty days from now.'

The man snorts. 'It'll be fine, as long as we schedule time for funerals straight afterwards.'

'If it's yours, no problem.'

'I was thinking of these kids.'

Furey closes her eyes briefly, then she straightens her shoulders and tries to adopt a more official look. In the flesh, she somehow seems too much like a whirlwind to fit neatly in a uniform. Her tie is wonky, one button is loose on its threads, her boot straps are flapping undone and she's got an unsmoked choke tucked behind one ear, and yet . . . when she speaks her voice has a quiet and undeniable authority.

'Welcome, everyone. My name is Marina Furey. This is Marton Fenlon, allegedly one of the best engineers in Rodina. I'll get straight to the point. We've all heard the Victory reports and we all know our Nation will eventually defeat the Crux menace. Unfortunately, we're encountering some . . .'

'. . . Catastrophic complications . . .' mutters Fenlon.

'. . . some unexpected abnormalities. Problems with technical function and bioweave structures.'

'Things are falling apart.'

'*Thank you*, Fenlon. Yes, to some extent, they are, quite literally, falling apart whenever they enter a certain sphere of influence. Whenever they approach the area known as the Morass.'

Lida raises her hand, somehow managing to seem insolent and patriotic at the same time.

'The Crux have attacked several towns near the Morass, like Hardhills and Noonsun. Is this going to affect our efforts to push the enemy back where they belong?'

Marina Furey rubs her eyes. She doesn't look like a Hero of Rodina Nation, she looks tired. 'The Crux are not retreating in the direction we'd like, or as quickly as Aura predicted.'

'You mean, they're advancing?'

I see Henke and Rill look at each other. I can't imagine what it must be like for them, having their home and family in Hardhills destroyed and knowing the enemy are still out there, undefeated.

'Let's move on,' says Furey. 'Aura's scientists are taking innovative new steps to combat the problems, using a chemical compound called Slick. That should eventually control and contain the Morass effects. In the meanwhile, we need to have some way of containing Crux forces infesting lands near the Morass. All of you here have been specially selected to help. I can't emphasise strongly enough how dangerous this project is. If you cannot commit then quit. Now. I mean it. Go.'

Not one of us moves.

'Good. What you're about to see and hear is also highly secret. I can't even tell *myself* what work we're doing here.' She laughs humourlessly. 'Come into the hangar. Watch where you're treading . . .'

We follow her through double doors from the hut to the hangar, which is bitterly cold. There are fragments of wrecked plane across half the vast floor. Not broken bioweave, but wood.

'I know this plane,' I whisper to Zoya. 'Remember, back at the lake? This is the remains of the Crux fighter that shot us down.'

More than that, I know the boy standing in the centre of the debris, watching a large corvil batter its wings against the hangar ceiling. My heart stops. How can *he* be here? He's absolutely immaculate in his white uniform. Absolutely beautiful. He sees me, he must see me – why doesn't his expression change?

Zoya tugs my sleeve. 'Look, Pip, it's that Scrutiner from the forest.'

'Ssh!' says Ang. 'You're not in school now. Pay attention!'

'You know the Scru?' whispers Lida, impressed despite herself.

'This is Reef Starzak,' Furey explains. 'Our official squadron Scrutiner. He's been responsible for recovering the wreckage of an unusual lo-tech Crux fighter plane, called a Catapult. Primitive technology appears to function fairly normally near the Morass. From the pieces of the Catapult our engineers have been able to design a similar prototype plane.'

'Not similar, *superior*,' corrects Fenlon.

When I glance over, Reef's eyes are on me. Is there a hint of *hello* on his lips? Above us the corvil keeps flying against the hangar roof, looking for a way out.

Fenlon tramps over to a lumpy shape at the far side of

the hangar. He hauls away a massive tarpaulin to reveal an extraordinary contraption – a thing of rods, flaps and nails. He plods round it, as if even acknowledging its existence is a deep low-point in his life.

'Well, get on with it then,' says Furey. 'Time is precious.'

'Time is an abstract concept,' Fenlon counters. 'So. Despite my improvements, the aircraft's structure is all horribly basic, as you can see. Beneath Rodina's dignity, if you ask me . . .'

'Which no one has.'

Lida raises her hand. 'Excuse me, can I just confirm . . . you're calling that an *aircraft*?'

'Yes,' snaps Fenlon.

'And is it airworthy?'

'In theory.'

'And in practice?'

'That's where you lot come in. You're the lab rablets. The test squad. You get to find out if it flies or not.'

Yeldon snaps to attention and shouts, 'We're ready to do whatever our Nation requires of us to defeat the enemy!' The rest of us are in total agreement. I think Furey's pleased at our loyalty.

Fenlon just sighs.

'I'll take you through the design, for what it's worth. There's no bioweave at all – one of the essential requirements for the zone you'll be working in. The same goes for all your flying gear. Basically, the plane's got a wooden framework covered by plant-fibre fabric that's been treated

76

with chemicals that rot your brain if you breathe them in too often. We're currently having to stitch the fabric by hand until we've designed machines to do it. The sewing is a difficult and painful process probably leading to bone distortion and severe joint pain in later life.'

Furey glares at him. 'Focus on the plane, Fenlon, not how you made it.'

'It's operated with foot pedals and hand controls. No Aura at all. Yes, yes, I thought it was an insane idea too, but hush muttering, I'm not done. The metal moving parts are crude and liable to break, leaving you with zero control of the plane. Navigational instruments . . .' He pauses to shudder. 'Enough said. All in all it's a flying death trap with the speed of a beard-trimmer and the manoeuvrability of a hair dryer.'

Furey takes him to one side but we can still hear the conversation.

'Fenlon, if you think this is all a complete waste of time, why did you even volunteer for the job?'

He looks startled. 'Who said anything about a waste of time? I'm bored of bioweave. This insanity will actually require intelligence and, who knows, it might even be what we need to beat the Crux. Count me in!'

We all study the plane, totally stunned we've been selected to work with it.

Four wings, one pair above the other, supported by thin struts. Two seats, one behind the other. A four-blade propeller. A tank for liquid fuel. It's like something a kid with too much time and too few friends would build from a kit. Crude. Clumsy. Intriguing.

I concentrate on these details and tell my heart to slow down when Reef comes just a bit closer. If he can play it cool then so can I. I hope.

Marina Furey ruffles her hair as she addresses us again.

'So there you go. This is our new weapon against the Crux. Right now you don't need to understand specifically why we need a new weapon, and why it has to be as basic as this. We're calling it the People's Number One Storm, since the prototype was brought down during a storm of some kind.'

Zoya nudges me meaningfully. I glance at Reef again. He's looking right at me. For a moment I'm back in the snow roses at the edge of the tree-eaten rift. Then he turns and leaves the hangar. So much for the wonderful reunion I've been fantasising about.

Furey smiles as if that alone will make everything super-fine and dandy.

'It seems we have a very short time to get you trained up and operational. We're starting with just nine aircraft, crewed by a pilot and navigator in each, plus a tech team and armourers. The Storms are to be used for scouting and bombing Crux positions in and near the Morass. Don't get me wrong, this is no heroic path to glory. We're dealing with a slow, massively flammable plane with limited range, uncertain capabilities and an untested crew.'

'*Now* you're talking my language,' says Fenlon with a grin. 'But tell them the worst bit.'

Zoya and I swap a quick look – *What could be worse?*

Furey says, 'I was coming to that. It concerns our tactics for overcoming the Storm's obvious limitations. On the one hand we're borrowing the Crux innovation for non-bioweave structures, so it shouldn't suffer effects near the Morass. On the other hand we're adding a twist of our own that the Crux haven't thought of yet. The fact is, in daylight you'll be sitting targets for Crux anti-aircraft guns or fighter planes. So you won't fly by day. You've been picked for your youth. For the ability to retain some vision in the dark. You'll fly by night.'

Instant consternation. *Night flying? Did she say night flying? How will we survive without bright lamps? That's sick. Do you really think she means it?*

I think back to the flash image I saw just now in the crew-room – the black birds flying across a night sky. I sneak a look at Furey's face, so strong and honest. Yes, she means it.

Our chatter dies down as Fenlon coughs and says, 'Er, that wasn't quite the worst bit, Furey.'

She sighs. 'I know. The fact is, our choice of flight instructor is rather unusual. He's the only person we have who's ever flown one of these things before, though I use the word *person* in the widest possible sense . . .'

Reef's back. He's not alone.

Lida swears quite loudly.

79

'That is unexpectedly one of the enemy,' states Dee, as if we can't see for ourselves thanks to the hideous cross shaved on to his scalp.

'Yash Crux!' mutters Yeldon. 'Your soldiers burned my grandpapi's village on the border. He's *homeless* because of you!'

From the corner of my eye I see Henke grip his sister Rill's hand so tightly it must hurt.

'Murderer!' he cries out abruptly. 'You bombed our home town. Our parents are *dead* because of you!'

It's Steen Verdessica.

They've got him in tight handcuffs, and he's looking warmer than he did in the forest, but there's no mistaking that weird Crux style of cropped hair and non-bioweave gear. I suppose some people might say he's handsome. Attractive even, if he wasn't so *Crux*. He manages to saunter across the hangar as if he's inspecting us, not the other way round. Reef stands guard.

'For the record,' Steen drawls, 'I'd like to point out I'm brought to this backwater against my wishes and strictly under duress.'

'Your objections are duly noted,' says Furey through gritted teeth, 'and your demands are being fulfilled as far as possible, not least your absurd request that we keep you alive, which very much goes against my wishes.'

'*Duly noted*,' mimics Steen. 'Good – you brought the pilot I mentioned. If anyone can fly your version of my Catapult, it's her.'

Overhead the corvil fights the roof so hard black feathers fall down. If only the lights here weren't so bright! I suddenly need a dark, dark corner to hide in because every single person in the hangar is following Steen's gaze to stare at *me*.

TEST FLIGHT

Quite a crowd turns out to watch the first actual flight of a Storm. They want to see what bizarre experiment has earned the great Marina Furey's time and expertise. Aura sends a message rippling with reassurance – *victory is near! be calm and confident!*

'I wish our new uniforms weren't one-size-fits-nobody,' Zoya complains as we stand by the hangar at dawn, watching Planet Umbra slowly sink below the horizon. 'At least everyone in our squadron has to wear them, so we all look awful together. I can't believe I got issued boots for two left feet! The only reason they don't pinch is because they're two sizes too big.'

'You sound like Ang Two-Times!' I tease. 'Did you stuff them with spare socks, like Petra suggested? You're lucky you haven't had to roll your trousers up a million times just to see your own feet, like me.'

The test plane is wheeled from the hangar out to the runway. Its wood glows a warm, dawn orange, while the metal parts sparkle. Some of the crowd sneer with contempt. I don't blame them. The Storm looks very small and silly compared to real bioweave bombers.

Ang glares at me and taunts, 'Time for your moment of glory, Pip. Everyone's been asking why *you* get picked to fly first, when some of us have tons more flying experience. I suppose it's because you're more disposable.'

Zoya bristles, but I hold her back.

'Don't you want to *kill* that girl?' she hisses. 'Everyone else does. She nabbed the best bunk in the dorm, she drapes herself over Yeldon like he's a coat hanger and did you hear her when you last went in the flight simulator, *Oh, but I've had to wait twice as long as everyone else for a turn?* You can't help it if Aura's got you doing extra sessions in the sim. I just wish I knew why . . .'

'Hey, Pip, there's your boyfriend . . .' calls Lida.

I squint into the rising sun to where Steen Verdessica is a kneeling silhouette, praying to the light of the rising sun. Reef is, as ever, close by as guard. He smiles, subtly, when he sees me. My heart sings and suddenly the sun does seem worth celebrating.

Reef messaged me just once that first day in the hangar, as we were leaving to be shown dorms and things. I'd connected to Aura for updates and instead got a bloom of white flowers unfurling into my mind, the colour of the Morass in winter and the shape of wild snow roses. They were tagged with a message – *found you.*

Lida folds her arms – usually a sign that trouble is brewing.

'Why has that Crux pilot got a thing for you, Pipsqueak?

83

I saw how he squashes up close in the flight simulator. Mates, are you? Maybe sweet on each other? Lovers?'

Does she have any idea how much I *hate* it when Steen presses against me in the sim, or the way he slides his arm round me to point out some detail on the control panel?

'Everybody knows Pip hates Steen!' sparks Zoya quickly. 'She's loyal to Rodina – *One of Many*.'

'*One of Many*,' we all echo.

Lida flushes. 'Are you calling *me* disloyal to the Nation, because if you are . . .'

'You're disconnected!'

'No, this whole setup is disconnected! *Yash* planes, a Crux instructor, Cadets for crew, no Aura and *night-flying*! It stinks.'

'Not as much as your moaning,' says Ang, wading into the quarrel.

'I'm not moaning, I'm just saying, don't you think—'

'I don't think,' pipes up Dee. 'That's what Aura's for. If Aura says I need to fly that wooden plane thing for Rodina, that's what I'll do and that's what Rain's doing. Right, Rain?'

I nod and Zoya nods too. Thank goodness I've got her as my ally.

Lida leans in. 'OK, Pip, but you still haven't explained why the Crux singled you out from all of us.'

Zoya flares up again. 'She doesn't know and she doesn't like it any more than you do.'

'Can't she speak for herself, Zoya, or does her big cousin always have to look out for her?'

Mossie throws her hands in the air. 'Girls, girls! Untwist your knickers. We're supposed to be working together, not against each other. Lighten up – here's Furey.'

Still fastening her uniform buttons, Marina Furey walks over to Steen and whistles for him to get up.

'Wearing your knees out in prayer, Crux? Anyone think to point out to you that the sun's just a ball of hot plasma interwoven with magnetic fields?'

'Prayer to the Light Bringer is calming,' Steen replies, without his usual sneer.

'We civilised people prefer to connect.'

'Yes, perhaps that is a kind of religion to you, giving blind obedience to the hub of collected information you call Aura. How much happier you'd be if you let us convert you all to the light.'

'*Conversion?* Is that what you're calling your invasion? Five more towns were bombed in West Rodina yesterday – thousands of casualties. Stray missiles landed on Sorrowdale. How can you live with all these deaths on your conscience, Crux?'

There are rumours, just whispers here and there when Scrutiners aren't listening, that Crux are sacrificing babies on god-altars. That they blind all captured soldiers and civilians. That we may not even win Victory before Long Night.

Steen's angry now and about to spout off some self-righteous lies about the war being started because of Rodina's persecution of religious believers. I've heard it all before, during our tutorials in the sim. Thankfully Reef gives him a shove in the back and says, 'Time to get to work.'

Steen rises to his feet in one fluid movement, like a dancer, but more dangerous. I shudder as he passes me, certain I hear him say, 'You live in lies and shadow. You should set yourself free . . .'

'I don't like this setup,' Fenlon growls from somewhere under the fuselage of the Storm. 'How do we know we can trust this Crux in a plane? What's to stop him going straight over the border back to his own kind?'

Reef's eyes narrow. 'There are a hundred captured Crux soldiers being kept hostage who'll be shot if Steen fails to collaborate. Aura's ac-reqs are clear – Rain Aranoza flies under his instruction, end of story.'

Furey agrees. 'There's too much at stake to argue. If Aura's calculated the Storms are necessary for Victory then we have to have them in combat soon. What is it now, Fenlon?'

Fenlon crawls out from under the plane, holding something in a fuel-stained hand. 'Found this tied to one of the landing struts. Anything to do with you, Aranoza?'

He thrusts a strange twist of coloured threads at me, all knotted in intricate patterns. I step back from it quickly and shake my head.

'Looks Lim-ish,' says Furey. 'Folk in Sorrowdale used to pin them on trees sometimes – can't remember why. Actually, it's like that braided belt the canteen cook wears, that Lim girl, Haze. Is it some sort of Old Nation good-luck charm, maybe?'

Good luck? More like a *bad*-luck charm. Just looking at it makes me feel uneasy, like I'm trapped inside too-tight skin. It can't be coincidence that Haze has a job here on the airbase, can it? I haven't seen her face to face yet. Everyone says she's the best cook ever, but the first time we ate in the canteen Zoya shovelled her soup in while I had to push my bowl away, because it tasted funny.

'Tastes fine to me,' Zoya said. 'Everybody else likes it. Don't you want yours?'

I let her gulp it down. It was only bioveg and herbs – but the herbs were horribly bitter. I actually felt sick just from the smell. My canteen tea was the same. Mossie asked *are you OK, you look pale?* Petra said I should go to the medic. I just gripped the edge of the table and said I was fine, absolutely fine. When I finally let go of the table it looked as if I'd dented the bioweave, which is impossible, of course. Once bioweave is set it won't change shape until regeneration. Since then I've taken to making my own tea in the crew-room and living off vending-machine snacks.

Now, seeing the knotted charm, I finally remember the second of Pedla's rules for staying safe in the forest – *Be very careful what you eat.*

All three rules run through my head.

Be very careful who you meet, be very careful what you eat and don't step off the path . . .

No matter how intense training has been, with marching, sports, tests and sim exercises, the Morass is never far from my thoughts. In the dorm, listening to Ang's hefty snores and the little whimpers Zoya makes as she dreams, I also imagine I hear the sounds of corvils calling and, once, beyond the frost-flowers scratched on each pane of the dorm window, I thought I saw a flash of silver as a wolf ran past.

Out on the airstrip Fenlon shakes his head. 'We can't have civilians tampering with the plane. Here – this is Scrutiner business.'

'Let me see.' Reef's right at my side. I feel him come close without even needing to see him there. He smells nice. Clean. Warm. He examines the braid then tucks it securely in a pocket. No one dares ask what he thinks of it.

Furey turns to me. 'Ready to go, Aranoza?'

'Mm.'

I look over at the rest of the squadron. There's Yeldon, stretching his muscles out; Henke tapping a tune against the side of his leg. Mossie's still rubbing sleep from her eyes and Petra's cramming a cap on her sticking-up hair. The two of them stand really close together, fingers brushing when they think no one's looking. Dee just blinks and tries to keep her fringe straight in the morning breeze. She's lost her cap and hasn't yet figured out that Lida threw it up on the hangar roof after a bet with Ang (who said she could throw it twice as far, but actually couldn't). Ang frowns at me with envy. Zoya waves. Most of the crowd just stare, sceptical that the Storm will even get off the ground.

A lump of anxiety bulges in my throat. Mama always said I should never put myself forward. Papi knows I'm not good at anything. What if I let everyone down today? Why does it have to be *me* singled out, like that weed that sprouts and needs yanking up?

'Don't worry,' Furey reassures. 'Our charming Crux instructor here can pilot via the dual controls if you get into difficulties, which I doubt you will. I've no idea why he specified you to pilot the test flight, but you're a natural on the simulator. Stop looking so scared! It'll be an adventure. If it was me, I'd be up there like a shot.'

'I've made this for you,' says Zoya just before I leave. 'It's a scarf, because you'll freeze in that open cockpit. Haze in the canteen's been teaching me how to knit like Lim people do. I'll ask her to show you too, if you like? Why not? You might be good at it.'

Why not? Because there's something about the pattern of coloured threads that makes my eyes feel funny, that's why. I say *thank you* and take it anyway, but as soon as she's not looking I pass the yarn scarf to Mossie and ask her to keep it safe for me.

'Are you coming?' Steen asks, holding out a hand for me to climb on the wing of the Storm with him.

'Keep your distance, Crux,' comes Reef's warning, dark and low. 'And keep your mind on what will happen if you try anything abnormal up there.'

Reef offers me a hand up instead. I'm in flying gloves, so no danger of touching his skin and getting a vision, much as I'd like to hold his naked hand. His words to me are neutral – 'Safe skies, Aranoza' – but he gives my hand a quick squeeze before letting go.

Steen drops into the back seat of the Storm while I scramble into the front. Zoya throws up the pad I need to raise the seat high enough so I can see out of the cockpit. I also have to have blocks on the foot pedals. Embarrassing but true – I'm just too titchy. I test the clumsy controls. Will simulator training be any use at all in this *flying coffin*, as Fenlon calls it?

'Good luck, Pip!' Zoya calls. 'Everybody says you can do it! If it works we can all fly Storms and win the war!'

No pressure then.

Just like my sessions in the sim I press the top of the control stick to release fuel to the Storm's engine, which goes from a grumble to a roar. So far so good. Fenlon heaves the propeller into motion. The whole plane starts to shake. I tense at the change in vibration and the following rush-back of air into the open cockpit.

'Are you ready for this?' Steen shouts from the seat behind.

I look over to Fenlon. His face is grey, like I'm dead already.

'Are you?' I shout back to Steen.

Fenlon scoots to a safe distance. Chocks are pulled away from the wheels and we start to roll forward. We pick up speed . . . lift off the ground . . . wheels bump once, higher now – we're off . . . We're actually airborne! This crazy contraption works!

What an amazing sensation, to be rising up like the morning sun, with light on our faces and lungs full of fresh, cold air! This could not be more different from my last flight – cooped in the noiseless aircon atmosphere of a closed cockpit in the People's Number Fifty-nine Tutor Plane. I climb higher, aware that Steen has hold of the dual controls, with a corrective touch here and there. I don't need his interference. Flying this plane isn't so difficult once I let myself feel how it responds. I like it. I love being open to the sky. Soon my friends are little specks and the sky is a glorious invitation.

'Fantastic, isn't it?' Steen calls. 'Shall we try a few tricks?'

Performing manoeuvres for real is nothing like the artificial judders and dips of the simulator. It scares the skin off me at first, knowing my actions are responsible for this wooden wonder's diving, turning, climbing and rolling. Soon, though, I wish I could jettison the plane and fly like the sun-sleek corvils suddenly streaming alongside our wings.

Zoya was right. It is really cold, but I like the way the air whips away my worries. Up here the only gaze is the sun's golden glory. If we just went high enough, far enough, there'd be no more war, no more eyes watching, just us, just me, free . . .

'Rain!' Steen sounds alarmed. 'Not so high.'

War is clearly visible from above. The Lim lands of West Rodina are patterned with puffs of smoke and explosive flashes. Up here my eyes seem sharper than ever before because I swear I spy out the nasty, scrabbling shapes of traptions on the move, and specks of black that could be platoons of soldiers marching. Convoys of military trucks crawl to the border . . . or where the border used to be. Transnation trains rush along their tracks with hospital markings on the carriage roofs.

South-east is the awesome spread of Sea-Ways City, shrunk now to a blur of toy buildings edged by the endless blue-grey of the ocean. South-west the sun skims over the thick mist of the Morass. I'm shocked to see how much of the forest has been scabbed by the brown, Slicked bioground of normalisation.

'Shall we go closer?' Steen calls. 'Legend has it the greatest god-house ever built was near the shores of a lake in the forest. I'd like to see it.'

That makes me think of the stone blocks I saw at the edge of the rift, and the snow-flaked picture of a god or saynt with blazing hair.

I shout, 'Why waste time looking for god when there's no proof god even exists?'

'Faith doesn't need proof,' he replies. 'I *know* there's a Light Bringer. People in Rodina will soon know it too, once we've converted them.'

'Or killed them.'

Needles on dials tell me it's time to descend. It takes a

couple of circuits to line up with the runway to land. I panic and throw up the air brakes too hard. We descend quickly and the plane's wheels hit the ground in an uncontrolled rush. We jolt repeatedly. The Storm shudders a bit then stops. I kill the engine. The propeller slowly spins to a halt. I sit there, motionless, sad there's now ground beneath our wheels.

'You did it,' Steen murmurs softly.

'Why pick me to fly?' I ask quickly, while no one is listening. 'I'm just *One of Many*.'

He gives a funny laugh. 'You really have no idea, do you? Let's just say, I've seen what you can do in a storm.'

'You did it!' scream the squadron, running up to meet us.

Fenlon trots over, frowning. 'It worked. It actually flew.'

'How was it?' shouts Zoya, climbing up on the wing.

How was it? I take a deep breath. A smile so big it could be sunshine breaks out. I actually laugh out loud, and there are even tears in my eyes. How was it? Forget all that business of sprouting weeds getting yanked out, I can't keep my enthusiasm hidden.

'It was brilliant!'

Furey slaps me on the back as I jump down. 'What did I say? You're a natural! You made that look easy.'

Did Reef watch how well I did? He's nowhere to be seen. No, wait – there he is, at the edge of the airstrip. I almost stop breathing when I realise that the man next to him is the Scrutiner who came to my home in Sea-Ways –

the white-clad, nail-nibbled Clint Roke. Both just stand there watching.

Clouds cover my smile. Furey turns sombre too as she addresses the whole Storm squadron.

'Make no mistake, this is only the beginning. Aranoza has shown that Fenlon's designs are, contrary to all expectation, sound. Now we know it *can* be done we have to work day and night so it *will* be done in time for Aura's deadline. Flying is a wonderful experience, my friends – the best in the world, I'd say – but we are not here for the fun of it. Tens of thousands of Crux soldiers are pushing across the west foodlands. Untold numbers are creeping through the Morass. Our Nation is in terrible danger. Fifteen days, that's all we have before our first mission. Make every hour count!'

A WITCH THING

Going up by day is one thing. We all get good practice buzzing about in Storms while the sun's out, no matter how much the 'real' bomber crews point and laugh. But night-flying is a whole new world of worry. We've hardly had a handful of starlit sorties before orders come through to muster for the first mission.

It's just not natural, waking up at twilight and deliberately waiting for the sky to darken. Usually the sight of Umbra above the horizon is our signal to go indoors and tell the lights to go up . . . not to switch them off. The whole of Loren Airbase is under new blackout orders, so all the other personnel are stuck inside where it's nice and bright.

I wonder if this sort of dread is how it'll be when the Long Night comes. I'm too young to remember the last Eclipse. I was only a baby then and Zoya just a toddler. We know all about it though, thanks to things we hear from older kids, and sometimes our parents, when they don't know we're listening. It's *bad* – that's the simple summing up. When I was little I had nightmares about it, about being snatched up by a shrieking wind and tossed around in a storm of black feathers. I told Mama once and she said I was to stop making things up, so I told Pedla Rue instead and she said Long Night is when witches come out to fly.

'They're the most repulsive monsters,' she elaborated, enjoying the absolute horror of the description. 'The hideous opposite of everything normal. They steal babies and make them slaves or *eat* them.'

I scan the skies over Loren for flying monsters, and see only clouds and the occasional corvil.

'You OK, Pip? Nervous?' Zoya asks. 'I'm not. Much.' Her fingers go tap tap tap against the side of her thigh.

'You should be petrified,' says Fenlon, slapping her on the shoulder as he walks past. 'I know I would be if I was young enough and dumb enough to fly a Storm at night. All right, people, gather round. Time for some last-minute advice on light. Light is, perversely, going to be one of your greatest enemies from now on. Once your eyes have adjusted to darkness it's important they stay that way. Keep the cockpit dim – just bright enough for the navigators to map-read. Navs, you've had your training on how to plot a route via stars or ground illumination.'

Zoya has her map all ready, folded into a waterproof, transparent pocket on the knee of her flying suit. It's made of paper, like the god-book I found near Steen Verdessica.

Fenlon continues. 'You've got a green light on your port wing and a red one to starboard. If you get lost, the trick is to keep flying between them . . .' Only Rill laughs at the joke. 'So . . . if the worst happens and your engine fails –

despite my brilliant team of technicians – then you'll have to glide to an emergency landing.'

'How will we know where it's safe to land?' asks Dee.

'Look out for the floodlights of a sports stadium, or a lit road that's not too busy. Keep clear of dark patches if you can, unless you're certain it's a nice flat field. Chances are, dark spots mean water or trees. In either case, if you land there you'll be dead and I'll be short of a Storm, which are harder to replace than crew right now.'

'And if we have to land somewhere dark, how can we see if it's safe or not?'

With a twisted smile Fenlon replies, 'Put your landing lights on. If you like what you see, marvellous. If you don't, switch the lights off again.'

It takes a while for Dee to figure out what he means. When she does her face goes pale.

'One final thing . . .' Fenlon squints at each of us in turn. 'You're all at a funny age. Young enough to see in the dark . . . but your night-sight could go just like *that*.' He snaps his fingers. 'We'll test you every evening before you fly. First sign of hazy vision, you're off the squadron – is that clear?'

We all blink, suddenly desperate to prove we can stay airborne.

Fenlon hauls open the hangar doors so we can all see the Storms lined up in rows by the runway, slowly being swallowed by shadows. Planet Umbra is streaked with clouds – not enough to alter plans, Aura assures us. While we wait Henke plays a song on his balika, about the ending of winter and the hope spring brings; about the chill of the Long Night being followed by the warmth of the sun's reappearance. It makes me imagine flowers in the forest unfolding fat petals, and trees sticky with new sap. My skin tightens and my heart thuds.

Suddenly Rill says, 'How does a night-blind pilot know when to take off?'

'I don't know,' we all reply. 'How does a night-blind pilot know when to take off?'

'He keeps going along the runway until all the passengers start screaming.'

We groan. It doesn't deter her.

'How does a night-blind pilot know when to land?'

'We don't know, Rill, how does a night-blind pilot know when to land?'

'When the guide dog's leash goes slack!'

Henke mimes cracking Rill over the head with his balika then carries on with his tunes.

Yeldon drops to the hangar floor and does a few speedy press-ups, right where Zoya can see and admire him.

'I'm ready for whatever the night brings,' he says, back on his feet and punching the air.

'*You* don't have to fly,' sniffs Zoya. 'Everybody else is in much more danger.'

'Hey – it'll be nothing spectacular, just a series of quick fly-and-bomb runs, that's all. Absolutely zero to be worried about. You've all trained non-stop and read maps and things. You got on OK with your first night-flights. I can't see why everyone's so tense.'

'*I'm* not tense,' snaps Lida.

'Me neither,' says Ang quickly. 'I'm relaxation incarnate.'

'Why are you digging your fingernails into your palms then?' asks Dee.

'Shut up!'

Ang is paired to fly with Dee as her pilot. They're both finding it quite torturous, particularly since Ang thinks pilots get too much respect compared to navigators. Henke is nav to his sister Rill. Lida has Petra as her navigator, but right now Petra's squinting through the twilight to keep tabs on Mossie, who's over by the Storms with Yeldon and Fenlon, doing last-minute checks. Being night-blind, Fenlon has to use a head-torch. He forgets he's wearing it, and keeps dazzling people when he looks at them.

'I never thought I'd say this, but I wish the sun would hurry up and finish setting!' Zoya sighs, shoving her hands in her armpits. 'Pip, you look toasty. Can I borrow your flying jacket just till we're ready to go? It's big enough for two of you, so it should fit.'

I do feel hot. Feverish even. Taking off my jacket is a huge relief. The nausea fades.

Zoya rootles around in my jacket pockets. 'Have you got any spare gloves? Ugh, what's this? Is this actual *animal* wool? Na – is this a *bone* stuck in it? Pip . . . ?'

I back away. 'It's not mine, I swear – no, don't give me

it, *I* don't want it! Someone must've hidden it in my jacket when it was hanging in the crew-room. There was something like it on the Storm the day of the test flight, too. Reef – the Scrutiner – took it.'

'Seriously? Did he say what it was?'

I shake my head. 'Furey said it might be a good-luck charm.'

'It's like those gross artefacts they have on display in the People's Number Ninety-four Museum back home – Old Nation stuff that's banned now.'

'Let me look,' comes a quiet voice. Rill pushes past Zoya to examine the object. We expect a bad joke, but she's serious when she speaks. 'My brother knows songs about people using amulets and prayers and herbs. There are fey-tales too. I don't know exactly what this exact charm means, but I do know it's a witch thing.'

'No such thing as witches,' is our chorus, with me chanting extra loudly.

'I'm not saying witches exist,' Rill adds quickly. 'But my mama said you have to do whatever you can to guard yourself against them, even if it means using protection that's called Old Nation now.'

It all sounds a bit like Papi's attitude when I caught the train at Sea-Ways – *No such thing as witches but guard yourself against them anyway.*

Zoya splutters, 'I can't believe you'd even say something like that, Rill. We should absolutely report this to *Eyes in the Dark.*'

'Report what?' comes a voice from behind our huddled circle. Reef is right beside me.

'It's not mine,' says Zoya anxiously. 'I just found it.'

'Where?'

She hesitates, not wanting to get me into trouble.

Dee answers for her, honest as ever. 'It was in the pocket of Rain's flying jacket.'

Reef's eyes are focused only on me now. 'Is this true?'

I nod and colour up. 'I don't know how it got there.'

'The wool is like that embroidered belt Haze in the canteen kitchen wears – sort of a Lim design,' says Lida. She suddenly looks taller, as if she'll be responsible for the group. I like that about her, even if she does keep calling me Pipsqueak.

Zoya frowns. 'Why would Haze make something like this? You shouldn't accuse people without proof.'

Lida says, 'I'm not *accusing*, I'm just making an observation . . .'

Reef holds up his hand. 'Enough talk. We have the Lim girl under Scrutiny. We have you all under Scrutiny. Forget about this now and focus on your flying.'

'Forget what?' comes Marina Furey's voice.

I look up at Reef with a mute *please don't tell* in my eyes.

Reef hesitates for a moment . . . then he slips the bone-wool thing away. 'They're to forget their fears,' he tells Furey calmly. 'Their Nation needs them.'

'Absolutely,' she replies.

I breathe out slowly and wonder if I dare message *thank you* to Reef.

Furey looks more dishevelled than usual, and angry too.

'Updates just came through,' she begins. 'It's not good. Crux have captured Sorrowdale. Yes, yes, it's impossible. But they have. I don't need to tell you that Sorrowdale is an important gateway from West Rodina across the foodlands to Rimm, Loren and eventually Sea-Ways itself. If Sea-Ways falls that leaves Corona vulnerable and it'll only be a matter of time before Crux are marching through our beautiful capital city . . . and right to the doors of Aura's laboratories. Which is *not* going to happen. You're going to stop them.'

'Why have they even got that far?' Lida asks, speaking for all of us. 'The Crux are just superstitious fanatics. Rodina has superior technology and more disciplined ground forces.'

'When our technology *works*,' answers Fenlon gruffly.

Marina shrugs. 'Normalisation squads are spraying Slick as fast as factories can produce it, but obviously it's not enough to guarantee bioweave won't unravel. Which is where our Storm squadron comes in. Now is the time to show the Nation what you're capable of. In a moment you can connect for coordinates and flight plans, but I'll tell you straight out, your first mission is to wipe out every last Crux in Sorrowdale, even if it means flattening the town.'

We all start clapping, while Ang mutters, 'If only we could start with that smug streak, Steen Verdessica . . .'

No one will argue with that.

'You're acting tough, but I'm guessing you're all afraid of what tonight will bring,' Furey says starkly, looking at each one of us individually . . . pausing for a moment longer when she comes to me. 'I don't blame you. You're going up into a night without lights, your wings weighted with bombs. Don't give in to your fear! Your Nation takes great pride in your efforts tonight. You're not just one person, you're *One of Many*.'

'*One of Many!*' we chant in response.

I look around. I still don't know the names of everyone on the squadron, and those I am getting to know well – my new friends – they're always bickering or bragging. Can we even pull ourselves together to work as a team?

Furey continues.

'I knew from the moment I first got airborne it was in my blood. If I could fly blind with you tonight I would. Instead, being stupidly too old for night-vision I pass my ambitions on to you. You have all taken an oath of loyalty to defend the Nation, so let's vow once more, together, to fight to our last breath in defence of our beloved homeland. The Crux come here to force us to return to Old Nation ways. They've stolen our territory, our peace, the lives of our people. Now the time has come to fight for harsh retribution. Rodina is the greatest Nation to fly the flag of civilisation! Stand in the ranks of the warriors for freedom! Success to you and combat glory!'

Forgetting our shabby outfits, our squabbles, our fears,

we all draw taller and shout as one, 'To combat glory!'

At Furey's signal we break rank. We sprint from the hangar, feet flying. First to the plane will be first away. Lida's long legs have her in the lead. Her propeller spins to life. Petra leaps into place behind her. Henke and Rill are fast too, if not quite first in the line to take revenge.

'Wait for me, Pip!' pants Zoya in her oversized boots, so I slow . . . long enough to catch sight of Marina Furey lighting up a choke to smoke with trembling fingers. I hear her swear and mutter to Reef, 'They're only *kids*!'

'Never underestimate what a young person can do,' Reef replies calmly.

She coughs and laughs at the same time then throws her choke away. 'You should know, Starzak, you should know. I've got clearance to see your record, remember . . .'

Know *what*? No time to wonder. Our Storm is waiting!

Just before I stow my keypad for take-off a message comes through from Reef.

hey rain

hello reef

i'll be thinking of you on your first mission – good luck. Then, after a pause, he adds *rain, perhaps i shouldn't tell you this, but i think of you all the time*

I smile inside . . . then I get a flashback to the sight of Reef standing with Roke, two Scrutiners together, at the edge of the airstrip after my test flight. I start to wonder, *what* does Reef think of when he thinks of me?

✕2

BOMB RAID

Airborne.

I patch into the primitive communication system Fenlon has installed in the Storm's cockpit. You have to speak into a tube and hear voices through two lumpy receivers inside the flying helmet.

'Hey, Zoya, can you see the map OK to navigate?'

Zoya's voice crackles loudly in my ears.

'Not a problem. That's Rimm over there, and those are the lights of the westbound Transnation railway. We're on target for Sorrowdale. You know what? It must burn Furey to know we're going to bomb her home town.'

'What do you mean? I thought she lived in Corona?'

'Yeah, since she got famous, but she comes from Sorrowdale, didn't you know that? Guess you and her have something in common.'

I want to turn and look at Zoya to see what she means, but the wind is getting pretty strong and I have to keep firm hold on the control stick to steady us with each buffeting.

'I'm from Sea-Ways. I've never lived in Sorrowdale, you know that . . .'

'Maybe I got it wrong, but I once heard my father say you guys moved from there when you were small – *smaller*, ha ha – to get away from Lim lands. I'd do the same. Being so near the Morass would creep me out. Do you think . . . I mean, have you wondered about why we got picked for the Storm squadron, since we're not really experienced for anything? Do you reckon it's something to do with what happened after the crash?'

I sense, rather than see the dark mass of trees and mist that is the Morass, not far to the south of our flight path. Up here there is no Aura, there are no Scrutiners. We can speak freely. Trust each other. I could tell Zoya all about the weird things – the way time stretched in the Morass, the death visions, everything.

'Pip? Did you hear me? Is this stupid speaker relay working?'

I could tell her about the normalcy test I took with Roke, about the black feathers, about Papi giving me Pedla's bane-metal protection charm. It would be wonderful to share all these abnormal things and know Zoya's on my side.

'Pip? I *said*, do you think there's something about the Morass that means we're on the squadron?'

I take a deep breath. 'Honestly? I've no idea.'

'Doesn't Reef tell you anything? He must like you. Everyone's noticed he's always watching you.'

I gulp emotions down. 'Not really.'

Before Zoya can ask any more questions I see the faint wing-lights of Lida's Storm drop altitude ahead of us. We're close. Oh god, this is real. This is actually going to happen. Suddenly our engines seem painfully loud in the night's silence. Surely the Crux will have heard us – *seen us* – coming? The Storms really are lumbering toy planes compared to proper technology.

'Can you get a fix on the target?' I ask.

'Dead ahead,' Zoya answers.

There it is. Sorrowdale. A Rodina town crawling with Crux soldiers. Can our little Storms make a difference when the Nation's best bombers have failed?

Lida's Storm drops even lower, then *up*! Bombs away!

She gains height rapidly and banks round to the right. I hold my breath. The night explodes. We cover our eyes against the sudden flare. Has she hit the town? I can't tell; can't make sense of the confusion on the ground.

The second plane approaches. New bombs fall. Henke and Rill make it through, trailing the echo of wild words in their wake – *Death to you all! Death for the death of our parents!*

Our turn next. I'm sick with tension. This is it! I hear a few feeble spurts of anti-aircraft fire as we dive. Zoya lines up the weapon sights and releases the wires, just as she's done a thousand times in the simulator – bombs away! It's like sowing seeds of death, not life.

I give us a surge of power to climb, curve and escape.

The blast follows but doesn't catch us. We whoop and cheer like we've just won the whole war in one go . . .

We've barely touched down at Loren again when Yeldon's at the plane. He's stripped down to a vest so his biceps show better.

'Thought you said it'd be dangerous!' he shouts to Zoya over the noise of the propeller. 'You haven't even got any bullet holes anywhere.'

Zoya sticks her tongue out at him.

'Hold steady while we refuel and rearm.'

'Same again!' Zoya sings, as I throttle forward and off we go . . . a black bird-machine heading back to war.

Halfway to the target on our second sortie the sky splits open and sharp splinters of rain spike down. Aura said it would be clear!

I hate spring rain because it's thick with sticky tree spores drifting from the Morass. When I was little Zoya used to tell me if you didn't wash the spores off straight away they'd root in your skin and grow into a forest. She also told me if you kissed a boy with thick eyebrows you'd give birth to furry rablets, but I spotted *her* doing that once and no rablets appeared, so I learned not to believe *everything* she said. Come to think of it, Yeldon has quite thick eyebrows . . . but now is not the time to think of kissing, or I'll be right back on the subject of Reef Starzak, that half-hidden smile on his lips, and his soft message – *i think of you all the time.*

I flick a switch that sets the wipers swiping across the

low windshield at the front of the cockpit. They can't keep up with the downpour. They sweep, I peek, then water pelts again. I feel it running down my neck and spine and pooling round my boots.

I want to ask Zoya what she meant about my family being from Sorrowdale, but daren't. Not when I'm on my way to bomb the place again. Not when my parents have always said I was born and bred in Sea-Ways.

All night we fly. All night we bomb, until dawn comes teasing the skyline, then we strip, dump our sodden gear and collapse into our bunks, too wired to sleep, to tired to talk. Come evening we're ready to go and pound the enemy again.

Just as before, Lida and Petra lead our formation. They reach the target, drop bombs and veer away. Everything's looking good for Henke and Rill's run-in until a sudden blade of light stabs the sky. A search lamp! Steen Verdessica would just love the religious poetics of this – bringing light to the unbelievers.

Nothing poetic about what happens next.

Like a lightning bolt, I think – *Don't look at the light*, but there's no way to warn Henke and Rill, caught in the lamp's beam.

Rill's Storm seems to skid in mid-air. It tips over and begins to spin. Rill must be blinded, Henke too. Unconnected, they can't tell which way is up quickly enough. They'll have no chance to come out of the stall in time.

Zoya shrieks, 'Rain – break formation! Abort the mission!'

Her words mean nothing to me. I'm pushing the Storm to its maximum airspeed, urging it on, willing the seconds to stretch so I can somehow break through normal laws of time and motion to catch my friends before they find the ground.

3
SEARCHLIGHT

I start to shake. The plane shakes too, worse than normal engine shudders. I see nails working loose from wooden panels. Screws untwisting. Fabric unstitching. Light burns on my face from the search lamp. In this strange dance of slowed-down moments I feel as if I can count the photons spreading out in a wave of dazzle. The plane's not the only thing unravelling. I feel this tremendous pressure pushing from the inside outwards until it seems as if I'm unpeeling like fruit skin. Some strange power sings, *Let me out! Let me burst free!* I clamp it down, struggling, almost literally, to hold myself together. I am normal, normal, normal.

Below us Henke and Rill are turning, diving, falling . . . hitting a Sorrowdale house – *bam*. Time zooms back to normal. Their Storm blooms into a hideous flower of orange fire that rain quickly batters into foul black smoke.

My voice is loud but rough from the ash in the air. 'We're close enough to the target, Zoya, release the bombs!'

'They're shooting at us!'

'I know! Release the bombs!'

'I can't, the wires are jammed!'

'Then fly the plane for me!'

Thank god – or Fenlon – for dual controls. While Zoya pilots the Storm I strip off my bulky flying gloves and heave myself half out of the cockpit to find that the bomb-release wires are totally twisted. Only one thing for it. Before I can talk myself out of such madness I'm climbing on to the lower left wing. The Storm tilts. I grab a wooden strut for support. It creaks . . . but stays firm. Zoya gets control; I get my balance. The search lamp swings round towards us.

'Don't look at the lights!' I call.

'Don't fall!' Zoya screams.

I think . . . *If you don't know you* can't *do something, maybe you can*. With my eyes closed I feel for the bomb wires. They're taut and strong. I yank them hard. Nothing doing. If only I had a knife, like the one Reef used in the Morass. That's too bad – I don't, and these bombs have to come off *now*. I pour all my anger into my hands. Wires cut, blood wells out, but they . . . almost . . . nearly . . . yes – *snap*! A wire-end whips past my head, cutting the fabric of my flying cap. One by one the bomb cylinders fall.

'Pull up!' I call. 'We need height!'

'Get in the cockpit!'

'More height!'

I hang on tight, drinking in the back flow from the propellers, then hoist myself into the pilot's seat once more. Our bombs land and burst and the search lamp goes dark for ever. How's *that* for poetics, Steen Verdessica!

We get away. We live. For now.

Marina Furey comes squelching across the sodden bioground of the airstrip, holding a lo-glo lamp that casts a weak circle of light around her. Her uniform is sodden and her hair is plastered to her scalp. An allergy to spring spores has made her eyes sore and her nose turn red.

'Power down!' she shouts hoarsely. 'That's enough for one night.'

The ground crew come slogging over to see what's going on. I can't bear watching while they're told the news. Henke and Rill – dead. I can't believe that's all there is to it. One mistake and you're gone for ever.

'With all due respect . . .' says Lida.

'Yes, keep it respectful,' Furey warns.

'Sorry, but . . . what are we supposed to do? Let the Crux get away with it? That was *Henke and Rill* who went down. We can't just grab towels, dry off and go back to bed for the day as if nothing's happened! We could manage several more sorties – really pummel the murderers to pieces.'

Furey shakes her head, scattering drops of water. 'Aura says that's it for the night.'

'Aura's wrong.'

I slap my hand over my mouth as soon as the words come out. Oh god-who-doesn't-exist, how could I even *think* such a thing, let alone say it out loud, in front of Marina Furey of all people?

Quickly Zoya jumps to my defence. 'She means, Aura

113

doesn't have a complete picture, since none of us could connect at the time. Right, Pip?'

I'm wanting to die and thinking, *I am a weed sprouting, I will get yanked out* . . .

'S-something like that.'

Furey folds her arms and glares at me. That's enough to wilt a grown man, let alone this weed.

'If you've got something meaningful to say, Rain Aranoza, I'm willing to hear it.'

I hear Papi's words in my mind – *Don't look at the lights* – and I remember the silent swoop of corvils in the forest.

'I think . . . and we can check with Aura, obviously . . . but I think I know how we can surprise them again . . .'

It's not a genius plan, just a cheeky one. We set off with only two Storms in the next sortie. If my idea doesn't work, then . . . then Papi can turn up to my funeral saying, '*Told you she couldn't tell ground from sky*' and Mama can cry for the rest of her life, saying, '*She wasn't good enough.*'

Lida's face is grim as she gets back into her Storm.

'We'll call this plane *Revenge* from now on,' she says.

In the orange circle of an outdoor light I see Mossie checking bomb wires before catching a quick kiss from Petra, hopefully not the last one ever.

'What'll we call our plane?' asks Zoya. 'Shall I ask everybody?'

Call it *Anger*, I think in secret. 'Call it whatever you like,' I answer aloud.

Lida insists on flying as head of our mini formation. Just as before, the first Storm has the element of surprise. Petra releases a lovely sprinkling of bombs that land on a herd of traptions gathered in Sorrowdale's suburbs. Anti-aircraft fire flares up, then silence. They're listening for the next bomber. They won't hear me and Zoya. Some way from Sorrowdale I cut the Storm's engines, with the only sound being the sweep of wind on our wings.

Lower, lower, lower we glide, like a corvil scouting for meat. The white cross of a Crux flag flutters from an old god-house tower as we pass over. I could almost leap from the plane and land on a rooftop. There are trees in the town, real ones, that shouldn't be growing so far from the forest. Some are bomb-splintered stumps, others are tall, black silhouettes. We slice their leaves and make the branches shiver. When our latest batch of bombs fall I've barely time to flood the engine with fuel and climb to safety.

Do I hear Crux cursing the smoke-choked sky as they run from the flames?

'Witches!' they spit at us as we rise. 'Night witches!'

We fly, we glide, we bomb, until Umbra slumps below the horizon, stained with plumes of black ash. My last view of Sorrowdale is of a few Crux survivors retreating over roads and fields. The town is ours again – what's left of it.

Back at Loren I land our Storm but don't let the propeller blades swing still. Now it's light the real bombers are being towed from hangars to fly missions away from the Morass. I'd like to see them do what we've done! I sense Zoya shivering in the seat behind me, from cold or shock or both. Stiff-legged and pale-faced, the rest of the squadron are gathering near the hangar. Reef stands tall amongst them, eyes only for me.

I can't speak to him yet. There's something needs to be done.

'Zoya?'

'Pip?'

'You OK?'

She pauses. 'I think so. That was scary.'

'I know, only . . . there's one more sortie we have to fly.'

'There is? Did you get ac-reqs from Aura already?'

I shake my head. 'We'll need a spade.'

4
SORROWDALE

Zoya stares at me. 'Shouldn't we wait for orders?'

I shrug. 'No keypads in a Storm . . . we can't connect.'

'We could ask Furey.'

'Night's over. Furey won't let us leave now.'

Her mouth drops open. '*Go without permission?*'

'For Henke. For Rill. We can't just leave them there.'

'But . . .'

'If no one's told us *not* to go, it hasn't been forbidden. You don't have to come. Stay here with everyone else.'

Zoya scowls. 'You're my cousin – you're *family*. I won't let you go alone. My father said . . . your papi said to keep an eye on you.'

'If we're going, we go now . . .' Before habits of logic, reason and normal obedience kick in.

I suppose because Storms have been buzzing around all night, no one really registers our engine noise until we're already bumping along the runway and our wheels are off the ground. What can they do? Shout at us? Yes – violently. Shoot at us? No – thankfully.

I force the Storm up into the brightening sky and back

117

towards Sorrowdale. It's outrageous, I know. So is dying young, when you should be playing music, or studying for school, or hanging out with friends, or just being *alive*.

I don't really need Zoya to navigate, not with this nagging, dragging need pulling me back to the bomb-zone, but I'm hugely relieved she's with me, even if she blisters my ears with worries – *Have I gone completely disconnected . . . Do I realise how much trouble we'll be in when we get back . . .*

The Storm cuts through streaks of black smoke to circle the town. It looks like the Crux aren't the only invaders – forest plants are rampant in the ruins. Sorrowdale used to be civilised. Now rambling bushes of thorn-vines curl round ugly mounds of bomb-mangled traptions, and trees send out spores with every sway of their branches. It's oddly wonderful to see a once winter-bound forest spread out for a spring revival, even if it's not at all normal for trees and plants to grow in towns.

I pick a field and we land with no more than the usual jolts. The early spring biofood crops have been slashed then burned by Crux soldiers. I taxi over the stubble to where new woods will shade the plane a little. The propeller blades slowly stop.

Silence. I close my eyes and smell the air – ashes, explosives, death and defeat. And something else.

Expectations.

'There's no one left,' I say. No one alive, at any rate.

A breeze rustles the broken crop stalks. I've a crazy urge

to bury my hands in the soil to feel if new life is sprouting from forest spores. When I look down at my palms I see faint red marks from where the bomb wires cut my skin to ribbons last night. The gashes are almost completely healed, despite the fact I never thought to spray medicine on them. Has Zoya noticed? She's just looking shocked we're even here.

Any other day, any other place, the morning light might seem cheerful. Now the sun is a great eye watching us as step by step we cross the burned field to town. Where are the foodlanders who once tended these crops? Where are the trucks that once hummed down these streets? That school there, where are the children and their screens? Who last shut that yard gate, tended that withering bioweave, played with that deflated ball?

Zoya whispers, 'They were all evacuated, weren't they? Our people, I mean – they did get out of town before Crux came?'

'They all got away safely,' I whisper back as Aura isn't here to answer, and who knows – it might be true.

We walk on, round rubble, bomb craters and Crux corpses, one careful footstep at a time. I wish Sorrowdale didn't have this faint feeling of *familiar* about it.

Zoya's got her scarf pulled up over her face against the stink of death and burnings.

'Our bombs did all this?' she asks in a hoarse voice. 'You couldn't tell from up in the air. If I was a scientist I'd figure out a weapon that could just pick off the enemy all nice and neat without this . . . this mess. My father's always saying it would be a much more logical way to win a war. It's what all his research is about. Everybody would be so much better off, don't you agree?'

She peers at me like a Scrutiner.

'Sure. These corpses are disgusting.'

I suppose if I were Steen right now I'd be scanning mottled faces, looking for people I knew.

I ask, 'Do you reckon Steen Verdessica has any family or friends in the war?'

'Who cares?' replies Zoya. 'If he does they'll all be dead soon, or prisoners like him.'

'I wonder if they know he's alive?'

'What's it matter? He'll be executed as soon as he's stopped being useful for the squadron, if he even is any more. I don't know why they let him hang around. Anyway, why are we even discussing him? Shouldn't we be looking for something to dig with?'

That's true. We've got friends of our own to seek out. First I ask, oh-so-casually, 'So what's that you said about my family living in Sorrowdale once?'

'It's true. I heard my father talking about it with some Scrutiner man who came round, a while back. It was just after the Eclipse. You were still a baby.'

'I never knew. Where . . . where do you think we lived?'

Zoya stands on a door in the middle of a street, hands on her hips. 'Take your pick – they're all ruined now.'

The only sign of life is the sudden swoop of a solitary

corvil. It settles on the roof of a half-ruined house at the far end of the street and begins preening.

Black feathers drift through my mind. I shake them away. They won't be shifted.

We walk on, wafted by eddies of spring spores. Hyper-aware, I can count each one, well into the tens of thousands. Most will fall and die. Some will root and thrive; some will root and be weeded. That's the way it goes. We survived the night; Rill and Henke didn't. Life is life.

Rain . . .

My name comes blowing over the burned fields. I twist round, scaring a whole flock of corvils now lined up on the guttering of the end house. Who's there? Who's calling me? It's an ancient voice – the tremor of an old woman.

Rain . . .

I seem to hear footsteps running along Sorrowdale's streets. Prayers from a god-house. Mama's voice reading the bedtime screen – *Look, Rain, look at the wicked wolves waiting in the forest . . . Always be a good girl, Rain.*

Reaching the end house I imagine Mama's here, in the open doorway, with me wrapped tightly in her arms – *Welcome back, my baby, my precious sweeting. I promise I'll never lose you again.* She takes me into the kitchen where I smell a fresh batch of spring cakes, hot from the oven. On the tree branches in the yard yellow paper suns are smiling and turning on their strings.

There, that's where Papi sat, looking at me with a mixture of joy and confusion once I'd been rescued. *Rescued from what?* There, that's where I was set once, in a beautiful bioweave cradle with a blanket that smelled of some other baby. *Who?* Over there, that's the window where Mama watched me as I played in the yard at the back of the house . . . making sure that the forest didn't come to steal her child again.

All illusions, of course.

There's a shed at the end of the yard. I yank the door open and yelp as a rustle of furry rablets run for darker corners. I spot a spade – made for gardens, not graves.

'Pip?'

I almost leap out of my skin. 'Zoya! You nearly gave me a heart attack.'

'You went off without me and didn't answer when I called.'

She's standing outside what would have been a kitchen, looking through the gap where a yard door would have been. Crux soldiers have obviously scoured the place for food or fine things. Cupboard doors swing open on to emptiness. A hateful white god-cross has been slashed on one wall, like an obscene kiss.

'Sorry, I was . . . looking for a spade. I got one.'

Zoya scuffs her boots in the mess on the floor. 'This place is dead. Come on. Let's get this over and done with.'

We find the wrecked Storm soon enough. Find Henke and Rill. Find the courage to pull them from the burned wood. Zoya's sick until she's got nothing left to heave up.

'Where shall we bury them?' she hiccups.

'The old god-house is close. There'll be a body-field next to it.'

I know where the god-house is without even looking – how abnormal is that? I can see, without needing eyes, the street leading to the burial plot, except in my memory the body-field isn't edged with a brittle lattice of modern bioweave. In my memory, bulky bushes of some nasty plant guard the bodies of the dead. The word *feybane* sneaks into my mind.

Now these bushes have been uprooted, but narrow wires of red metal still criss-cross the cemetery, dividing rows of grave markers.

Zoya kicks some of the metal. 'I read about these, or Rill told me, or someone did. They're more of that bane-metal stuff. Meant to keep witches away.'

'No such thing . . .'

' . . . as witches. *I know*.'

I start digging, careful not to trip over the wires. The sun is unfairly hot for this early in spring. Heat, effort and emotion make me feel sick inside and out.

The nearby god-house casts shade, but not on us. I'm surprised it's still standing. Most were pulled down once people learned from Aura how to think properly. They were converted into food stores or schools. Standing here now, looking at the garlands of paper prayers Crux have pasted round the door, I think I remember the day the witch-warning bells came clanging, ringing, falling down, leaving dents on the cold, stone floors. Trucks took them away because there were no such things as witches, so no need to warn against them.

Are these real memories or is it the sun? The trauma? Should I have kept the bane-metal charm Papi wanted me to have for protection? What if there really are witches? What if they're waiting for me, just on the edge of common sense and science?

Rain . . .

Spores make me sneeze – a welcome distraction. Keep busy, that's the best answer. Dig.

Our hearts are heavy as we hack into the wet ground to make a final resting place for Henke and Rill. I hardly knew them, apart from the last, intense days of training together. We never messaged. I never took Henke up on his offer to learn some balika tunes. Never asked Rill what sort of stuff she liked connecting to. Now he won't play music ever again and she won't churn out bad jokes. We may have given them the respect of a burial but it seems horrible just to leave them in the ground, alone and unknown.

'Can't we put something with them? Some goodbye present?'

Zoya frowns. 'Sounds a bit Old Nation. What would Aura say?'

'Aura doesn't work here any more.'

I notice a tangle of thorn-vine bushes crawling up one side of the god-house. The warmth of the sun has made their buds burst open into flame-coloured flowers, and there, alone in a bed of twigs, is a speck of glossy black – a baby bird with a miniature beak and fluffy feathers sprouting. I hear a whirr of wings and the grip of talons on branches. Too late I remember what Reef said about corvils killing to protect their kin, but the birds higher up on the vines don't attack. They're watching me, seeing what I do next.

I pick four of the thorn-vine flowers, one for each eye socket. I can't explain why. Then we say *goodbye-and-go-well* to the brother and sister. *Goodbye and go where?* I wonder. Steen would say something like, *The dead are gathered to the lap of the Light Bringer.* Aura would send intricate explanations of how the body is broken down through decomposition and its molecules recycled into the surrounding ecosystem.

I'm sure Henke would've liked music, but my voice is dry. It will not sing, despite the tune I've got going through my head with snatches of lyrics –

Light the white light, burn the red flame;
Blows the wild wind, snuffs all out again . . .

Who used to sing that dismal song to me?

Rain . . .

Zoya steps over the bane-metal and starts heading towards the fields. 'We should go. The Crux could come back . . .'

I'm right behind her when down from the sky comes a flurry of feathers and claws, straight at me. I cover my face.

Feather-tips brush past and there, when I look down, is the baby corvil, set at my feet. It peeps at me. I step over it. Two corvils swoop again, driving me back.

Zoya takes off her cap and starts flapping it at them. She looks so funny I can't help laughing. The whole joke goes on until I scoop the baby bird into my cupped palms. Then the corvils fly away.

'You're not keeping that,' Zoya says.

I run the tip of my forefinger over the bird's shining head. It peeps again. 'Life is life,' I say.

'Can I stroke it?' she asks. 'Ow! It stabbed me with its mouth!'

'It's called a beak, I think.'

She glares. 'Beak, then. I'm bleeding!'

'It's only a little cut. It'll be fine.'

'Since when did you train as a medic? Right about the time you started stealing planes and kidnapping me?'

I don't know what to say apart from a general *sorry* that's meant to cover a whole ton of disgraces. While Zoya complains – *Sorry isn't good enough . . . Don't ever pull a stunt like that again . . . I can't believe you just brought me here we could be in so much danger and I promised your papi I'd look after you* – I pluck some thorn-vine leaves and make a bed for the baby bird in my jacket pocket.

Not long after we take off the sun dims, clouds gather and rain starts again. I realise I've left the spade. Too bad. It would be handy for digging us out of the trouble we'll be in once we get back at base.

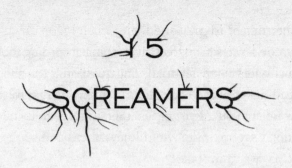

5
SCREAMERS

You only realise how comforting a crowd is when it squeezes you out.

From the moment our Storm lands back at Loren there's only Roke and Reef waiting. An official un-Welcome Committee.

I shrivel up inside to see the cold expression on Reef's face.

'What were you *thinking*?' he demands to know, while Roke is busy questioning Zoya. 'You stole a plane!'

'I brought it back.'

'You took off without orders.'

'To find Henke and Rill!'

'They were already dead.'

'We had to bury them.'

'And who'd bury *you* when you got shot down, flying into the war zone in broad daylight?'

'You don't have to shout at me!'

'I'm not shouting!' he shouts, then he calms a bit, rubbing his eyes as if they're sore. 'You should've connected for ac-reqs from Aura. You wouldn't have been permitted to go.'

'Do we always have to do everything according to Aura?'

Reef stares at me, stunned. The question is too abnormal to need an answer. 'Look, Rain, I didn't . . . *people* didn't know where you'd gone or whether you'd even come back. No, don't say anything else. I knew it was a mistake . . .'

'What was a mistake?'

'This . . . Everything . . . Us . . .'

He steps away and closes his eyes. The black *Eyes in the Dark* tattoos show on his lids.

Zoya is in tears once the Scrutiny is done and I feel like a monster because it's all my fault. We're given our keypads back and told to go and get breakfast.

'You're grounded until further notice,' says Roke with a certain amount of unsmiling satisfaction.

'We shouldn't have gone,' moans Zoya. 'I shouldn't've let you talk me into it. What's everyone going to say? Marina Furey must think we're awful. I want to *die*. They won't tell my father, will they? He'll kill me if I mess up here.'

For once she lets me go into the canteen first. I take a deep breath – nearly retching on the stink of the herbs Haze still insists on cooking with – and then, with my hands deep in my pockets and my gaze to the ground, I head over to our usual squadron table.

People – strangers – start to point, murmur and message. The Storm squadron go silent when they see us. What's worse is the sight of the breakfast table still set with places for Henke and Rill, as if they'll just come bustling in any moment to sit down to eat.

I link arms with Zoya, sensing she's about to turn and run. She stuck with me in the Storm, I'll stick with her now. This has got to be faced.

One by one the Storm crew scrape back their chairs and stand. I almost faint. Don't tell me *they're* going to cut and walk out on us!

At first no one speaks, then Mossie, red-eyed from crying, nods towards a seat. Petra pushes a plate of bread closer. Dee lines up two mugs. Yeldon pours tea.

Zoya gives a little sob. 'You mean we can join you?'

'Are you crazy?' says Mossie.

'Probably,' mutters Dee to no one but herself. 'They'd have to be to do what they did.'

'Are you *crazy*?' Mossie repeats. '*Of course* you can join us. You're both one of us. *One of Many*.'

'*One of Many*,' they all echo.

'What you did,' says Lida in a pretend-not-to-be-tearful voice, 'it was brave, as well as demented and disobedient.'

'Yeah,' says Ang. 'And I wouldn't worry about getting Scrutiny for it. I got detention my first week in school. Twice.'

A group of men comes to loom over us, each with an emblem of the People's Number Nine Bomber Squadron on their uniform.

One says, 'Hey, we've heard about you lot, buzzing around playing war games when the rest of us are trying to sleep. They say the Crux are calling you *night witches*.' He prods my shoulder and says, 'Aren't you the kiddie who stole one of those wooden jokes this morning?'

The Storm squadron closes ranks.

'No,' says Lida firmly, arms crossed. 'She's one of the kids who kicked the Crux out of Sorrowdale because *your* planes weren't up to the job.'

Grounded.

It's like a prison sentence. Before I ever flew it didn't bother me to keep both feet firmly on the ground, with maybe just my head in the clouds during a really boring class at school. Now I'm itchy, twitchy *aching* to be back in the air again. What use are we to the war if they don't let us fight? All day we have to wait in the crew-room, watching Victory reports that can't hide the fact the Crux are flattening resistance.

'They shouldn't be winning!' says Fenlon, bursting in on us one day. 'We absolutely outgun and out-tech them *and* they're all just homicidal religious junkies. I'd feel sorry for them coming up against our armed forces if it wasn't for the fact that they keep churning out more troops and traptions.'

'Isn't it our superior technology that's the problem?' I ask tentatively. 'They're using machines that aren't affected by the Morass. If we had more Storms and some traptions of our own . . .'

'Ha! Try telling that to the scientists! We've got the go-

130

ahead for more Storms at least, but up in Corona City they're waiting to develop some sort of super-weapon that's going to turn the tide of war.'

'Worse than Slick?'

'Makes Slick look nice enough to pour on your porridge, I heard. In the meanwhile, keep your kit bags ready packed, kids. It's only a matter of time before Loren is in range of Crux missiles.'

He's right.

'It's not a retreat,' everyone says as Loren Airbase is dismantled and boxed up. *Not a retreat*, as trucks are loaded floor to ceiling. *Not a retreat*, as Storms take off in search of a safer home for the night-bomber squadron. The official term from Aura is Strategic Withdrawal.

Otherwise known as *running away*.

Still grounded, Zoya and I have to travel by road, like techies. Zoya goes on ahead in a truck with more ground crew and Roke as guard. I'm to be watched by Reef.

'See you there!' Mossie waved as they set off. She tossed me a packet of cookies, somehow knowing I wouldn't want the pack-up Haze made for everyone.

I crumble one cookie now and feed the baby bird in my pocket. I checked Aura and discovered you call a baby bird a fledgling. I'm going to name mine Eye Bright, because that's what its eyes are like – alert and beady and full of life. I feel its feathers rustle against my hand. Aura says there's a word from Old Nation days for animals you keep and look after – *pets*. Eye Bright is my pet bird.

A life saved when others have been lost.

I was going to call it Lucky, but that would be stupid, because clearly that word would never stick with me. I'm unlucky, unhappy and under observation, here in the back of a convoy of trucks crammed with canisters labelled *Slick*. I've got Steen Verdessica on the seat next to me and Reef Starzak on guard opposite. Reef is sitting with his feet up so there's more room for my legs but Steen isn't as considerate. Our legs are so close I can feel the heat of his thigh even through the fabric of my trousers.

Worse than that, wedged between canisters just behind the driver is one person I've been hoping to avoid. The canteen cook, Haze. The girl they say has got my face.

How could anyone confuse *me* with her? Haze is big and stocky, like most foodlanders – bulked up on a stodgy diet and lots of muscle-based work. Her hair's cropped round her ears and high across her forehead. She's lumbered by a full-length skirt that divides and is bound round the ankles by embroidered bands, then at the waist with a decorated belt. Her sleeves are rolled up to show strong arms; her sun-browned skin is laced with fine scars.

Haze glowers at me, Steen looks under his lashes at me, Reef observes everyone and I look at the floor.

Where are we going? Nowhere fast, thanks to the mud.

Spring thaw is the worst possible time to be travelling, especially in foodlands, where biograss struggles to hold the ground together once the rain-storms have flooded down. Aura reports worse snow-melt than usual this year.

Questions are churning in my mind, like wheels in wet mud. I'm getting nowhere, answers-wise. I want to know why no one told me we used to live in Sorrowdale. Why's this Lim girl, Haze, set on leaving witch-thing charms for my protection? What's Steen's interest in sticking with the squadron – something he wants so much he's rumoured to be feeding Aura information about the Crux Air Force to keep himself out of prison?

As for Reef, I'm trying not to think about him at all, just in case Scrutiners can read your mind. Whatever tentative connection we had, I've utterly wrecked it. Like he said, *us* was a mistake.

The truck skids through yet another bad patch, flinging me sideways on to Steen, who grins as I flinch.

Reef says, 'The roads get better after the bridge.'

Which bridge? I try and remember what I can about the route we've taken so far from Loren. We're heading south-east, so that means towards Sea-Ways, which means the bridge will be over the river that runs through the city to the ocean – River Seaward.

A sudden wave of nausea hits me and I have to put my head down to my knees.

'Rain? Are you OK?' I hear Reef but can't answer. What's wrong with me? The Slick stinks, but I thought I was used to that. This is worse – a definite *bad feeling* for no logical reason.

'Travel-sick, bless,' says Steen sarcastically. 'And here I was assuming roads in Rodina would be so civilised – it claiming to be such a sophisticated Nation.'

'Shut up,' says Reef – not eloquent, but to the point.

'She doesn't want to cross the river,' says Haze abruptly. Her voice is slow and thick, as if she's not used to talking much. No one pays any attention to her, thank god . . . thank *whatever*.

With a great grinding of gears we come to a stop.

'Mud!' Reef pushes open the carry-go door and leaps down. 'Crux – come out here and help.'

Steen's eyebrows shoot up. 'And be lynched by every Crux-hater within a ten-klick radius? No thank you!'

'I'll help,' says Haze, bundling up her fat skirts. 'It's all I'm good for, after all. Do this, fetch that, cook this, clean that. Not like little softie city girls with mothers and fathers to work for them . . .'

Reef nods and starts to take off his pristine, white Scrutiner tunic. I try not to stare at the shape of his muscles.

'I can help too . . .'

He raises an eyebrow and looks at me, shaking his head. 'Stay in the truck.'

Do I really look so pathetic – such a pipsqueak – next to Haze? I twist round and peer through the mud-spattered windows. The roadside is thick with refugees – hundreds, perhaps even thousands of silent walkers slogging through the mud. Some are dragging carts loaded with boxes, some balance bulging suitcases on their heads, some have little children straddling their shoulders. On they trudge, round our convoy, not even bothering to stop and ask for a lift.

Squinting forward I can see the bright paint of a school bus just ahead of us. I also spot the great arch of the upcoming bridge and the shapes of more military vehicles from Loren crossing over.

How did it happen, that one day there was peace, the next day war, and now this?

I flick a quick look at Steen. A Crux. Cause of all this misery in motion. He won't meet my eyes.

Our engine whines with fresh effort until the truck is finally sucked free of the mud and we hear a faint cheer from outside. Then comes a stranger noise, quiet at first then louder and louder until it seems the sky must be shrieking in agony and we have to cover our ears.

Steen bangs into me, shoving me down to the floor. 'Screamers!' he shouts. 'Take cover!'

Screamers!

The name doesn't do the sound justice. I feel as if my ears are being shredded by poisonous blades; as if hot wires are slicing my brain. We know from Victory reports that Screamers are crude Crux dive-bombers, fitted with filters on their wings that literally screech as the planes hurtle down, unbelievably fast, to fire. How many are there coming our way? Two? More? An explosion rocks the truck. The door flies open.

'Get out, get out!' Reef shouts, dragging me from under Steen by my jacket sleeve and pulling me into the sludge of a roadside ditch, where Haze is already hiding. A second Screamer cuts the cold air and grey bombs fall between the rain of bullets. Reddened mud sprays out.

Refugees cower alongside us, arms wrapped round their children or just over their heads. I hear babies squalling . . . and the scary sound of *praying*. Reef flings his arm around my back and covers me with his body. I wish I could melt into him and feel all wrapped up for ever.

Nearby a large woman trembles and mutters, 'We should never have pulled the bells down in the god-houses, after the last Long Night. I said no good would come of it, and no good's come, see? Bells were our protection – look what happens without them!'

Haze is utterly eye-wide with fear. She stutters, 'It's the witch in the woods, come for me. First she sent wolves, now these!'

'Quiet!' shouts Reef, and because he's a Scrutiner everyone obeys.

I want to tell Haze, *There's no such thing as witches*, but I can't speak. I'm staring at a puddle of dirty, brown water in the bottom of the ditch. It vibrates every time a bomb falls. In between the ripples I snatch sight of a vision – a crippled bridge and a drowned girl.

The corpse I see is me.

6
RIVER RUNNING

Reef connects as soon as he can wipe the mud from his keypad. For a moment he doesn't speak.

'What do we do? Where do we go? Will they come back?' babbles the big woman next to me.

Reef checks his updates again and slowly stands. I'm chilled when his body warmth leaves mine. He jumps up on to the side of an overturned truck and shouts for attention.

'Listen to me, everyone! Our priority is to get any military vehicles that can still be driven over to the far bank of the river. Push them across the bridge if you have to. Get those wrecks out of the way! Carry cans of Slick by hand if you can! You all heard me – *move*!'

Haze hauls herself out of the ditch, trailing revolting green weeds that shouldn't even be growing this far from the forest. 'That's right, get to the river,' she echoes Reef. 'River running, witches retching . . .'

She makes me think of that thing Pedla Rue said, about how, if you need to get away from a witch, you must ring your bells and run to the river. But it's the Crux who are coming, not monsters from the Morass.

I scramble after Reef. 'It'll only slow people down, pushing trucks and lugging Slick. Shouldn't they just run . . . ?'

'Empty that school bus and push it into the ditch if it won't start!' Reef shouts into the crowd.

'Out, out, out!' calls a teacher from the bus, and tiny evacuees come popping out of the bus and falling in the mud.

'Give us a hand back here!' yells a grey-haired woman from the back of the bus. 'All push together!'

'Can someone help me with the children?' the teacher asks.

I head for the evacuees. 'Clear the road or carry a canister, Rain Aranoza,' Reef commands.

'But . . .'

'Aura's orders!'

'But those Screamers could be back any moment, and I'm sure I can hear traptions nearby . . .'

'Heave!' grunt the people pushing the bus.

The big woman stumbles into the road. 'Did you say traptions? Are there traptions coming?'

'Keep together! Everyone hold hands and follow me,' the teacher calls to the kids.

'Push!' rasps the woman behind the bus.

'Save the Slick first!' Reef shouts to the teacher.

I know you shouldn't question a Scrutiner's orders or tug on his tunic to get his attention, but I'm utterly, devastatingly certain something terrible is about to happen, so I do anyway, insisting, 'We've got to get everyone across the river fast!'

Reef shakes his head. He won't look at me. 'I told you – Aura's orders. The Slick must be saved.'

'Before children?'

'You heard what I said, the same as everyone else!' He jumps down from the upturned truck, sets his shoulder to the bus and starts to push. There's no way they'll shift it. I muscle into a spot myself.

'Heave!' we all chant together. 'One, two, three, *heave*!'

Strength flows out of me. The bus starts to shift. It topples at the ditch edge . . . then slides down into the water with an obscene kiss-smack noise. Reef grabs the grey-haired woman to stop her skidding down after it. It's the first time I've seen him truly dirty and dishevelled. He's been hit by shrapnel. A thin line of blood trickles down his forehead and stains the inked tattoo on one eyelid.

Next he directs people to a cascade of Slick canisters fallen from a truck, telling them to drag or roll them to the bridge. 'You too!' he shouts at the teacher, who is desperately trying to look calm so the kids – some of them so tiny they're knee-deep in mud – don't get even more scared than they are already.

'Stay together. Keep away from the traffic,' he tells them. 'Get to the bridge if you can. I'll be back for you soon. I've just got to help move those cans.'

The children stand there, petrified.

I drop the can of Slick I'm carrying and wade towards them.

'Rain!' Reef comes right behind me and grabs my arm to stop me. 'I don't like it any more than you do, Rain, but Aura knows best how to win this war . . .'

I shake him off. 'Does Aura know how it feels to have a Screamer firing at you? To get crushed under traption tracks? To get blown to pieces like, like . . .' I wave my hands at the nasty lumps of people-shapes left in the mud by Screamer attacks. 'Like *them*?'

'I can't ignore Aura,' he says quietly.

'Can't, or *won't*?'

Time slows. There are just the two of us balancing in the mud.

Reef takes a deep breath. He stares at the Slick. At the kids. At me. 'Rain, you've been deafened by the Screamer noise.'

'No, I—'

'And your keypad is too wet to connect.'

'No, it's fine . . . Oh. You mean, you think I'm a bit shell-shocked? Not quite responsible for my actions? And you're too busy salvaging Slick to stop me disobeying orders?'

He nearly smiles. 'You're confused and panicky.'

'Right.'

He bends down to my ear and murmurs, 'But still very lovely.'

Then he's straight and tall again, directing operations on

the road. A subtle hand gesture from him tells me – *Go
– go!*

I remember images of River Seaward from the stream-
screen – a placid stretch of calm, covered in canoes and
rowboats. Now, after all the rain and snow-melt, Seaward
is in full spring flood, a surging torrent of brown waves
tossing tree trunks around like toothpicks.

I herd evacuees this far. Now all I have to do is get them
single-file across the bridge without anyone being squashed
by rumbling trucks or dutiful citizens lugging canisters of
Slick. On the far side of the bridge a group of soldiers has
arrived, and they're already setting up anti-aircraft guns.
Better still, I hear the unmistakable sound of People's
Number Forty-eight Fighter planes coming to our rescue,
harrying the Screamers, hurtling in for the kill. Hurrah for
Rodina! I hustle the evacuees forward, *quick, quick, quick.*

'Don't be afraid!' I shout at the running children. Me,
I'm terrified. There's no way I'm leaving land. I don't care if
traptions come gobbling mud, or witches even, whooshing
through the clouds on black-feathered wings. Let them
come! I won't cross that seething water!

On the far side of the bridge I spy Haze gathering up
children who've made it over safely. She pauses to stare at
me – a gaze of pure malevolence. Then she points and
laughs. 'You can't cross!' she mouths.

Can't. Won't. As the sky-battle boils above, I cower
below. I think I hear Reef's voice through the chaos.

'Run, Rain! Get to safety!'

What about him?

'Get on the bridge!'

His words explode as more bombs tumble down. The bridge is hit. Girders are blown apart, stick-figures fly high and fall, and the whole structure tips sideways with resentful groans.

Not everybody falls.

Halfway along the tangle of toppled girders is a little girl in school uniform, the last of the evacuees. She's clinging to a railing and screaming screaming screaming. She won't be able to hold on for long.

What can I do? What good would Aura be if I bothered to connect? There'd just be a message, something like *status update: situation precarious, please wait for action-requirements, please wait, please wait, please wait*

If not Aura, what about praying? I close my eyes and make something up.

Oh god-that-doesn't-exist, I need to get over this river . . .

Where are the saynts with wings, swooping down to carry me to safety? Where are the bolts of god-light and bell chimes of jubilation? All I get is a sudden swirl of black birds flying in a noisy corkscrew overhead.

There's just me, and what I need to do.

'Hold tight,' I croak to the girl. 'I'm coming!'

I step on to a twisted girder. It's no good. Even when I close my eyes I can still hear the wild water of River Seaward. There's an awful lurch as the bridge wreckage drops lower, groans, shudders . . . and holds. How is it that climbing on to the wing of the Storm was nothing to me, but this bridge-crossing is agony?

'Hold tight,' I say again, more to myself than to anyone else. Oh god, the Screamers are returning – the *noise* . . . ! The girl's howls are drowned by their far more monstrous wail.

I don't know how I reach her but I do, just as the bridge is peppered with bullets. I should be able to stay balanced and get us both across. I should . . . but I can't. Panicking, the girl fights me like she's a whirlwind, or like I'm a wolf. My head spins, my feet slip, and the best I can do is hold on to her as she pulls us both off the bridge and down into the flood.

We plunge.

It's like hitting a broken wall; being a salad tossed by a tornado; having a bath in angry ice. Which way up? I want to breathe. Can't breathe. Want to swim. Can't swim. Want to hold on to the girl . . . can't hold her. Got her coat, her collar . . . got nothing but her coat. She's spinning away under the waves. I stretch and kick and stretch again till I've got it – her hand, her cold, bare hand. Images tumble round my head like the river water – visions of an old, old woman lying in bed, dressed in tubes and a hospital robe.

The girl doesn't die today!

That gives me the strength to surge up and, quick, breathe – suck all the sky in at once. I fight the water, fight the water, fight the water . . . lose the fight, get dragged down, down deeper, down darker, a strange turmoil. Ears are screeching, heart is breaking, hand-hold weakening, then . . . PAIN – as if my hair is being torn out! Let go of me, let go of me, let go of me . . .

'Let go!' I cough, turning to sick up Seaward water on to the riverbank.

Steen Verdessica is straddling me, sodden from scalp to socks. 'I'm giving you the kiss of life,' he says, wiping the back of his hand over his mouth. 'I'm not sure you've properly recovered yet . . .'

'Get off me!'

I shove him away and grope around in cold mud for the still little body at my side. 'Is she . . . ?'

'Alive, don't worry, thanks to you. And you're alive, thanks to me.'

I gather the girl up and keep her close for warmth. She's breathing at least.

'You dragged me out by my hair!'

'Good job it's long then,' Steen replies, tweaking one of my wet braids.

I notice he's shivering and his wrists are bubbling red.

'What happened to your handcuffs?'

'Burned off, thanks to a truck fire. Bioweave stinks when on fire. I thought it best to be mobile, given the situation on the road. Traptions aren't subtle machines. I didn't rate my chances of convincing them I'm on their side.'

'What about Reef?'

144

Steen pulls away from me. 'I don't care about him. It's you I was worried about.'

'You . . . *meant* to jump in and save me? Why would you do that? We're the enemy to you!'

He looks at me with pity in his eyes. 'Crux worship light, not death, Rain. Just because I fight in a war doesn't mean I glory in the death-toll. And the girl . . . she's just a kid.'

I wish I had something scathing to say about that but I don't because I'm vomiting again, with Steen holding long hair out of my face.

'As for you,' he says wryly, 'isn't it obvious I would die for you?'

THE BATH-HOUSE

Soldiers come. There are medics and Scrutiners. Hospital tents and heat lamps. Lights to keep a new night at bay. Eventually Zoya finds me and bundles me in a hug, along with the billowing silver therma-wrap I'm wearing to fend off hypothermia.

'Pip, you lunatic, I thought I'd lost you! Our trucks got over long before the bombs, so we're all fine. Are you going to eat that food bar, because if not . . . ? Thanks. So. Are you OK now? You're shivering.'

Damn right I'm shivering. My head is full of visions of death for each of the three medics who've laid hands on me since Steen dragged me to safety. I saw one medic get shot by friendly fire; one wastes away from an old-age disease. The third one, a female, I sense is growing a baby, which will live far longer than its mother.

Enough, enough! I don't want to know these futures! I don't want this torrent of life and death! I shrink away from Zoya too. My best comfort is having one hand in my pocket to stroke the quivering ball of feathers nesting there. My bird. I'm amazed Eye Bright survived the river.

When all clothes are dry and all reports completed I meet the rest of the ground crew to continue our Strategic Withdrawal east. We're jammed into yet another truck – I notice it's got a flattened wild rablet stuck dead on one tyre. Zoya squashes between Yeldon and Haze, leaving me the only free space, next to Mossie, who tells me she's so happy I'm safe, then promptly falls asleep on my shoulder.

We're dumped at a set of monumental gates at the edge of an industrial estate somewhere west of Sea-Ways. A screen that's dying for lack of power streams a sign: *People's Number 41 Biopolis*. Beyond the gates great bio-vats march across the horizon, blocking the sun. These are the towers where bio-fibres are woven, ready to be formed into whatever the Nation needs. Now they're as empty as the other factory buildings. The workers have had their own Strategic Withdrawal, to sites on the east side of the city, where it's safer.

This, then, is the home of the new Storm squadron. The planes are under camouflaged nets along one side of a long strip of patchy bioground.

'It doesn't look like an airbase,' Zoya says doubtfully. She connects for reassurance from Aura. 'Oh no! Check your updates, Rain. We've got to report to Marina Furey. I bet she's still mad at you for taking the Storm . . .'

Aura directs us to the new HQ. Before we can even knock to enter, an office door is yanked open and Marina Furey stands there looking magnificent and terrifying, with hands on hips and a half-opened packet of chokes sprouting out of a pocket. We haven't seen her since we set off for Sorrowdale that last, illegal time.

'Do you two have *any idea* how much trouble you're in?' she bawls. Her anger echoes round the Biopolis and lasts until she runs out of energy, then she rubs her eyes, gives one final lament about insubordination from one of her most promising pilots, and tells us to clear out.

'Go and get something to eat. Get a bath too. You look filthy.'

Did she mean what she just said? Did Marina Furey, the world's greatest aviator, call me *one of her most promising pilots . . . ?*

'We're free to join the squadron again?' I ask.

'Yes, Aranoza. You're more valuable to us as a pilot than a prisoner, *not* that this means any more abnormal behaviour will be tolerated in the slightest.' Her expression softens. 'You were wrong to take the Storm to Sorrowdale, but under the circumstances all charges have been dropped. It was the least I could arrange after what you did for Henke and Rill . . . and for me.'

I glance at Zoya – *What does she mean?* Zoya looks just as confused.

Furey snaps her fingers for the nearest stream-screen to power on. She scrolls through some images until one face fills the screen.

'That's the girl on the bridge,' I gasp. 'She's not wet in that picture,' I add lamely.

'No,' says Furey, with a bit of a sniff, 'she's not wet any

more. She's one of the evacuees from People's Number Twelve Young School in Sorrowdale. Her name is Tilly Furey and she's my daughter – the only family I have left in the world.'

I'm dizzy-glad that happiness came out of the horror of River Seaward. My heart would be a lot lighter if I knew that Reef was doing OK, but that's Scrutiner business and Aura won't let me access updates about him. Of course, he could message me himself. But he doesn't.

Once we're ejected from Furey's office Zoya declares she's famished. She heads off to see if there's hot food.

'Everyone will be in the canteen,' she says. 'Aren't you coming?'

'In a bit. I need to get some clean gear on. Scrub up a bit.'

'OK. Don't be long – everyone will wonder where you are.'

I want to wash any lingering traces of the river away and I get Aura to direct me to the Biopolis bath-house.

It's an Old Nation building that's been modernised with decent plumbing and hopefully hot water. Apparently there are sweat-rooms, dry-heat rooms and a cold plunge-pool. The first two sound wonderful, but when I get to the bath-house they don't seem to be open for business. The changing-rooms are empty, with just one forgotten sock in the corner.

I figure I can at least shower. I undress quickly. It's silly to keep looking over my shoulder as if someone's watching me, but I do anyway. Taking care not to disturb Eye Bright, who is a ball of sleeping fluff, I fold my clothes, grab a towel – grey and scratchy as if it's been murdered in the laundry, rather than washed – then tiptoe into a shower cubicle. The floor is cold. I say, 'Shower on.' Nothing happens. Again, sharper: 'Shower on!' The nozzle leaks water like a runny nose. Cold water. Nothing to do but pull the towel tight and nip to the next cubicle. 'Shower on.'

Not even a dribble.

Showers, sauna, steam-room – all cold. I try the sinks outside the row of toilet cubicles. Joy. One tap spits out enough water to fill a basin before choking dry. I drop my towel round my waist and manage a rough strip wash, wetting my hair and soaping that too. Maybe I should cut it off after all. It tingles from where Steen grabbed it to haul me out of the water. I still can't believe he did that. Why would he? He said he'd die for me. How idiotic.

There's a mirror over each sink. In mine I see a stark reflection. A girl who keeps surviving catastrophes.

I look normal enough. Uncomfortable, obviously. It's funny being more or less naked in the open like this. I seem healthy enough – I always have been, until the recent bouts of sickness. Maybe my body needs a bit more padding. Bigger breasts? Will I grow taller? What will I look like as I get older? What would Reef think if he could see me now? Na! That makes me shiver! I imagine his eyes on me . . . My skin tightens. Nipples go hard.

Colder water required.

Even when it's been scrubbed clean my skin still feels wrong. Stretched too tight. Itchy. Is it my face? I get one of those moments when you stare at your reflection and it's like looking at somebody else's face through a pane of glass. You wait for the other face to do or say something. You frown. It frowns. You blink. It blinks.

When I open my eyes the light behind me is flickering, *on-on-off, on-on-off*. Not the sort of power glitch you expect in Rodina.

'Is anybody there?'

Silence except for the sound of invisible water trickling. If I had fur my hackles would rise.

On-on-off goes the light.

I look in the mirror again. For a flash moment there's no reflection – I don't exist. Then there's my face again in the sink water – an oval of fear framed by black hair.

A single droplet rolls from the tap into the sink. It falls without a splash into the basin. A second drop goes the same way. A third drop is as red as blood. It blossoms in the sink and spreads, making a grim sunset on a pale horizon. Dark shapes appear against the red – a phalanx of planes in formation. Bombs scatter down, fires flare up. Then I see a shape in the flames – a burning god-house and a girl with lightning for hair . . .

Enough!

On-on-off. The light reminds me where I am. I plunge my hand into the water. The pictures swirl into soapy grey and are gone.

Off.

All the lights go off.

Utter darkness. Not a glimmer.

'Who's there?'

I don't need to ask. I can actually see in the dark, not just the light shapes and shadows of normal night-vision, but as clear as if all the lights are on. They're not – I check, and they're dead.

Haze keeps her distance. She's afraid. Of me? Of being without light, most likely. She twists the end of her embroidered belt nervously. If there were lights, what would she see looking in a mirror now – her face or mine? She shuffles in the dark, approaching me around the walls.

'I know you're there,' she whispers. 'You're hiding.'

'I'm not hiding. There's a power outage or something. The lights will be back on again in a moment.'

'You hide in the light too. You lie and steal. Thief!'

'Hey – you can't go around saying things like that!'

'Can,' she says stubbornly.

'It's you, isn't it, who's been leaving those disgusting charm things on my Storm and in my jacket? I know you probably think they're for protection or something, but I don't believe in witches, so I don't need charms against them.'

'No.' She gives a funny laugh. 'You don't need charms against them.'

'So you won't leave any more around?'

'You can't tell me what to do! I'm not your servant! I'm nobody's servant now!'

Her anger makes me flinch. 'No, I can't tell you what to do, but I could tell the Scrutiners about you and your superstitions.'

She draws back. '*Eyes in the Dark* are nasty.'

'Exactly. So keep away from me, or I'll tell them everything.'

'Everything?' Her voice takes on a cunning tone. 'All *your* secrets too?'

'I don't have any secrets . . .'

'Lies, lies, *lies*! I want it back, you know, all of it.'

'All of *what*?'

'My life. My family. Everything you stole.'

'Honestly, Haze, you're mistaking me for someone I'm not.'

'No.' She's almost crying. 'No – *you're* mistaking yourself for someone you're not!'

She runs out of the bath-house.

The lights flash on all at once – too bright! I slide my hand into the sink and pull the plug. Water gurgles down the pipes, leaving the sink spidered with a few long, black hairs.

8
CONTACT

One of the factory meeting-rooms has been converted to a dorm with bed-slats on the floor and windows shuttered blind for the blackout. I rescue my kit bag from a pile dumped in one corner and dig through it, looking for clean clothes and a comb. I'm shivering and itchy and going half crazy from Haze's words bouncing round my head.

How dare she creep up on me like that! Now I just feel wrong, wrong, *wrong*. I scratch my nails along the skin of my arm, just to remind myself I exist. Long, red welts appear. I gouge deeper, glad of the pain's distraction and fascinated by the bright blood that appears. What if I found a knife? What could I do then! The pain of the cuts would surely be better than the pain of all this abnormality.

Calm, Rain – keep calm. It's not normal to cut yourself.

Zoya's not back yet. Is she avoiding me? No, that's paranoia.

Just because you're paranoid doesn't mean they're not out to get you, is what Fenlon likes to say.

I should stop being so anxious. Zoya likes her food. She'll just be getting seconds in the new canteen block, wherever that is, eating more of the nasty stuff Haze produces, and being with the rest of the squadron, like normal. Like I should be.

I towel my hair dry. So far I've avoided the regulation military haircut by hiding my braids in my cap. I tip my head forward and begin to brush vigorously. I daren't use a mirror, too scared I'll see something – or nothing – reflected. I'm so focused I barely notice a door opening. Someone walks over.

'Hello, Rain.'

I fling back my hair. 'What . . . what are you doing here? I mean, hello. You're alive! You made me jump.'

He smiles. Reef Starzak. Right in front of me. I try and smooth the static black around my face.

'Sorry. I was just . . .'

Reef looks around the dorm. Now I'm conscious of how old and grey the bioweave is; how thin the blankets; how stark the unshaded light.

'So, this is where you'll sleep.' He sits on the bed-slats opposite. The dorm's pretty tight for space so our knees are almost touching.

'How are you then? Reinstated to fly, I hear. I'm glad you're OK. You are OK, aren't you?'

Why's everyone asking if I'm OK when I'm absolutely falling apart?

'I'm fine. Normal. What about you? You look . . . well.'
He looks gorgeous.

Reef runs a hand over his hair, embarrassed at the

compliment. This is the first time we've been properly alone together since the Morass. It's quite painful, and wonderful too.

'I'm feeling a lot better since Aura told me you'd survived your fall from the bridge. My hopes that Verdessica had drowned were premature.'

'He . . . pulled me out of the river. Saved me, really. I don't know why.'

'You don't?' Reef gives a wry smile then looks down at his boots for a moment. 'I guess you have that effect on people. You really . . . you're really . . . Na – I shouldn't, being a Scrutiner and all that, but I like you, Rain. You remind me of the forest in late winter, so still but so ready to burst into life. Thinking of you makes me wonder what the Morass is like in spring, when the snow's gone and everything is shaded green from new leaves.'

The Scrutiner is gone. He's real now. Open to me. The slice of space between us seems to get whisked away until we're so close I breathe in the air he's breathed out. I love his smell – washed hair and warm skin.

'Rain . . .' His voice is husky. His hand brushes nothingness because I've moved away.

'Sorry.'

'No, I'm sorry,' he says. 'I shouldn't . . .'

'You should. It's just . . . I can't.'

'You're with someone else?' He looks like he's been slapped.

'No! No one. It's this thing. I can't . . . I

156

don't . . . It's . . . I'm not feeling well. A bit feverish. Maybe I'll see a medic.'

What else can I tell him? That I have visions, hear voices, snap bomb wires with my bare hands . . . that I'm *not normal*?

He's worried. 'You don't look ill. You look . . . nice.'

'I'm fine. Not contagious.' Spreading my arms out with a nervous laugh I suddenly panic about the scratch marks on my arms but, strangely, the skin isn't red, scabbed or even cut any more. Everything is whole and healed.

Out of the blue Reef asks, 'You haven't found any more of those Old Nation witch-bane charms, have you?'

'Witch-bane?'

'It's an Old Nation metal used in the knots and bone artefacts you found. They're supposed to keep witches away.'

'But there's—'

'. . . no such thing as witches. So we're told.' His voice trails off and he's lost in memories, where I can't follow. They're not happy memories, I can tell that much.

'Was it Haze who made the charms?' I ask.

He nods. 'She seems to have had a difficult and sheltered life, skivvying for some old grandmother type. She hadn't ever used a keypad or connected before I found her in the forest. We're keeping an eye on her, don't worry. She's got a healthy fear of Scrutiners.'

'She was acting funny in the bath-house earlier, saying stupid things.'

'Like what?'

'Like . . . oh, nothing. She was a bit crazy really. Said I'd stolen something, but I haven't, I swear, I really haven't.'

Reef smoothes his hair again. 'Listen, Rain, all sorts of abnormal things have happened to you recently – the Morass, the war, the night-missions. You're under a lot of pressure, and it's going to get worse. It's not fair, I know. I want to help if I can. If there's ever anything you want to tell me, anything at all, no matter how abnormal . . . come to me *first*, do you understand? You do know you can trust me, don't you?'

I want to. I truly want to. This time when he leans closer I don't pull back, I just set my hand on his sleeve to hold him away. That's when the lights go off. No warning, no blinking. Utter blackout. Not even back-up lo-glo lamps.

Reef doesn't move to connect for updates about the power cut; neither do I.

My hand moves up his arm, just grazing the sleeve, then my fingertips touch his chest. His muscles are hard under the smooth weave of his white tunic. Mesmerised, I spread my fingers so my palm is right over his heart. It beats very quickly. I'm rigid with fear in case we touch skin and I see some nasty death-scene – Reef blown to pieces by a traption gun, Reef devoured by carnivorous trees, Reef in hospital hooked up to machines, Reef all white-haired and shrivelled at the very end of being old. His heart mustn't stop beating! He must stay alive and beautiful, whatever it takes!

We breathe. We breathe. And we breathe.

'Rain . . . I want to tell you something about me. About how I became a Scrutiner. Something you shouldn't hear from anywhere else . . .'

The door bangs open and in comes Zoya, chomping on a sugar bun.

'Mmn, sorry, I'll just . . .'

Too late.

Reef leaps to his feet and straightens his clothes. Those fingers that should be touching me graze a keypad to connect. He bows to me slightly and leaves, every atom a Scrutiner again.

9
SPRING CAKES

Sun-gold light streams in through the dorm windows. I count specks of dust hanging in the air and wait for the others to wake up. It's too hot. I shove my covers away and look down at my body in its crumpled grey nightshirt. It *is* my body. It moves when I tell it to. It feels heat, cold, pain, pleasure. So why does it seem to be something apart from me, up to things I can't control? How can I keep walking round in it as if everything's normal?

Pulling on my uniform helps. It reminds me I'm *One of Many*. Except I'm not. For all it's been fantastic to see the girls again I can't shake the feeling of being *one*, while they are the many. I don't know if Zoya's said something about finding me with Reef, or about me being rescued by Steen, but I'm sure everyone's looking at me funny, sort of sideways, when they think I won't notice.

A shadow passes the dorm window. An aroma wafts by. Zoya unburies her head from a pillow.

'I know that smell!' she says, sitting up and sniffing. 'Pip, do you remember when we were little your mama used to buy spring cakes and make us windmill suns?'

'Sounds boring,' grunts Ang as she wakes up too.

'They were brilliant,' answers Mossie sleepily. 'I remember them too. They were these sun shapes you put on sticks and they used to go round and round when you ran about with them.'

That makes me think of the memories – I mean, *hallucinations* – I had in the ruined house in Sorrowdale . . . Glimpses of dappled light on paper suns strung up and twirling from tree branches, and Mama singing as she swept winter out into the yard and welcomed full spring in.

What yard?

Nobody sweeps anything in People's Number 2032 Housing Block in Sea-Ways. Or sings, either, come to think of it. This morning I've got some of Henke's tunes running round my head with unsung words of my own – *Spring is love is life is change is dying is winter is dead is cold is warm is spring is love is life* . . .

Lida laughs and stretches. 'Na – we had windmill suns too when I was a kid. A bit Old Nation, I know, but we'd only just got Aura then so we didn't know any better. Most of you will be too young to remember a time when we couldn't connect.'

'I can,' says Ang stubbornly. 'Just. I was born before the last Eclipse. My family were one of the first to get fitted for connection.'

Lida's still lost in nostalgia. 'We used to have spring cakes too, baked in bird shapes . . .'

Petra leaps up and pads to the door. 'Someone here,' she mumbles. She's not a morning person, though she sends a sly kiss Mossie's way as she passes.

'Happy spring!' beams Haze from the doorway. She's holding a cloth-covered tray. When she lifts the cloth we see rows of bird-shaped cakes.

'Haze, you're amazing!' cries Zoya. 'I'm so glad you stayed with the squadron.'

Haze gets one hug after another. Not from me.

'Aren't you eating?' Mossie asks, handing me a spring cake.

'Not hungry, thanks.'

Haze smirks.

Spring is on us with a vengeance. When we hustle outside to prep the Storms for the night's missions we're greeted by the sight of saplings – real ones – waving thin branches insolently across the makeshift runway. Pushing up through mats of biograss are bright-green shoots – real grass.

'Some of these plant things are taller than you, Pip,' says Petra with a grin.

'That's not hard,' laughs Lida, but I don't mind the banter so much now. Being teased means belonging. I *will* squash strangeness and be normal like everyone else.

Zoya looks uneasy. 'This isn't supposed to happen. They should get Slick on it all.'

'No Slick's been delivered yet,' replies Lida. 'Not enough

to go round everywhere that needs it. We'll have to take care of this ourselves.' She grabs one of the saplings and pulls. It takes two hands and all her strength to yank it out of the ground. Tufts of grass are torn up too. 'Weird, look. I read trees are supposed to have roots, right? This one doesn't.'

'Witch weeds,' says Haze, standing on the far side of the group from me with her strong arms folded.

I roll my eyes. 'No such thing as witches.'

'Not witches. *Weeds*. They don't need roots. They grow next to another plant, grass or grain. Stick claws into the other plant's roots and use them to suck up life from the soil. The grass will soon die. Witch weeds don't care. Witches take what they want.'

I snap, 'Haze, you can't keep going on about witches! Everybody knows they don't exist.'

'So you keep saying.'

'She's right,' says Lida. 'That sort of talk will have Scrutiners down on you like Slick from a spray can.'

We all get stuck into the weeding. It's a good excuse for Yeldon to flex his muscles. I edge over to Zoya.

'Anything happening with you and Yeldon?'

'You kidding?'

'He seems all right.'

'He's not bad.' She looks down at the limp plant in her hands. 'You know my father would never let me come home with anyone less than a multi-award-winning scientist.'

163

'Last I looked, Uncle Mentira isn't anywhere on this airbase.'

Zoya glances around. The Scrutiner Roke has come out to squint at us all. 'He still wouldn't like it. Anyway, Yeldon probably kisses like a sink plunger, so what's the point?'

'How does a sink plunger kiss?' asks Dee, bumping into the end of our conversation.

'Ask Ang,' says Zoya. 'She's probably already tried it – twice, knowing her.'

'You really think so?' And off Dee goes to see if it's true.

'You feeling better?' Zoya asks me after a while.

I hesitate, wondering what the right answer is. Out beyond the stark curves of the bio-vats there's a war waging. Tonight we'll be flying that fine line between life and death. In the meanwhile, we're all working together against a different enemy – these sprouting weeds that need yanking out. I won't be one of the weeds. I won't sprout. I'll be nice and normal like everyone else.

'I'm good. Why?'

'You know I'm here for you, right? I promised to take care of you. Ugh, look over there. They've dragged the *Crux* out here to graft. Hope he stays well away from the rest of us.'

Roke doesn't join in with the weeding. He keeps nipping at his nails nervously. Steen strips down to tunic and boots and stretches out to feel the light. Prayers over, he attacks saplings with an angry concentration. I stare at him, trying to figure out where he fits into things.

164

'Wait, Moss, I'll get that!' Petra is trying to wrestle Mossie away from a particularly big sapling.

'I can manage,' Mossie gasps. Her breath has gone shallow and her lips have an eerie blue tinge. Even as I look over she sags a bit.

Petra catches hold of her, pretending not to panic. 'Take it easy. I'll get a medic update from Aura . . .'

'No! It's nothing. It'll pass.'

'Doesn't look nothing to me.'

I move in front of them both, to block Roke's view. 'What's wrong?'

Mossie flaps her hands as if to shoo us both away. 'Stop fussing! I'm hot, is all.'

'You're freezing!' mutters Petra. 'I'm telling Aura. You should take the day off . . .'

'When . . . Storms are operational . . . tonight? We need all . . . the techies we can get.' Mossie can hardly speak, she's labouring so hard to breathe.

She looks bad, like when Zoya's mama got a heart attack and nearly died. Mossie can't die!

'Let me feel.'

I say the words without knowing how I can possibly help. Petra frowns but Mossie seems to pick up on my unexpected self-assurance because she unfastens her jacket and pulls her top down a bit.

I rub dirt off my hand as best I can. Am I really going to do this? Yes.

Without knowing why I set my hand flat on the skin

over Mossie's sternum, the bone at the front of her ribs. First I feel her fluttering pulse, then I hear the rasp of oxygen crawling into her lungs. Fainter still I sense cells dividing and dying, chemicals flashing. Through my fingers I actually see her heart. There's no jolt, like with the other visions I've had. I simply feel her heart grow calm, full and strong again. Life, life, *life* flows from me to her!

Petra pulls me away. 'Watch out. Someone's coming.'

'What's going on?' calls Zoya, simultaneously cramming her mouth full of ration crackers.

I colour. 'Nothing. Just . . .'

'Just weeding,' says Petra calmly.

'Rain was doing something to Mossie. I saw.'

Mossie fastens up her jacket. 'We're only messing around, Zoya, no big deal. Are you guys just going to watch while I do all the work?' She yanks out the nearest sapling and dares anyone to argue. Her cheeks are flushed with health again.

'There's nothing wrong with your heart,' I whisper when I can. 'It feels fine. Amazing, in fact. Full of life.'

A shadow falls on us both. Reef is right there. How much has he seen? What has he heard? His face is as blank as only a Scrutiner's can be.

To the others he says, 'Concentrate on the largest weeds only. A new consignment of Slick has just been delivered, ready to be sprayed – sparingly – where it's most needed. Aranoza, come with me.'

It's not a request.

I follow him off the airstrip and round the base of one of the huge factory towers. I'm surprised to see the browny-green runners of thorn-vines prising bioweave apart with their sharp tendrils and spreading leaves wide to catch whatever sun makes it through newly massing clouds.

Reef stops abruptly once we're out of sight of the others. He ruffles his hair. Takes a deep breath. Blows it out again.

'Why did you lie to me, Rain?'

'Lie?'

'Right to my face, in the dorm last night.'

'What lie?' *Which one?*

'Oh come on, don't mess me around. You said you felt ill, but I checked your bio-updates. You're fine. Completely normal. Fantastically healthy, in fact. So why wouldn't you . . . didn't you want to . . . you know?'

Thorn-vines, please crack the ground open and let me fall into a deep chasm.

'Oh. That. Sorry, it's just, I don't know, I mean . . . things have been pretty strange since . . . since the Morass and meeting you.'

He closes his eyes briefly then laughs. 'I know exactly what you mean!'

'You do?'

His eyes are so warm when he looks at me I feel like running into rivulets of snow-melt.

He says, 'I'm supposed to be coordinating the Slick dispersal and connecting with teams of normalisers to figure out why these Morass plants are so dominant, but

167

you're on my mind all the time, Rain Aranoza. I know it's wrong. I'm a Scrutiner and you're air crew. It's not supposed to happen . . . but there's just something about you that stops me thinking sensibly. It *is* strange, not having the proper rules for how to feel. I don't like it. I like you though. I just can't tell if you . . .'

Quickly, 'I do. I like you too.'

He grins and it's all I can do to stop myself leaping right into his arms. But duty clamps down on him almost instantly.

'Good. That's sorted then. You'd best go back to the others. We need the runway clear for tonight's mission.'

Steen edges up to me when I start work on the weeds again. I edge away. Closer still he comes until we're almost shoulder to shoulder at the task. I can see Yeldon measuring his muscles, wondering whose are biggest and who'd win in a fist fight.

'See those,' Steen says suddenly, as rays of sunlight push through the clouds. 'God's fingers, we call them. Aren't they beautiful?'

'How can you Crux even know what beauty is?'

'We know it when we see it,' he answers, looking right at me. His voice drops to a murmur. 'Rain, I've been looking for you all my life. I could worship you, worship the very ground you—'

'Shut up!' I glare at Steen, conscious that Roke has stopped chewing his cuticles and is now staring at us both.

'Why are you even here?' I hiss. 'Why are you still collaborating?'

Steen raises his hands as if to touch the sunrays. For once his grey eyes don't flash defiance and his voice doesn't cut as sharply as usual.

'I'm just staying alive as long as I can. Didn't it occur to you that I have family I want to see again? That there are people who love and miss me? We're not monsters, you know. We just wanted to be left alone to worship in our way.'

'So why invade? What could possibly be worth so much death and destruction?'

'Light,' he says simply. 'If you shine enough light there'll be no more darkness.'

'We have our own light in Rodina,' I object.

'Artificial lamps. Pretend light. Real light comes from faith, that's where power is. That's the god I'm looking for.'

The intensity of his gaze disturbs me. Up above, clouds thicken. A flock of corvils fly over, quickly followed by fat stones of ice-cold hail that pound the ground wherever they land. I shield my face, then, along with the rest of the squadron, I run under a Storm's wings to escape the worst of the bombardment.

Steen licks his lips and shouts after us, even as the hailstones pelt him.

'It'll get worse, you know. The saynts all predict this – a season of extraordinary weather. The ground will burst, trees will spawn like never before and in the depths of the

Long Night a dark light will shine to blind all unbelievers!'

I scrape his words out of my ears but I can't erase one low, thrilling phrase – *I could worship you.*

20
BLACK FEATHERS

How many missions a night? How many nights?

I'm sure Aura keeps tally of them all, and Marina Furey too, brooding through the night hours with her lights on full. Me, I've lost count. Eight, nine, ten a night . . . or more. Some in rain, some in clouds, some in clear nights with only Umbra-glow to light our way. All are a duel between fear and excitement. A dance of life and death.

Out here in the Biopolis, between the city and the war, we've forgotten how to do anything but fly. Each night is a blur of sensations – the creak of the plane's wooden frame, the stutter of an engine stalling, the flap of fabric torn by bullets, the thunk of our parachute packs when we finally get to unclick and drop them at dawn.

We're getting good. Accuracy is improving with every bomb drop. Roads, railways, towns, traptions, we blow them all to pieces then curve up and away with the Crux shouting curses. 'Night Witches,' they call us. The name sticks. Trouble is, no matter how good we are, the Crux keep coming. All the Victory reports in the world can't hide the fact that the enemy are now in control of the forest's northern borders and edging closer to Sea-Ways every day, for all we make them crawl into hidey-holes and graves by night.

The Biopolis is a strange haven between missions. New recruits crowd into neighbouring dorms, staring at us like we're grizzled veterans . . . and I guess we are. New planes are delivered from factories far from the front line. New engineers arrive to maintain them. Fenlon bullies those that Furey hasn't time to shout at. She's unstoppable, and so is her smoking habit. I see her lighting up another choke while she argues with clerks who can't get her supplies and with officers who won't stop sending her untrained recruits, and while she pleads with her daughter Tilly to go to bed when she's told.

Tilly hasn't spoken since the bridge bombing, though she seems healthy apart from that. I watch her sometimes, just keeping a little eye on her. She watches me too, not smiling, not waving, just looking. Whenever someone suggests Furey should send her away to a safe house in Sea-Ways, Marina just hugs her daughter close and says, 'Nowhere's safe except with me.'

I like that. My mother would be the same. As spring slumps into a heavy, humid summer, Mama messages more and more.

are you sure you're all right, rain?

mama, i'm fine. aura would let you know if anything ever happened

the war, the victory, it's taking so long and i saw pictures of

*those traption things and i worry about you, i don't know where
you are or what you're doing*

mama, i can't tell you anything about war work

*that's exactly what i said to your uncle mentira when he
asked if you'd been in touch. as long as you're all right and
you're sleeping and eating properly?*

Sleeping? Eating? Hardly.

They give us uppers to keep us awake through all the
long nights, and downers to help us rest in daylight hours.
Both sets of pills churn our stomachs up. I try not to take
them too often. I feel messed up enough with other
things – like when I catch a glimpse of Reef somewhere
across the airfield, or I get a message and I think it's from
him, or someone says his name, or something that sounds
like his name.

Is he thinking of me? He once said he thinks of me all
the time. Now he's actually come out and said he likes me
it's as if that's got to be enough. He's pulled away. Afraid to
admit he doesn't like me any more? Afraid he might like
me too much?

As food stocks run out – thanks to Crux capturing
foodlands – Haze cooks vats of something called kasha, a
thick Lim porridge so filling even Zoya can only manage
two bowls at a sitting. Since new rations only allow one
serving per person I let her eat mine.

'Don't you like it with salt?' she asks, seeing my
expression when she stirs some in. 'Or is it just Haze's
cooking you've got a thing about?'

173

'I've never liked salt on my food.'

I swear I see Haze smirking every time I push the bowl away.

not much food in the shops here, Mama messages, *and these awful weeds growing in the parks and streets, aura says we're on a waiting list for something called slick, you spray it and the plants die but what about the animals, they're everywhere, it's horrible, all these birds and rablets and rachnids. there was a rachnid in the shower this morning, all hairy legs and eyes it made me jump and papi called in the new pest control people . . .*

mama, i'm sorry but i've got to go zoya says hi by the way

love you, sweeting, take care and be a good girl

I know all about the rachnids. Ang's developed a phobia about them, which is the joy of Zoya's life. She loves hearing how Ang's been scared by one that's *twice* as big as anything anyone else spots lurking in a corner.

I've discovered wormlings – little pink wiggly things that live in real soil. I have to go out grubbing for them when no one's looking because it turns out my pet Eye Bright can't get enough of them. I tried making it a nest in a quiet spot but the bird's only happy when tucked up in my pocket.

Haze spots it one day as she's snooping around.

'Is that a corvil?' she hisses at me. 'I hope it pecks your eyes out!'

I wait till she's gone before I start feeding it again. 'You wouldn't peck my eyes out . . . would you?'

Eye Bright gulps down the last wormling then jabs its beak into my palm, wanting more . . . wanting meat.

It's a stab-tail summer. These horrible insects love the long, hot days every bit as much as we hate them – because there are fewer hours for us to go night-bombing. Stab-tails make hives in neglected nooks of bioweave, but fly wherever they like in search of blood. We learn to check our boots to make sure none have crept inside. When she sees her first stab-tail Zoya cries, 'Aren't they pretty?' That's before she gets bitten (though Ang gets *twice* as many bites) and Haze has to show everyone how to make fly-swats from woven witch-weed stalks.

'Make a pattern of knots and swirls,' she instructs, as she twists the stems with calloused fingers. 'Witches get tangled in them.'

Haze is the worst of all the summer's infestations. One day she stamps a jar of stab-tails on the canteen table. 'I've got a present for Rain,' she says.

Zoya pushes her chair back quickly. 'Don't put them near my food, Pip.'

'I caught them,' boasts Haze. 'Now they are in prison. They don't like it. I wonder what will happen if I turn, if I open, if all the stab-tails fly out?'

I shove hands in pockets to stop fists finding her face.

'Take them away, Haze.'

'They're so angry, angry all the time.' Slowly, Haze turns the jar-lid. The stab-tails go wild, flying, swerving, beating themselves against the wall of their prison.

A calm voice interrupts, 'Have you ever been stung by a stab-tail, Haze? No? It's more painful than you can imagine.'

Haze whips away the jar and scurries back to the kitchen.

Petra smiles down at me. A friend.

Haze has got one thing right. I *am* buzzing inside like a tribe of trapped stab-tails.

you looked tired in the canteen before you set off, are you all right? Reef messages one time, just after we're back from a pretty dreary night of cranky planes and foggy skies. It's the sort of morning when the sun can barely be bothered to rise.

I think up about fifty draft replies before messaging back *i'm fine, how are you?*

thinking of you

My fingers hover over the keypad, tingling. Oh, why not? I message *maybe we could meet?*

There's a heart-squeezing pause before his reply comes through *i'd like that*

tonight? before missions?

sooner? can't wait that long

now?

got a report to finish and then i'm all yours

All mine! There's just time to shower before I see him. I'm shaking by the time I get to the bath-house. I strip my grubby kit off and stand in the shower with lukewarm water pooling round my feet because the bioweave of the plughole is all gunged up. At least the showers work now – kind of. I look down. It's a funny view between the wide valley of my breasts, past my belly, all the way to my toes. There he is, a vision of Reef in the water, spattered with new-falling drops. I stop breathing. Turn the shower off. The water settles and I see every detail of him as clearly as if he was really there. The gloss of his hair. The curve of his cheek. The warm spot behind his ear. He's leaning forward across a desk, staring at a screen. Then something catches his attention. He looks up. I freak and splash the vision away.

'Where you off to?' Zoya asks, coming into the bath-house as I'm just leaving.

'Nowhere. The Scrutiner's office. I'll tell you later!'

I run as far as the office block then slow to a walk. Mustn't look too keen. The door's open. I take a deep breath. There he is, in the office, leaning forward across a desk, staring at a screen, just the same as in my vision. I could touch his hair, his cheek, that warm spot behind his ear. Then I see whose face he's staring at so intently on the screen. Mine.

He looks at it as if he'd like to memorise every detail. Because he likes me . . . or for some more sinister reason?

I catch my breath. He hears the sound and looks up. I'm gone – just the memory of a shadow in the doorway.

Later I message *sorry I was so tired I fell asleep* – and I hate myself.

After that it's more awkward than ever before. Reef's distant; I'm embarrassed. Just when I think he'll give me up altogether we'll meet by accident and he'll smile at me and my sun shines. Then Steen will appear, or Roke, or some other surplus person. The smile vanishes, the sun fades. My skin tightens to bursting point and I want to scream.

Flying helps. I can run to the Storm, leap inside and feel free for a while, up in the night air. When we're on a bomb run I don't care that Steen stares at me all the time; that Reef is mostly stuck with his Scrutiner face on; that Haze has got this crazy vendetta against me.

There's one really bad night that brings a mid-air collision between two Storms flown by newbies. I nearly crack then because I never even knew the names of the kids who died.

'One parachuted out,' says Petra sadly. She saw the whole thing happen. 'He got shot while floating down.'

Our only consolation is that further Storms took their revenge afterwards, with the biggest bombardment in the squadron's short history.

'Folk in Corona City are sitting up and taking notice!' Marina Furey tells us.

'Wish they'd take more time to respond to all the request messages I'm sending,' grouches Fenlon. 'The Glissom company are querying my orders again. If we're to keep up this level of mission intensity we still need more crews, more planes, more spare parts . . .'

'More bombs at this rate!' Furey grins. 'I'm proud of you all, Storm squadron. You are making a difference to this war.'

' . . . even if it feels like you're just slogging your guts out before they get blown out,' Fenlon concludes.

Inside I might feel like a bomb-blast, with questions as sharp as shrapnel, but the main thing is to keep everything calm and *normal* . . . on the outside at least. If I can just stay within my stretched-tight skin, everything will be fine. Absolutely fine.

Until it's not.

'That was a truly awesome spree!'

Zoya signals the end of another night's bombing by pulling off her flying visor and helmet and giving her hair a quick going-over so she won't look like a battered bush back in the crew-room. 'Did you see me spray that Catapult with bullets? It went down, right? You saw it go down? Everybody must've seen it go down.'

I rub my eyes, wishing sunlight wasn't so bright. Eleven raids, one after the other, stopping only to refuel and rearm.

'You hit the Catapult. It went down,' I say automatically.

'You sound tired,' answers Zoya crossly.

'Sorry. You're a *fantastic* shot, everyone says so. The best thing Fenlon ever did was fit Glissom guns for the navigators.'

'Yeah, being stuck just map-reading was too boring. I bet it was your mama and papi who made the gun at

Glissom's factory. Seriously, Pip, you look wiped. My father messaged me asking if you were OK. I said yes, but are you? Haze said you've not been yourself lately.'

'Haze doesn't know what she's talking about!' I snap, heaving myself out of the Storm.

Zoya jumps to the ground after me. 'Don't be so down on Haze all the time. She's just worried about you. You would tell me if anything was wrong, wouldn't you? You know you can tell me anything, don't you, Pip?'

'Absolutely. I'm just . . . tired. You know.'

She does know. We'll be far too wired to sleep properly this morning, no matter how many downers we take.

As usual, Steen Verdessica is out praying in a neglected corner of the Biopolis. He goes topless in the heat – pure arrogance. It's so tempting to go over there and . . . and do something violent, I'm not sure what. He turns and raises his hand to me.

Calm, calm calm. I must stay calm.

Somewhere on the edge of my mind I hear Zoya saying, 'Your hair's a complete mess, Pip. You should let me at it – brush some of those tangles out. Didn't you hear there'll be an inspection from someone senior soon? You don't want them to see you looking such a wreck. When we get back to the dorm, hand your hairbrush over . . .'

Out comes Marina Furey, tapping a choke against her trouser leg because even she isn't eccentric enough to smoke around the flammable fuel of the Storms.

'Welcome back,' she calls to all the crews as one by one

they taxi home for the day. She frowns and starts to count. 'One Storm short – who's missing?'

'Lida was right behind us,' says Zoya. 'I saw her last over the Rimm railway sidings, about three klicks from here. Enemy fire was pretty heavy but she was airborne last I looked.'

'She should be back by now,' says Mossie, covering her eyes against the sun to see if a Storm is near. There's no sign of anything except a few early-rising clouds. I glance at Zoya. She mirrors my worried expression. Where are Lida and Petra? This is not good.

Furey connects, then shouts at the response.

'*No information available*? *Status updating – please wait*? What sort of yash response is that?'

Now the choke is behind her ear and she's got her arms folded as she paces the edge of the airstrip, which still stinks from the latest spraying of Slick. I'm secretly glad there isn't enough to get all the weeds around the factory. The thorn-vine blooms are brilliant to see – so vibrant and alive.

All eyes turn to the sky. 'Come on, come on,' Furey murmurs. 'I've lost three crews; I will not lose another.'

We've been incredibly lucky to have no casualties apart from Henke and Rill, the mid-air collision victims and one poor guy who got cut from the squadron because he started losing his night-vision.

'I see Lida's Storm!' My eyes are sharpest. 'There, coming in above the seventh tower. They're low. Too low.'

'Are they OK?' squeaks Mossie.

'I've got them,' cries Furey. 'Definitely too low. Pull up, you idiots. Get some height!'

Too late. The Storm scrapes along the rim of the bio-tower.

'There's damage to the tail and the left wing,' I call out. 'She'll be lucky to keep it under control – the angle's awful for a landing.'

'Don't say that!' Mossie's face is horribly pale.

Calm calm calm . . .

Furey's already messaging for support and we hear the ominous sound of an emergency siren. The Storm trails black smoke. They must've been hit back near the target and I never noticed. *Nose up*, I tell Lida silently, wishing I could message her. *No no no, bank more to the right, keep your wings as level as you can. That's right, nose up – not that far up! You can't land on your tail!*

'They'll never do it,' Zoya murmurs.

'They have to do it,' says Furey emphatically.

Juddering wildly, the Storm touches down, jerks up, tips sideways and comes right off the runway, scattering ground crew and sand canisters, hurtling towards the wall of a nearby factory building, trailing flames in its wake.

I run. I'm there. I don't think about it, I just fling myself in front of the plane. They can't die!

Who knows what happens next. Some twist of the controls? Some flip of the wings? Some miracle, perhaps, that grinds the Storm into a mound of weeds so it slows and only grazes the building before crumpling up?

As soon as I can see or hear again I fight my way up through a rain of black feathers – *feathers?* – to where blood runs down from the cockpit.

Lida's dragging off her flying helmet and waving her arms.

'I'm fine, I'm fine,' she cries, eyes wide in shock.

She'll have to wait. I'm scrambling up to the navigator's seat to get at Petra, who's bent all wrong, with her safety strap straining across her neck.

'Na-a-a-a!' A scream rips through the crowd. It's Mossie – lovely, gentle Mossie – pushing people aside as if they're flower-dollies. 'Where's Petra?' she howls in a voice that's barely human. 'Where's my girl?' She flings herself on to the Storm to find me wedged into the well of the navigator's seat, cradling our friend.

'Pip, oh, Pip, is she . . . ?'

I shake my head. 'Alive.'

Petra's unconscious. She's no way of knowing that the minute I touched her face I was flung decades into her future, to a death by far softer and kinder means. That's why I cry. Whatever she's torn or broken today, she's going to be fine for years and years and years to come, oh thank you god-who-doesn't-exist!

Mossie slumps over the edge of the cockpit until we're all three wet with tears and blood. Medics and fire-crews jump down from a swarm of trucks closing in on the wreck. We're drenched in dousing foam. I hear shreds of words.

Did you see that?

Impossible!

What happened?

They were going to get pulped for sure . . .

I'm not letting go of Petra yet. She's so cold she needs me to warm her. I blow a black feather from her hair, the only one left to be seen.

'It's OK,' I whisper. 'I won't ever let anything hurt my friends.'

FORTUNE-TELLING

Maybe it's the heat, maybe it's the shock of Petra and Lida's lucky escape, or the strain of so many missions back-to-back, or maybe it's just some perverse mood that comes over the crew-room. I don't know how we ever dare get on to the subject of seeing the future, I just know I hate the whole idea right from the start.

It's when Petra and Lida have been released from the medics' care and I've finally been freed from yet another Scrutiny session with Reef. I love seeing him, but not when I have to sit there being questioned. Reef keeps breaking out of his Scrutiner role to ask, 'What were you thinking? Why did you run to the plane? You could've been killed!' Then he remembers he's doing a job and clamps down on his emotions. I sit there, twisting my hands and saying, 'I didn't think, I just ran. I don't know what happened, everything was just all right.'

As if the crash wasn't enough to deal with, there's an upcoming inspection from the man who runs all the armaments industries for Aura, including the gun factory in Sea-Ways where Mama still works – none other than

Glissom himself. In honour of the celebrity occasion the crews are all given a rare night off from missions.

'Enjoy the novelty of relaxation,' orders Furey, who hasn't had a day or night off since the war started. 'Fenlon needs to keep the Storms nice and shiny, which in some disconnected way is supposed to be more important than actually going out to pound the enemy. If we really impress the inspector we might, just *might*, get the sort of credit and resources we deserve for our work.'

So we're stuck, sweating away the hot dusk hours in the crew-room, mending uniforms, messaging family or slumped dumb with exhaustion, hoping night will bring a breeze. I try not to notice the tiny white flowers budding in dusty corners of the room.

Ang opens a cupboard door and squawks. 'Get it out! Get it out! There's a rachnid in there eating cookies!'

That has Zoya on full alert. 'There are cookies left?'

Dee trots over to the cupboard and looks inside. 'There's no rachnid here. Did you imagine it?'

Ang growls, 'If I was going to imagine anything it would be me winning a ton of medals, or the war ending, or you getting a sense of humour . . . *not* an hairy-legged insect.'

Dee pouts. 'I do have a sense of humour. I just don't laugh at *your* jokes.'

'If I ever wasted my valuable time telling jokes, they'd be so funny you'd have to laugh.' Ang slumps back into her chair. 'This inspection idea is all very well, especially since people need to know how good we are, but I want to be up where the action is tonight.'

Lida's bruised face shows she's seen rather too much action recently.

'Maybe we're all grounded because I crashed,' she grouches.

'It wasn't your fault,' says Petra, as best she can with new skin sprayed tight over the multitude of grazes on her face. 'Besides, you saved us at the last moment, else we'd've been jam on the factory wall now.'

'People are protein-based, so they can't be jam,' corrects Dee.

Lida won't be consoled. 'Yeah, but forewarned is forearmed and all that. I mean, wouldn't it have been better if Henke and Rill had known that searchlight would blind them? What about those kids who got killed in the mid-air collision – you think they wouldn't've kept a better lookout if they'd seen in advance what was going to happen?'

'You can't see the future,' says Dee emphatically. 'You can only work on probabilities.'

Lida scowls at her. 'You've heard Fenlon's predictions. They sound pretty accurate. He says we're all going to die young.'

'But you both survived the crash,' says Mossie quickly.

'Yeah, but I wish I'd known we were going to survive back when the engine failed, right, Petra?'

'Oh come on,' says Zoya loudly. 'Predicting the future's

not normal. What if you really did know when you were going to die – how would that be a good thing?'

'I'm not going to die,' announces Ang. 'Well, I know I will eventually – thank you, Dee, for being about to point that out – I'm just saying I feel really alive right now, so why should that change?'

'You don't know what's going to happen to you,' repeats Dee. 'You might get shot, or crash, or just skid on some Slick, or get run over by—'

'Whoa, steady!' says Mossie, ever the peacemaker. 'Can we all stop thinking about death? What about happier futures? It'd be nice to know how the good things in life work out. Romance, and things . . .'

I shiver at the thought of *Reef*, romance and things. Maybe it would be pretty good to know if we'll ever . . . whatever . . . something . . .

Zoya picks up a chair pad to throw at her. 'Everybody knows how things are working out for you and Petra,' she teases. 'Especially after Fenlon caught you both smooching behind the hangar.'

I wish she wouldn't talk about smooching. It just makes me think of Reef and how badly I want to kiss him.

Mossie throws the sofa pad back. It's pretty battered, with fluff spilling out of rips in the biofabric. We all stare at it, wondering if that's just how cushions go or if this is the first sign that the Morass effect is spreading to objects around us? It's a badly kept secret that conventional military machines are getting increasingly high fault rates.

'What about the war?' asks Lida after a pause. 'I'd like to know when that ends. Aura says it'll be over by Long Night, but the Eclipse will soon be on us and we've still not run out of targets to bomb, have we?'

That's where the whole topic might have ended if it hadn't been for Haze sticking her nose in.

'You want to know the future?' she asks, as she barges in with a tray of hot drinks. 'Why not ask a witch? They can tell fortunes, didn't you know that? It's a Lim tradition from Old Nation days. After sunset, girls and women go to the bath-house. They cover the windows and lock all the doors. No knitted or knotted belts allowed, or any kind of bells.'

'What if their trousers fall down because they haven't got belts on?' asks Dee.

Haze stares at her. 'That's not important. If you want a witch to come and do the fortune-telling you can't have them trapped by knots or scared away by bells. Not a real witch of course,' she adds quickly. She's been around Scrutiners long enough now to know how to watch what she's saying. 'It's just pretend, isn't it, Rain?'

'It's stupid, Old Nation and superstitious,' I reply.

'Totally,' says Lida. 'Who's got a better idea for how to spend the evening?'

'What if Aura knew?' objects Zoya. 'We'd get arrested instantly. Didn't you see those mugshots of criminals on the news-stream, who've been caught praying to god?'

'So don't connect.' Lida leaps up from her sofa. 'I'm sick

of doing nothing, or just doing as I'm told. 'Nobody needs to know . . . unless you're going to report us . . . ?'

'Of course not! As long as you don't believe any of it.'

'It's just for fun, I promise. Who's in? Pipsqueak?'

'Not me. Zoya, you're not doing it, are you?'

'No-o . . . Unless you are?'

Zoya watches the others to see who else is keen. Ang won't admit Lida's got the guts to do something she daren't, so she says she's up for it. Dee is confused, so she's sticking with Ang. Mossie and Petra look curious.

'Just don't let *Eyes in the Dark* find out,' Petra warns.

Mossie grins. 'We'll tell Reef we're having a girls-only orgy.'

'That's rude,' says Dee. 'Do you think he'd want to join in?'

'It's a *joke*, Dee,' laughs Mossie.

'It won't be a joke if we get caught,' I insist.

Zoya gives me a look I can't quite read. 'Oh come on, Pip, it's only for fun and everyone else is game.'

Haze stares right at me. 'What are you scared of, Rain Aranoza?' She says my name like it's a taunt.

'I'm not scared. I'll come if everyone else is.'

Lida says, 'OK, Lim girl, this is your show. What do we have to do?'

Haze looks triumphant. 'If one of you plays witch, I'll bring everything we need.'

The airfield is horribly quiet without the rumble of Storm

190

engines readying for action. I feel my heart hammering as if we're on a bomb run, not just sneaking round the bio-towers to the bath-house. Once there Haze spreads a blanket on the changing-room floor. In the middle she sets a metal bowl stacked with burning fuel blocks from the canteen. Next to it is another bowl filled with water and a pillowcase. At this stage the lights are still on.

'Sit in a circle,' she says. 'Everyone take a pen and paper.'

'Paper?' snorts Lida. 'I haven't written on *paper* since I was at pre-school!'

'Me neither,' says Ang. 'I bet you lot don't even know how to hold a pen.'

Barely.

'We used to write on connecting boards before Aura started streaming through the keypads,' says Zoya. 'We can manage.'

'I learned to read and write by myself,' Haze boasts. 'I only had books I hid from the Old Mother. You went to school, didn't you Rain?'

Dee is so fascinated by the pens it saves me answering Haze. 'Where are these from?'

'Fenlon ordered some from a museum in case connecting doesn't work one day. Do your best with them,' Haze replies, like some kind of teacher. 'Write a fortune on the paper. Put it in this pillowcase. Next, one by one, put a hand inside. Pull a fortune out.'

'See,' Mossie whispers to me. 'It's harmless, don't worry.'

We suck pen ends and slowly form letters on the paper.

191

We pass the folded notes to Haze.

Lida goes first. She sticks her long arm into the pillowcase, picks a paper and reads, '*You will be the best aviator on the squadron.*'

Dee complains, 'That was *my* fortune!'

Lida laughs. 'You're not supposed to write them for yourself, Dee.'

Zoya says. 'My turn. Huh, this is stupid, listen – *You will marry a foodlander and have fifteen babies.* Oh, *come on*! Mossie, why are you sniggering? Was that the fortune you wrote?'

'How many of the babies will look like Yeldon?' Mossie teases.

'Do you think they'll come out with ready-made muscles like their papi?' wonders Petra.

Zoya glares. 'You try *your* fortune then!'

According to the pillowcase predictions, Petra's going to inherit a fortune, Mossie is going to kiss Marton Fenlon – 'You can't make me!' she shouts – Haze is going to open a fashion boutique in Corona, Dee is going to run away with a tractor driver and I'm going to devote my life to knitting socks for soldiers.

At what point do things start getting serious?

Probably about the time Haze says to put the lights out.

'All of them. Right out. Firelight only. Think what you want to know about your future. The basin of water will show the answer.'

'It doesn't *really* work,' I point out, and Dee looks at me gratefully.

The others don't care. They're caught up in it all. Haze pulls the basin of water closer. She stirs it with a black feather and stuns us with a chant that conjures up every forbidden thrill of Old Nation superstition.

> *'Black Night's daughter*
> *Bright White's kin*
> *Let the lights go out*
> *Let the Witch come in!'*

22
THE FUTURE

'What can you see reflected in the water?' whispers Haze.

'I see the bath-house ceiling,' Dee whispers back.

'Whoever's jiggling the bowl, *stop it*,' says Lida. 'You're making ripples.'

Haze raises her hands. She's not touching the bowl. No one is. Little snakes of steam twist up from the water. Haze blows them away.

'Look . . .' she invites us.

Don't look! shouts my common sense.

Look . . . calls the water.

In my pocket the bird Eye Bright is stirring. It pecks and peeps but no one else seems to hear. Each of us moves closer to the basin till we're a ring of firelit faces with cold shadows leaning over our shoulders.

There are things I want to know, of course there are. Will Mama and Papi be safe in the war? Will I be safe? Will Cousin Zoya? My friends? When will we win the war – *will we win*? And Reef . . . what about Reef, my beautiful, impossible, not-happening-not-going-to-happen romance? Does he really like me? My nails press so hard in my palms they must be breaking skin. Does he love me?

Don't look . . .

I look.

First I see my friends, not as they are now in the bathhouse, but lined up on a windswept airfield, with a cloud-blown sky behind. One by one they turn from me, as Umbra swallows them all into darkness. All light disappears. I stumble around, blind. Whatever I touch burns. The skin on my arms blisters and peels away. My hair becomes a fiery halo. I fall . . . and the forest catches me. Ferns uncurl around my face. Spores burst from tree bark and drift across a stretch of silver water. I see birds – no, bird skulls – bobbing on the lake with flames for eyes. Not flames, bright-orange thorn-vine flowers, nestling in a dead woman's face. I reach down and lift the blossoms. The woman's eyes open.

Welcome, Rain, she says.

Flowers pour out of every corner of this vision, covering the ground with perfume and petals. Stone walls rise up and light shines through coloured glass. Now, spread face down at my feet, is a bare-backed boy. I crouch and stroke his hair. He lifts his face and kisses me but I can't see who he is because of a mazy white mist spiralling around us.

Enough! I want to get away! I turn. And turn. And turn again. My way is blocked by bane-metal bushes. As I yank them out of the ground my skin is torn to ribbons. I try to hold myself together with my hands, but they seem to become wings or wide rays of black light. Ground-eating trees soar up, winking their mirror leaves. A hundred thousand birds whirl round, beaks as sharp as cut diamonds.

Help me!

I shout but my voice is a trickle of pebbles on a waterless riverbed. The mist thickens. I flounder on. My skin is almost all gone. There's nothing but darkness inside and out, and the pain of something peck, peck, pecking me.

My corvil breaks the trance by stabbing at my leg. Startled, I lash out. My hand smashes the basin of water. The visions disappear and countless droplets of darkness spill out of the basin in slow motion. I watch them fly into the air. Each drop has an eye. Each eye has more darkness inside. There, in the bath-house, while the other girls are frozen, I curve and turn in a mad dance to catch every drop before it lands, pouring them into the bowl.

Then I stumble back into the circle.

And breathe.

And breathe.

And flinch as time speeds up to normal.

Sound slams into my ears.

The girls all move and speak at once. *When will it start? When will we see something? Has it happened yet?* Only Haze

196

is silent. There's a wet spot on her tunic, right over her heart – the one drop I missed. When she eventually speaks, it's to me.

'You saw something.'

'Me? No . . . oh, you mean, just *pretending*? OK, yeah, actually I saw lots of visions, one for each of you. There was Zoya to start with . . .'

'Make it good,' says Zoya, hugging her knees.

'Why wouldn't I? Er, you get free run of a luxury banquet in Corona.'

'Wait till I tell Yeldon! He'll be mad it's not him!'

'Petra and Mossie are going to stay lovey-dovey together.'

'Doesn't sound very probable to me,' says Petra, with her arm around Mossie.

'Sounds horrific,' Mossie complains, nuzzling Petra's neck.

'Who else?' asks Haze.

I could kill her for forcing me on. 'Let me see . . . Lida gets command of her own squadron, and Ang gets awarded the Hero of Rodina Nation medal – twice.'

Ang likes that idea. 'What about Dee? What's her future?'

How should I know? I scrape my brain for ideas and get an odd one. 'Dee will be very happy with a new hat.'

'Oh come on,' Ang complains. 'If I came up with something twice as good as that it'd still be pathetic.'

But Dee is satisfied. 'I need a new hat,' she points out to Ang. 'You threw mine on the roof again, and you still didn't

197

get it further than Lida could.'

'What about Haze?' says Zoya suddenly. 'Can't you give her a fortune too?'

Haze says, 'Yes, tell me what you saw for me, Rain Aranoza.'

'You don't really . . .'

'Tell me!'

Everyone must notice the sudden tension. I swallow. I've got an awful urge to reach out and touch Haze so I can foresee her death, preferably happening really soon, because right now I hate her more than anyone or anything in the world. She's bug, bug, bugging me all the time, for absolutely no reason I can think of. She wants a fortune? Fine – I'll think of one. I close my eyes, and that's when I see her, wrapped in a woman's arms, both of them crying with great, shaking sobs.

I open my eyes. I'm so surprised at the vision I forget I'm supposed to be making one up. 'You're going to meet your mama again,' I say slowly. 'She'll hold you.'

Haze's mouth tightens to a thin line. 'Hurting me?'

'No . . .' I've started this now, I'd better finish it. 'She loves you. She'll be happy to see you.'

'You're lying!' Haze screams, suddenly furious. 'Liar liar liar!'

Lida tries to calm her. 'Easy, Haze. It's just for fun, remember? Just fun.'

'She's making fun, talking about my mother! Ask her why – liar! Thief!'

198

All eyes are on me.

'Oh come on, I've no idea what she's talking about, honestly!'

Mossie shivers. 'I think we've all had enough fortune-telling for one lifetime.'

Dee frowns. 'It's not fair. We all had a fortune except Rain.'

I laugh that idea off. 'That's OK, nothing ever happens to me. I'm just little Pip, right?'

It's no good, I can't sleep. I'm still having wide-awake nightmares long after the others have settled for the night. What is *wrong* with me? Maybe I should connect and see what a medic says. I could just be sick from some completely normal problem, like optical nerves jiggling during stress, causing hallucinations. Apparently that happened to Ang's brother. I could handle that. Except then they wouldn't let me fly and that would be the worst thing that could happen.

I watch Zoya sleeping, on her back with her mouth open. She says I'm too secretive. That I keep everyone at a distance. If I push all my friends away *that* would be the worst thing that could happen.

'Zoya?'

She mumbles something and rolls over.

'Zoya, are you awake?'

Of course she isn't, and I should let her sleep while she can. I reach for my keypad, thinking Aura will know best. Best for who? The keypad stays under my pillow. Easing myself silently into clothes and boots, I nestle the baby corvil in a pocket and creep between the beds to the door. Dee gives a funny mew as she stirs.

'Rain?'

'Ssh, don't wake the others.'

'Where are you going?'

'To get some air.'

'But there's plenty in here, else we wouldn't be breathing.'

'Go back to sleep, Dee.'

Power-rationing and blackout rules mean the Biopolis is mostly submerged in shadows. There's very little light from nearby Sea-Ways either. Stars wink whenever there's a break in the clouds. I wander between empty bio-towers, listening to the rustle of rablets and rachnids when the wind lulls. Out here more plants have colonised the bioweave. Only after sunset do their tiny flowers unfold white petals almost too small to see with the naked eye.

I take Eye Bright from my pocket. Growing bigger every day the bird now grips my hand and spreads its wings to feel the air.

'Are you going to fly?' I whisper.

At the first drops of hot summer rain Eye Bright creeps back inside my jacket.

A streak of lightning cracks the sky, followed some time after by deep thunder and a downfall. I don't care. I wander on, letting the storm play out. I find I'm near the place where Steen's imprisoned – one of the big bio-vats that are open to the sky. I hope he's getting rained on. I hope lightning strikes him dead.

I could worship you, he said.

I press against the bio-vat wall, wondering if I can hear him breathing.

I turn. A silhouette appears in a second lightning flash.

Reef Starzak is out night-walking too. He's silver-sleek wet. If Zoya thinks *I'm* secretive, that's nothing on Reef. He's solitude in solid form. I've never heard him speak of family or friends. He walks alone and sleeps alone. At least, I hope he sleeps alone. I think it would be so restful just to lie down at his side, arms wrapped around each other, as white snow or white blossoms drift down.

He sees me. No point trying to run or hide. He must know Aura hasn't authorised my wanderings. I just stand there, watching rain trickle down his face and his throat; watching the wind flatten his clothes against his body. My hair is loose and runs like a river along my spine.

Suddenly a shape streaks between the towers, not far from Reef. Wolf! In one fluid motion he's raised a gun to fire.

'Don't shoot!'

My words can't be more than a whisper, but Reef hesitates. The wolf pauses too, breathing out clouds of white. Now there are three of us sharing solitude. Reef is the first to move. He holsters his gun unshot and the wolf runs free. Life is life.

Reef reaches for his keypad. I spread my empty hands to

show I don't have mine with me. He shrugs and gives a little smile as if to say, *Here we both are, breaking rules . . . what now?*

He said I could trust him. Out here in the darkness and rain, I believe him. I am so tempted to walk over and spread my problems at his feet. He'd tread carefully, I know he would . . .

A door opens and a square of light shines out. Someone coughs from indoors – the engineer, Fenlon.

'Go blow your choke smoke outside! Why don't you quit those vile things? They kill you slowly.'

Furey steps into the doorway. 'One advantage of dying young is I'd be shot of you nagging me,' she replies. 'Life's got to have some pleasures, now I've had to give up flying to watch over this die-hard bunch of adolescents. I'll quit the day the war ends – happy?'

'Quivering with joy,' answers Fenlon.

'You? Joyful? That'll be the day I truly do quit.'

Fenlon comes to the door, takes one look at the weather and retreats. 'What's there to be happy about? You, me, kids and wooden contraptions with wings are all that stand between us and total domination by the Crux. Not to mention all the Eclipse coming up. I've a feeling this Long Night's going to be even more depressing than last time.'

'Look on the bright side,' says Furey. 'I might strangle you before then . . . put you out of your misery and do the Nation a favour.'

I can't be sure but I think I hear Marina Furey thumping Fenlon when she goes back inside. Zoya would take that as a sign she really likes him.

The door shuts. I look to Reef. Now can we talk? He shakes his head, motioning for me to go back to the dorm. My secrets are unspoken, my lips are unkissed. Tomorrow. I'll talk to him tomorrow.

As soon as I'm back in bed I message him that we need to meet, then I drop all my wet clothes in a pile on the dorm floor and lie naked between the sheets, wondering . . .

23

INSPECTION

By morning I'm certain. I'll confide in Reef and he'll help me. Somehow he'll understand and everything will be all right. First I'm summoned to see Marina Furey, who is a whirlwind of energy and bad temper.

'What, I ask for the millionth time, is the point of sending an inspector *today* when we're supposed to be spending our time terrorising Crux, not buffing our boots! Fenlon – have you seen my . . . oh, thanks. I thought I'd lost it.'

Furey finishes buttoning her smartest uniform jacket and pins on her Hero of Rodina Nation award.

'How do I look?'

This time she's speaking to her daughter Tilly, who's been given one end of a desk for her schoolwork and play-space. Tilly looks her mama up and down then, without a word, gets up to give her a hug. Furey kisses the top of Tilly's head.

'Aranoza, is that you? Come in. Tilly, you remember Rain, don't you?'

Tilly hides behind her mama. I don't blame her. Who'd

want to remember that awful swim in the river?

'Silly widget!' says Furey. 'Go and play now while Mama makes order out of chaos.'

Tilly goes back to her keypad. Furey's already connecting on hers. She waves for me to find a seat. 'Shan't be a mo – got Aled Glissom himself messaging about security for the inspection, mustn't keep the big man waiting . . .'

She waves to Tilly and nips to the next office, where the Scrutiners work.

I'm too nervy to sit. Is that Reef in there with Furey now? I move a little closer. If I concentrate I can just about make out fragments of a conversation between Furey and the Scrutiner Roke. Scrutiners usually prefer to keep things messaged, for privacy. Furey is infamous for liking face-to-face confrontation.

Furey's asking, ' . . . and we can definitely trust him?'

Roke replies, 'No question.'

Trust who? I edge closer to the door. Tilly stops connecting to watch me. I fake interest in a screen streaming images of immaculate troops marching to the front line.

Furey rasps, 'I don't have a problem with him, apart from the fact he's far too young to be involved in all this Scrutiny business.'

My heart flips. They're talking about Reef!

Roke's voice is oppressive. 'Glissom shouldn't be so paranoid. We have security for the inspection in hand. As for Starzak, I vetted him myself. He's loyal to the core.'

'Yes, yes, aren't we all,' replies Furey.

'He's more loyal than most,' Roke insists dryly. 'You may not be aware of this, but even as a young boy he showed an exceptional sense of duty. He was responsible for the denunciation and arrest of both his parents.'

My heart is a stone. It sinks. Reef denounced *his own parents*? That's appalling! But legal. Commendable. Wouldn't anyone loyal to Rodina do the same? Every day the screens stream lists of criminals convicted of praying or spreading superstitions. What idiots we were to play at fortune-telling in the bath-house! What an idiot *I* was, to think it was safe to confess my own secret abnormalities.

Furey doesn't sound surprised to hear the news. 'Yeah, so I've been informed. Still have a sneaky bit of faith in god, did they?'

'Worse than that. The evidence and their guilt were overwhelming. They were convicted of believing in witches. Both were imprisoned for life. These days the punishment would be lethal injection, of course.'

'Right. Of course.'

'Rain?'

I truly do feel as though I leap out of my skin when I hear Reef say my name. There he is in the office, in the flesh. Nothing dishevelled about *his* appearance for the inspection. He's white, throat to feet, and as beautiful as ever. I trip over my own feet and bump against the stream-screen, sending it fuzzy for a moment, then the soldiers march on in ranks again.

'You're early for our meeting,' he comments. His eyes are smiling. 'Are you excited?'

'About . . . about what?'

'Hasn't Furey told you yet? Out of the whole squadron you've been chosen to fly the display plane for Glissom's visit.'

'That's . . . great. I mean, why me? Lida's good too. I'm nothing out of the ordinary. I'm just *One of Many*, right?'

Reef's smile deepens. How can he look so honest and trustworthy when he's so . . . so . . . I can't stay here!

'Hey, Rain, where are you going?'

'To tell the others. About the flying. The inspection.'

'Didn't you want to talk?'

I shake my head violently. 'No. Just . . . nothing. I'd better go.'

Marina Furey comes out of the next office. She's crackling with frustration.

'Morning, Starzak. Aranoza – wait, not so fast.'

Reef says, 'I've already informed her of the decision about the display flight.'

Furey raises an eyebrow. 'Well, that saves a job.' She turns to me. 'Aura will send ac-reqs for timings; I'll leave the choice of stunts to you. Just promise me not to dive-bomb the inspector, no matter how obnoxious he gets. Think you're up to it?'

I nod. It's safer than trying to speak when I'm still trying to process what I overheard about Reef. His parents! His own mama and papi! He sent them to prison for *life*.

'Good,' says Furey. 'We'll see what the big boy from Corona City has got to say about our modest operation here. Maybe he'll dig deep to get us better resources and recognition.'

Dismissed, I dodge desks to leave, hearing Furey laugh to Reef, 'Thought that'd stun her. Poor kid needs more confidence. She doesn't know how good she is.'

'No,' says Reef. 'She's got no idea.'

No idea, no direction, no focus, no *clue* what to do now!

All this time I've been thinking maybe, just maybe, Reef is more of a friend than a Scrutiner – more than just a friend even. That he's interested in me because of *me*, not thanks to some ac-req from Aura to play spy. Obviously he's the last person I should be trusting. Last in a long line of people I can't turn to now.

It's not fair! It's not my fault all these things are happening. I didn't ask to be like this, or to have these abnormal streaks in me. Maybe I was just born this way and it doesn't matter how many times people tell me to fit in and behave and be *good*. Haven't I tried? Haven't I done everything I've been told? Why can't I just be allowed to be *me*?

What *is* me?

I find I'm running and have to force myself to slow down. That's right, just walk normally, Rain, one calm footstep after the other. I put my palms over my face until it's a mask. I bury all the aggravation deep, deep down, where even ground-eating trees couldn't find and devour it.

'Hey, hey, hey!' cries Mossie as I come into the crew-room. 'Here's the girl herself – stunt pilot supreme!'

Everyone cheers, even Ang, though she's quick to point out that she could've done a stunt display in her sleep. Everyone laughs. Ang still needs to live down the hysterics she had when she found herself airborne with a rachnid in the cockpit.

'Big as my fist,' she said it was.

'This big,' Dee told everybody later, showing a tiny span with her thumb and finger.

I look around the crew-room. 'Where's Zoya? I messaged her.'

'She left something back at the dorm,' says Mossie. 'Her hairbrush or something.'

Newbies watch me head across the Biopolis to the hangar. They're so squeaky clean. New uniforms. New haircuts. Nervous smiles.

'That's her . . .' one of them whispers.

That's her *what*? What stories are people spreading about me?

'The one Marina Furey chose to do the display today?' asks another. 'Wow. Do you think we'll ever get to fly that well?'

It's a gusty day with clouds scudding across a sky the colour of dirty dishwater. The Nation flag snaps in the wind. Fenlon does the pre-flight checks with me.

'Well done getting picked for this,' he says. 'One day we might even make a good pilot out of you, if . . .'

' . . . if I don't die first, yeah yeah.'

Once I'm in the Storm I sigh with relief. I know where I am now. There's me, the plane, the sky, nothing and no one else. Zoya's been told a nav isn't needed for these stunts, and I haven't even got Eye Bright stirring in a pocket, since I didn't want it to peep when I met Reef.

Huh. Reef who's been sending *good luck, fly-girl* messages all morning. Reef who'd snap cuffs on me and haul me to prison the second I seemed superstitious.

The wind blows the noise of a limousine engine towards the runway. There he is. Aled Glissom, factory manager and, ultimately, my parents' boss. They've given him a podium in front of our improvised parade ground. His boots click on the podium steps.

'So these are Furey's heroes,' his voice rolls out. 'These are the so-called night-bombers. A bunch of badly dressed children! Not what I had in mind. Not what I had in mind at all.'

The Storm's engine growls into life and I'm spared the rest.

I begin by soaring high above the Biopolis. After a few exploratory passes to catch the inspector's attention I spiral down in a lazy corkscrew, then rise for a graceful figure-of-eight. The Storm works faultlessly. I loop the loop a few times then break free from the clouds and climb higher, higher, higher to where the sun dazzles and the air is clear.

Here, poised somewhere between planet and space, I cut the engine completely.

For a moment I glide . . . then the plane nose-drops, air rushes back in my face and I fall with wings in a spin – round, round, down, ground . . . towers, roofs, faces, fear . . . At the last possible moment I flood the engine with fuel, draw the control stick back, stabilise the wings and shoot away from the most perfect stall-turn I've ever attempted.

Are they clapping down there? Wait till they see this . . .

After more high-altitude manoeuvres I line up for one final stunt, approaching the airstrip level with the row of bio-towers, watching the needle on my airspeed indicator jostle to the very limit of the dial. It's fabulous to be so fast. There he is, the inspector, still on his podium. I fly so low I could practically crop his hair for him. His eyes go wide, he clamps his hand on his fancy hat and ducks. I swoop up, laughing, the best I've felt in a long time.

Then I have to come down to the ground, literally.

Fenlon is grinning when I land. 'Nicely done, Aranoza.'

I give him a little wave and trot over to join the rest of the squadron.

Glissom has straightened up. Two spots of pink glow on his cheeks. His trouser creases are so sharp you could cut bomb wires with them. His shoulders are square and his boot-caps are mirrors. When he speaks – and he's obviously in the middle of a long indulgence – his accent is pure Corona.

'. . . I've been sceptical of the reports about the squadron's successes, with grave reservations about the merit of such primitive technology. I daresay much of the kill-rating the Storms have allegedly scored is due to the fact that our enemy has been mortally wounded by *proper,* conventional weapons. Yes, I say mortally wounded because even as I speak the Crux are being forced to retreat. However, I will concede, in light of the display just now, that the Storm does demonstrate certain impressive capabilities – but I come back to my first point, Marina . . .'

Furey has to squint up at him because he's got the sun at his back and the extra elevation of the podium. She doesn't appreciate Glissom using first names, that's obvious.

'Which first point was that?' she asks innocently.

'About the use of *children* for such vital war work! I employ them in my gun factories, of course. They've got little hands for working with smaller-calibre pistols, shot-guns, rapid-fires and flame-throwers, but as we've clearly seen from those aerobatics, it takes a *grown man* – or woman – to manoeuvre an aircraft without Aura's fine guidance. Not some kiddie who can barely reach the controls . . . Yes, young lady?'

Following an ac-req from Aura I've approached the podium to be introduced to our inspector.

Furey keeps her face very, very straight. 'May I present

212

our highly gifted display pilot – Rain Aranoza.'

I don't need to be able to read minds to know what Glissom's thinking – *This pipsqueak was capable of flying like that?*

It's an exquisite moment, overshadowed by the sudden realisation that I'm going to have to clasp his hand. He looks equally reluctant to make contact. He's so smartly turned out, why isn't he wearing gloves? Why aren't I, for that matter? I must've pulled them off in a moment of job-well-done back at the Storm. Ugh, his hand is so hot, so damp, so . . .

. . . *limp, so sticky with blood, there are bullet-holes instead of buttonholes on his uniform, and so he dies . . .*

I'm stunned at the vision. Appalled.

'Nothing to say for yourself, hey?' Glissom blusters. 'Too young for all the attention, I expect. Precisely the kind of thing I've been talking about, Marina. Off you go, girl, back to your little friends.'

I slip into place between Dee and Lida. Lida smirks at me and the others send subtle signals of congratulations.

After a few more comments Glissom descends from his podium to inspect the crews. We watch his expression puff with contempt. He finds buttons too dull, tunics too crumpled, boots too cracked and trousers just offensively ugly. From the corner of my eye I can see Dee clenching and unclenching her hands, furious that Glissom said her hat isn't on straight when she, in her Dee-like way, is clearly a hundred per cent certain it is. It's a new hat and she was extremely pleased to get issued it in time for the parade. She's guarded it from the cap-tossing inclinations of Ang and Lida.

Glissom tuts. 'I see Marina has been quite the wrong sort of role model for you all. Have you no pride in your appearance? You – why is your cap so big?'

He stops in front of me. I fix my eyes on the front of his tunic as he reaches out to yank my cap off. Inside I'm buzzing like Haze's jar of stab-tails. *Don't think, don't feel, don't react, don't stand out . . .*

Down fall two black braids. He frowns, then squints. I think it's only then that he recognises me again as the stunt pilot.

'Ha!' We all flinch at his exaltation. 'Precisely the sort of thing I've been talking about. Aranoza here is the only girl in this parade who's actually retained a little prettiness. Why would you all want to cut your hair off? It looks plain and unattractive.' With the backs of his fingers he strokes a braid where it falls over my chest.

Don't think, don't feel, don't react, don't slaughter . . .

It's no good. I'm not sure how much longer I can hide my outrage . . .

Then up comes Reef. 'Excuse me, sir, perhaps you'd like to step over to the hangar to inspect facilities there . . .'

When Glissom hesitates Reef blinks once. Enough to show the *Eyes in the Dark* tattoo on his lids. Eyes that see everything, and if they don't like what they see, they report it. Then Reef winks at me.

214

He wouldn't wink at me, or rescue me from slimy officials if he knew all about me.

Just as Reef and Glissom move away my ears start to buzz. The noise gets louder. Drone, drone, drone. Is that Glissom's voice, or stab-tails I can hear? Or, unbelievably, *Crux*?

'Incoming!' I shout. 'I hear planes!'

Glissom swells with indignation. 'Preposterous discipline!'

Reef scans the skies. Can't he hear it? He's connecting, or trying to.

'Can't get connected? Sloppy tech,' Glissom sneers. 'Precisely the kind of thing I've been—'

'You're not in Corona now,' Reef snaps. 'Things work differently out here.'

'They don't seem to work at all! This is fuss over nothing! I'll continue the inspection now . . .'

No time for that. There it is. Unmistakable. A drone, a whine, a hideous wail. I cover my ears against the agony of the sound. Moments later others hear it too.

Crux Screamers!

24
DEE'S HAT

Two Screamers streak out of the clouds.

Furey cups her hands to shout, 'Scramble the Storms! Make for the emergency meeting point!' She practically turns her lungs inside out to make herself heard then she runs to scoop up her daughter Tilly and carry her to cover.

Set out on the airstrip and in the hangars, our Storms are sitting targets for the Crux attack. This far from the front line, no one's seen fit to issue us with anti-aircraft weapons, so there's no way we can defend ourselves.

The first missile explodes like thunder. The ground is caught in invisible claws and torn loose from the planet.

What are these dents suddenly studding the parade square? Bullets. What is that red mist dampening the air? Blood. What is this outrageous sensation in my chest?

Pain. I'm shot!

While everyone sprints for planes, kit and trucks I find myself slipping into a separate stream of time where moments are long enough for thoughts and decisions. I see the glint of a second missile being released and watch it fall, oh-so-slowly now. When it finally strikes I can actually

216

count the flecks of shrapnel spiking out in all directions. More bullets spit down. Unlike seeds or spores they burst into death, not life.

Round the Crux planes curve, sweeping in for a second attack. How did they get so close to Sea-Ways? How far behind is the rest of the invading army? Shots fire from a People's Number Five Glissom Gun – from Reef! One Screamer judders and whips away.

I run for the hangar. Dee is running too . . . straight to where a line of Screamer bullets will soon hit. I try to shout a warning. A missile detonates. The blast knocks her new hat off.

'Leave it!' I call, as she pauses to see where it fell.

She won't. She veers to scoop the hat up and, in stopping, misses the line of bullets. She looks at the puffs of air where the bullets hit. Looks at her hat. Looks at me. I know what she's thinking. Her point-to-point brain is joining the dots. She's remembering the fortune-telling in the bath-house last night, when I said she'd be happy with her new hat – a hat that's just saved her life.

One by one the Storms are powering up. People grab a seat where they can. Yeldon's trying to organise a convoy of trucks while Mossie decides what can be left and what absolutely must be taken. Like me, they're wondering whether Crux ground forces will be following the air assault. I look for Zoya. There she is, crouching under the wing of our Storm, vigorously signalling me over.

'Come on, Pip, we have to get out of here!'

217

I'm torn – save myself, or see what else can be done? 'You go – hurry!'

'Not without you, idiot!'

I dash across open space, then skid to a stop at the sight of Fenlon, fallen on churned-up ground, clutching a red-soaked leg.

'Leave me! Run!' he gasps. 'I'll be fine; I'm too old to die young.'

He's so heavy! I don't know where I find the strength to drag him over to the Storm but I do, then with Zoya's help I heft him into the nav seat where he sags to unconsciousness.

'There's no room for me now if you take the pilot's seat,' Zoya says in a choked voice.

'Don't be stupid. You can fly this plane as well as I can – get him to the emergency meeting point.'

'What about you? My father said I wasn't to—'

'I'll be right behind – go!'

We can hardly hear each other over the crescendo of a new Screamer approach. Zoya scrambles into the Storm's pilot seat. I heave her propeller into action and bang on the fuselage to signal *goodbye-and-go-well*. She taxis to the start of the runway where Storms are practically nose-to-tail for take-off.

Through all the chaos I hear someone yelling – Marina Furey. She's driving one of the bigger trucks, loaded with new recruits and techs. 'Jump on board!' she's shouting to me. A nearby fuel store is hit. Flames gush out. The truck swerves.

'I'll take the next one!'

As for Aled Glissom, he's already in his limousine, bumping across the airfield in search of safety. A bomb-blast shatters the windscreen of the vehicle. It calmly rolls forward and falls nose first into the crater, back wheels still turning. Glissom squirms out of a mangled door, waving for help.

That's when the bullets catch him, just as I foresaw, a line of holes along his city-tailored tunic.

The day darkens. Clouds are lit from beneath by all the fires and explosions. When I look up I can't believe what I'm seeing – Ang in her airborne Storm has hit and crippled one of the Screamers. Its shrill shriek kills my ears. It falters, falls, skims the flagpole and finally collapses down to furrow the ground. That girl deserves a medal!

I'm hypnotised by the turmoil of the crash – the churned-up roots, Slick-limp weeds and one pink wormling there in the middle of it all. Wormlings . . . Corvil! I dodge the mayhem and head for the dorm, knowing it's *stupid* to waste time saving a bird, but I can't just leave Eye Bright to its fate. Life is life. I left it nesting in my locker. Frightened, it stabs my hand when I reach for it.

'Come on, you poor thing, we have to get out of here. There's just time to catch the last truck if we're quick . . .'

As I sprint past the bio-vat towers my way is blocked. It's Haze. She's turned into a screamer as painful as the one still zooming over.

'You did this, Rain Aranoza! It's all your fault, all of it!'

'You're mad, Haze! Unless you've got some kind of death-wish we have to leave!'

'You already stole my life, why should I worry about losing it?' She lifts up one hand. She's holding a jar of stabtails. As I watch she smashes the jar to the ground. It shatters. The insects dart out in every direction. I swipe the air to keep them away from me.

'Why do you hate me so much?' I yell. 'We could have been friends. Everyone says we look like each other – we could even have been sisters. Whatever you say I've done, I didn't know I was doing it.'

'I saw you make Mossie poorly!'

'She wasn't poorly, she got better.'

'Look at your jacket. You've been shot, but are you dead?'

That gets me. It's true the front of my uniform is torn and the rips are red at the edges, but no blood runs now. The bullets have been pushed out and the wounds are closed.

'I know all about you,' Haze taunts. 'I'm the only one who does, though others are watching and wondering. I know where you're from and what you can do. *Monster!*'

Something catches my eye. Na! It's the Scrutiner Roke. Has he seen? Has he heard? He's reaching for his keypad. Let him not connect! Let him not tell the world what Haze has said . . .

Be careful what you wish for . . . A bomb shatters the tower beside us. Great blocks of bioweave fall in a cascade of grey, and that's Roke gone, almost every bone in his body broken, just as I saw in my vision that winter's evening, all those ages ago when he came to scrutinise me at home.

The blast catches me too.

There's a cry. A thud. Then darkness.

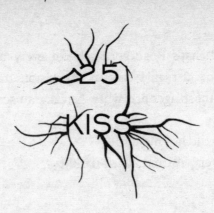

25
KISS

Here you are, thank god, my precious, my darling, my sweeting, you're safe, I've found you, I'll never let them take you again I swear . . .

Mama's arms pull me close. Lips kiss my face. Gentle hands brush feathers away.

I feel small and cramped, as if I've gone from being a meadow to being a flower. Suddenly there's no room in my mind for all the memories I need to hold. They start to shrink into a small hard ball that can be rolled away. I forget who I am or what I am. I begin again – a child, a mere baby. I fear, I need, I cry.

As if for the first time I see with eyes, taste with a tongue, feel with skin and nerves. Mama buries me with love. She wraps me in a blanket that smells of some other baby. Takes me to a house. Shows me to a man – calls him my papi. She crafts sun-shaped windmills and cakes that sparkle with honeycomb. Tells me she'll never lose me again, never.

The storm has passed, the light is back, my baby's safe, she croons.

222

Is this what *safe* feels like? I'm definitely wrap-trapped in something. I struggle out of dreams, memories, mad-thoughts, whatever they are. I'm not a baby. I'm me. I'm now.

I'm grown over with green.

Shoots twine in my hair. Flowers whisper in my ear. Grass tickles, leaves tease. It's a wonderful way to lie, lazy with life spread out all round me. If I didn't have this bulk, these bones and flesh, this body . . . if I was free of the whole lot I could easily coil and swirl with the vines. I could burst into orange flowers or spread through the sky with feather-light spores, or dig deep into the warm earth along with the roots. How lovely it would be to let go . . . not just to live life but to *be* life.

Whatever's gripping me squeezes tighter.

I open my eyes and start to thrash. Stalks snap. Stem sap stains my skin. Let me go! Plants growing around me shrivel away. Some are burning, catching sparks from the flames of bomb-blasted bioweave. I scramble to my feet and stagger around in a wild, orange-black world.

Night has darkened the broken bio-vats. Fires glare from fuel spills. Smoke chokes the airfield. It's ruined, all of it, wrecked by a few wild Screamer flights. My friends are gone. The Storms are gone. The flag has gone. The pole is whole but bare.

How dare they, yash Crux!

I start along the rows of bio-towers, dragging my nails

against the weave. *Pad pad pad* go my boots on the ground. Where are you, Crux? There, in that tower, behind that door there, the locked one, that's where the prisoner skulks.

Steen leaps to his feet as the door crashes open. Wasn't it locked after all? It's flat on the floor. I'm standing on it, fists clenched.

He's dressed in shorts only, slick with sweat and fear. Bare chest, bare feet. A bed, a chair, a table, a god-book . . . and smoke from the fires outside. His chair has fallen. He's backed right into the farthest, darkest corner of the tower with his manacled arms flung up to shield himself. Not so arrogant now! He's right to be afraid. I found him before the flames did.

'You!' I scream. 'They were *your* planes bombing us! *Your* bullets!'

He breathes half his fear out. 'Thank God – you're alive.'

'Very!' I shout. 'More than you'll be when I'm done. Have you been praying? Your god-talk won't help you now.'

'Kill me if you want,' he whispers. 'I'm yours, life and death.'

I stop in my tracks.

His eyes shine, even in the dark. 'You . . . you're everything that matters, Rain. You're what I've been looking for, dreaming of, praying to find . . .'

'Shut up! Stop talking! I'm not listening!'

No more words come out. Next thing I know, Steen's slammed up against the wall and I'm not afraid of touching

224

him because I've already seen how he dies back in that killer-cold day in the forest when he got cut from his 'chute and collapsed in my arms, so now I can press my hands against the bare skin of his chest; could push them all the way through his ribs if I wanted, grab his heart, squeeze it, squeeze the life out of it . . .

But I don't. I don't even push him away when his hands grab my arms – weren't they in cuffs a moment ago? – and his eyes light up with fear and . . . and something else. I know what else because I feel it too. Feel angry. Passionate. *Alive!*

Feel I have to kiss someone.

Kiss him.

This is more than a kiss, it's outrageous, awful, stunning, sensational.

From the way he presses hard against me I can tell he'd devour me if he could. I'm gripping the rough stubble of his head as if my hands will burn off the white cross shaved on to it. His mouth is on my neck, my throat. His hand reaches up, feeling my body and whatever monster is seething inside me.

Enough!

I push him away. Is that me, snarling? He's breathing furiously, and his expression . . . I've never seen a face so drenched in lust. I hate him. I don't want him. I want . . . I want . . . *I don't know what I want.*

'They're coming,' he whispers. 'My people. Soon they'll be here. Nothing can stop them – Sea-Ways, Corona, all of

Rodina will fall before the Light. Come away with me now to the forest, come be with me, let me take you home. Let me treat you as you deserve. Let me worship you . . .'

I hear a new sound – someone calling my name over the sound of crackling fires.

I stagger backwards. Crash into the toppled table. Can barely suppress my energy before I turn to see who's there.

Reef Starzak stands in the broken doorway.

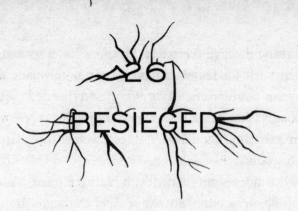

26

BESIEGED

'Reef?'

'Rain?' His face lights up with hope, but there's no light in his eyes. That's when I know for sure. Reef is night-blind. His lo-glo lamp is too feeble to shine into the vat's furthest corners. Steen's fingers grip my arm. I prise them off.

'In here! I'm coming!'

Let Steen go running back to all the other god-rotten Crux. I don't want him around me. Don't want proof of what I've done.

Reef is shaking when I reach his side. He's covered in strands of burned bio-weave and blinking away shock. He wraps an arm around my shoulders. 'Come with me,' he says hoarsely. 'Let me take you home.'

Home? This city under siege can't be Sea-Ways, surely?

I don't recognise my own home town. Traption trenches circle the suburbs, crested with repellent spikes. High walls bristle with anti-aircraft guns, watchtowers and troops. Soldiers defending the walls aren't the smart heroes we saw

227

marching through the streets all those for evers ago when we first left for Loren Airbase. These are civilians shoved into any old pieces of uniform and handed whatever weapons Glissom's gun factory can produce. There are old men patrolling the barricades; old women on sharp-eyed sentinel duty.

All windows are stained with blackout paint. Blast-bags are built up around doorways. *Sold Out* signs are pasted across every shop front. Swathed in drab camouflage nets, salvaged Storms line a school sports field. Reef leads me into an infant classroom painted with the gaudy colours of peacetime.

It's a subdued reunion. My friends are safe, but there were other fatalities at the Biopolis – more people I never knew, and now I'll never know. Perhaps someone, somewhere, mourns the Scrutiner Roke.

Zoya comes to squash up next to me. It's no use trying to sit on the infant chairs – our knees come up to our chins – so we perch on the tables instead.

Zoya's face is grey. 'How many lives have you got, Pip? We thought you were dead. Haze too.'

'Haze is alive?'

'Reef found her – sent her here. What happened?'

I shake my head. I can't think about it, let alone talk.

The classroom door bangs open and Marina Furey strides in, promptly knocking her head on a kid's arty mobile hanging from the low ceiling.

'Brilliant.' She scowls. 'Why do I suddenly feel like I'm a

228

teacher barging in to break up playtime? Of all the places I've been based, this really is the . . . Hey – is that a sandpit? Tilly will love that . . .'

The door slams open again. This time it's Fenlon. His overalls must've been cut off him during emergency treatment for his injured leg, and now the only top that'll fit his frame is a big teacher's tunic with *Hello Children I'm Here To Help* emblazoned across the chest. He limps into the classroom and makes a big show of stowing his walking sticks. We can't help laughing.

Furey holds up her hand to calm us.

'Fun's over. You'd have to be blind not to notice there's nothing much to laugh about now. Comms are patchy; reports are more like rumours. One thing's obvious. Sea-Ways is under siege. Hush! There'll be time one day to ask how this could happen. Let's just count ourselves lucky we got away as lightly as we did.'

'Easy for you to say,' Fenlon growls.

'Lives were lost from our squadron, and I regret this more than anyone. Thanks to Ang's excellent shooting, and quick responses from all of you, more lives were saved than lost and we've salvaged all of the Storms. Now the real fight begins. Some of you have been with me from the first. Some of you are new . . .'

She looks over all the newbies, who sit up a bit straighter, despite the childish surroundings.

'For the newest recruits, this siege signals the end of your training. For you the examination will begin in the middle of the battle. You will not fly in awesome machines and, to be frank, you aren't excessively awesome in appearance. However, desperate days are upon us and the Long Night draws near.'

'You're right about desperate,' mutters Fenlon.

Furey turns on him. '*Yes*, desperate! Do you think I'm not torn up inside, worrying what's going to happen to my daughter and all the other evacuees now sheltering in this very school? Do you think I don't know the Crux have siege weapons that can flatten this city before they convert us at gunpoint? Does that mean we just roll over and give up?'

Fenlon looks alarmed. 'Over my dead body!'

Furey's brow rises in appreciation of this thought.

Zoya nudges me, murmuring, 'She likes him.'

Furey swipes the art mobile out of her way and paces across the classroom.

'I bet you've all thought in secret, *What can I do in this war, against so dreadful an enemy? What use will my effort be – I'm only one person?* My reply is this – you are One of Many.'

'*One of Many!*' our response ripples.

'You, Ang – you're the best shot on the squadron. Lida, you've the gift of knowing how to get a team working. Zoya, Dee, Petra . . . all of you are dedicated and talented. Rain . . .'

I shake my head. *Don't look at me!*

'Rain, you fly like you were born to it. I'm counting on

you, *all of you*, to pull together now. Every supply dump wrecked, every siege engine crippled, every traption disabled, every unit of creepers kept on edge by the drone of our engines, *every* mission you fly in the Storms contributes to the downfall of our enemy. One of you alone cannot win this war. Many of us together *will* win, if we stay strong and loyal. Sea-Ways City must not, *will not* be conquered. At whatever cost, we and our Storms will protect it.'

First they jeer, civilians seeing us trundling along the sports field in our funny wooden planes. They think we'll be toys against the great siege machines circling the city. They don't see us gliding between searchlight beams to drop our bombs. They can't count Crux casualties as we fire down on enemy encampments.

Then the rumours start to spread. It's Storms that safeguard the only remaining railway into Sea-Ways. It's Storms swarming like stab-tails for air battles above the suburbs. It's Storms that send enemy planes crashing down in flames.

Mama messages *have you heard about them, these storms? all night they're flying, even though it's dark, can you believe it? last night i was awake and worrying about where you were, and down it came, this plane, right past my window, waggling its wings . . .*

I smile. That was me, of course!

I was going to buzz Zoya's apartment too but she said

no way, her father would be furious if she did anything so frivolous.

'You mean you told Uncle Mentira you're with the squadron? We're not supposed to let our families know what sort of war work we're doing.'

'Aura said it was OK.'

'The rest of us aren't allowed to.'

Zoya shrugs. 'He's a scientist. He needs to know things. Don't bug me about it, I'm tired. Eighteen times we went out last night, fifteen the night before. I could sleep right through the Long Night when it happens — how come *you're* always so full of energy?'

I can't answer that. I feel like a bag of chaos inside. I'm sloshing with sensations . . . the sweaty constriction of my flying helmet on hot nights, the scent of tiny white flowers pushing up through fine cracks in bio-fibre floors, the taste of bile in my mouth whenever we have to fly over the river running through the city.

The best and worst day comes when an unusual ac-req arrives through for the squadron.

'I don't believe it!' Lida is too angry to sit down and take the news nicely. 'They want us to risk our necks spraying *weedkiller*?'

'If I had two necks I'd risk them for the Nation,' says Ang stubbornly.

'*I'd* risk both your necks as well,' replies Lida. 'It's *mine* I'm worried about. Honestly, sending us off on a daylight mission to go Slick-spreading when we've only just got back from night-bombing! Hasn't Aura analysed the weather out there? You can't see the end of your nose visibility's so poor.'

Dee goes cross-eyed trying to test if it's ever possible to see the end of your nose.

It's hard to know what Aura can and can't see these days. When I connect for ac-reqs I often get nothing but a monotonous *please wait please wait please wait.*

Today a thick sea-mist has crawled up from the low-lying harbour. It smells of salty bones and fish eyes. It creeps through our warmest flying clothes, leaving us clammy and cold despite the summer season.

At the centre of the runway Yeldon stands tall with luminous batons to guide the Storms into position.

'At least we can't see how bad things are when it's like this,' says Zoya, as we wait for our turn to take off, wings weighted with cans of Slick. 'I hate looking down at all the Crux bomb-slingers and siege engines and traptions crusting the city edges, just waiting for a chance to come and trample us.' There's a crackle over the comms, then she says, 'Pip . . . we *are* going to stop them, aren't we? We are going to win the war?'

I can't lie. 'Not with Slick we're not.'

'My father says we have to do whatever we can to win the war.'

'And we both know your father is always right!'

I laugh, but Zoya doesn't laugh back.

'It's tricky to spot any landmarks,' she calls once we're over the city centre. 'Everything's so grey, just a few dim lights. Isn't that the big screen in the station square? That could be our school roof there. I think we're in position. Shall I start spraying?'

No! Leave the weeds alone! Let the grass grow, let the saplings shoot up, let the flowers blossom! I hate the thought of all that black poison raining down, spattering on rogue leaves and sliding down green stems.

To Zoya I say, 'Sure. Do it.'

I think I can hear people down on the streets putting up umbrellas as we sweep past. Why are we wasting time with this? Who is the greater enemy, the Crux and their killing machines, or the Morass with its mazy ways? Loyalty is such a funny thing. You think you know whose side you're on, who's on your side, and then . . .

'Pip!' Zoya screams as the plane jolts. 'Enemy aircraft!'

I snap back into focus and take control. 'Screamers? Catapults?'

'Unknown. I think we're hit!'

Dreaming in the mist I never heard anything approach. I take us up to break the mist and hope the other Storms have spotted the enemy too. The moment we emerge into morning sunshine sounds are sharper.

'Behind us, Pip!' Zoya swings her Glissom rapid-fire round to shoot at the Crux Catapult planes that have been waiting for us to appear out of the mist, like wolves watching a rablet hole.

234

Whatever I do to shake them off, however I turn, there's a shower of Slick following behind, some blown back in our faces so we're smeared in the disgusting stuff. The sun's eye is harsh and I wish I'd remembered my flying visor.

Zoya shouts, 'Drop altitude – hide in the mist again!'

Down we go, swooping low over long lamp-poles and rooftop washing lines, still trickling Slick from the under-wing canisters. A woman pegging things out to dry shakes her 'fist at us. She should be glad she won't have flowers budding in her 'blankets, though I think that would be rather lovely, sleeping with blossoms . . .

It takes all my concentration to dodge tall buildings while still keeping out of range of the Catapult. Finally I find River Seaward. I follow its sludge-green ribbon for a while. That brings up bad memories of tumbling into the water with Tilly . . . and being hauled out by Steen. I wonder where he is.

'Zoya – can you hear me?' My own ears feel full of mist and Slick.

'I'm right behind you – what's the plan?'

'We have to get the Catapults away from the city.'

'You mean out over the harbour?'

My stomach flips at the thought of the churning ocean. 'Definitely.'

'That might work . . . especially as they're right on our tail again now – *Pip*!'

I pull the nose up and whip around sharply before

turning towards the coast again. There are the harbour lights . . . the Catapults are too close!

'I can't lose them!'

'I can't hit them!'

A stutter of bullets shreds into the Storm. Wires ping and the plane begins to dance. I don't have control. More bullets. Zoya yelps. I twist round. She's disappeared from sight.

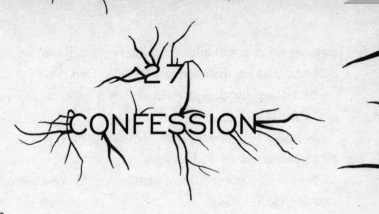

27 CONFESSION

No, no, no!

Sea-mist and shock cling to my body, slowing me down, just when I should be doing something dynamic. Why am I so sluggish anywhere over rivers and sea? The Storm twists and plunges like a twig on floodwater. Is this it? Is this how it ends – I die alone?

Not alone. Dee's Storm comes powering up, right on the tail of the Crux planes. Predators become prey. Ang shoots one Catapult right in the fuel tanks so it explodes in mid-air, creating a second sun. The other is almost out of range when she scores a direct hit on the pilot, sending that plane tumbling down into the mist.

I fall after it, dazed by my own uselessness. The plane just isn't responding. Wires must've been jammed or shot to pieces, because I don't have control. Without wires, what can I do? I keep jabbing the rudder pedal with my boot, as if that'll help . . . and, amazingly, something unsnarls. The wires run smoothly and the Storm responds to my touch again.

The sea doesn't catch me with its white-flecked

wave-tips. I'm not swallowed in nasty salt billows.

I hear a groan. Behind me a blood-grazed hand appears on the edge of the cockpit, followed by a thatch of pale hair and a scowl.

'No floor left!' Zoya shouts. 'I'm sitting on sky!'

I want to whoop with delight!

'You owe Fenlon a huge thanks for that extra-strong seat and harness belt.'

'I owe you thanks for the boot-wetting. I thought we were going under then.'

'So did I! Can you hang on till we reach the base?'

'Do I have a choice?'

I laugh, feeling suddenly light enough to fly without a plane. 'We won't need landing gear – you can start running when we touch down . . .'

'Don't joke, that might actually happen. Listen, Pip, thank you for not letting us die.'

'Thank Ang. Her shooting was inspired.'

'No, I mean it. It's true what everybody says. You really are loyal, aren't you?'

I tense. 'Why wouldn't I be?'

'It's just . . . There's something I shouldn't tell you . . .' Zoya's voice is strained, probably from the effort of hanging on to her harness.

'Can't it wait?' I'm squinting through curtains of gauzy mist.

'Yes, kind of, but not for long. It's about—'

'No, really, it'll have to wait – more Crux incoming!'

Soon the sky is specked with planes. I zip between them as best I can. Zoya hoists herself up to the cockpit edge but she can't hold on and shoot at the same time. Once again, Ang saves the day, eventually escorting us back to base before returning to patrol the skies.

Fenlon himself hauls Zoya free from the floorless navigator's seat. His way of congratulating her on surviving is to slap her on the back so hard she stumbles and would fall if Yeldon weren't there to catch her in a pretty hearty hug.

I start shaking. Delayed reaction, I guess. Someone hands me a towel. It's soon black with the Slick I've scrubbed from my face and hands.

I've long since scrubbed Steen from my lips. Reef's not so easy to slough off. He's busy with some Scrutiner business the day of the near-disastrous air-duel over Sea-Ways. Increasingly we get glitches with Aura connections – the Morass effect? – but he still finds time to message me.

rain, how are you today?

rain, i miss you

rain, are you avoiding me?

Avoiding him? Absolutely.

Other people are counting the days – not many now – till the Eclipse. I'm counting off each day I don't have to face Reef. Everything's so crazy I get away with it for ages until, trudging down a school corridor after another night in the sky, I quite literally bump into him.

239

'Rain! Finally! I've been looking for you.'

What have I done now?

'Here, come into this classroom. We need to talk.' He shuts the door behind us. 'I've just been sending updates to Aura. People in Corona are really sitting up and taking notice of the squadron. They're so impressed with the Storms' successes defending Sea-Ways that they're going to include one of the planes in the big Festival of Light parade in the capital. Guess what else the updates said . . . ?'

Bang bang bang – my heartbeat is loud but my voice is small. 'I'm in trouble because Steen escaped?'

'Forget Steen. With any luck he'll have been killed or injured trying to get back to his own lines, or he'll fall in some forest rift and get eaten by trees. I'm glad he's gone – I was sick of babysitting him. These updates were about *you*.'

'Am I in trouble about something else?'

Reef laughs. 'Relax! Trust me, all the reports were positive. Why wouldn't they be? You're an amazing pilot, a good team-player and a loyal citizen. Obviously there were observations I withheld from the reports . . .' I cringe. Here it comes – the denunciation. '. . . like how your eyes light up when you smile – which you don't do half often enough. How you twirl that bit of hair over your ear when you're thinking. How you stretch when you get out of your Storm, as if you're bridging the gap between sky and ground.'

How does he do that? Make my heart stop beating by saying something so sincere?

He looks straight into my eyes and I feel silvery threads drawing us close. I wish I could trust him. Wish I could waft off to the forest with him to sink into summer among the trees, with dawn cobwebs, heavy flowers, fat green leaves and the shiver of lace-wing insects . . .

. He pulls me closer. I feel all his body along the length of mine. I put my hands on his chest as if to push him away, even though I'd far rather trust the instinct to let him wind himself around me, like two thorn-vine shoots twisting together.

'You can't do this . . .' I whisper.

'I know.' His voice is hoarse.

'You're a Scrutiner . . .'

'Do you think I ever forget it?' His eyes darken. 'I sacrificed a lot to do this job. I've always done the right thing, even when . . . even when the right thing seemed horribly wrong.'

He won't look at me now.

'Your parents?' I ask quietly.

'You know?'

'A bit. Not the whole story.'

He straightens up and smooths his uniform. Now his voice his hard. 'I only did what was right. They were Limborn. They believed in witches – worshipped them even. They went out in the woods for days and nights, dancing, drinking, whatever people do in the forest, leaving me alone with only Aura to keep me company. They'd bring back branches full of leaves to put in the house, garlands of

241

blossom and fans of corvil feathers. They sang songs of . . . I don't want to remember. Then one day Aura asked where they'd gone. I told the truth. I never saw my parents again.'

'Do you feel guilty?'

'What do you think? How can I not!' He folds his arms around his body and stares at an invisible spot on the wall. 'But I was only a kid, doing what everyone said was my duty. They praised me for it. Took me away for training. Taught me how to spot signs of superstitious thinking. Aura's laboratories were my home. I told you already I knew your Uncle Mentira. It was his idea to send me to the Morass as part of the normalisation team. He said it would do me good to control the place that had made my parents so wild . . .'

'And did it?' I can't forget the way he so casually shot the wolf watching me on the edge of the forest rift . . . or how he couldn't bring himself to kill the wolf prowling around the Biopolis airbase.

He shakes his head. 'Yes . . . and no. It grows on you, the forest. Literally, these days.' He stops to pull up a small seedling that's dared to root in the wall of the classroom and twirls it between his fingers. 'Sorry, this must all sound pretty bad to you. I just wanted to explain, and there hasn't been a chance.'

I like his honesty . . . if that's what it is. His eyes search mine now, looking for acceptance, or accusation, or something else only Scrutiners know about . . .

I can't look away.

'Thank you for listening,' he murmurs. 'It's a tough secret to keep.'

'I won't tell anyone.'

'I know. And I want you to know you can talk to me in confidence any time you need.'

'Because you're a Scrutiner?'

'Because I want us to be friends, Rain. More than friends, whether that's right or wrong.'

'But you always do what's right. Like at the bridge – you followed Aura's orders to save the Slick when you wanted to save the evacuees.'

Reef stares at me. 'You don't pull your punches, do you? Just between us, maybe I was wrong at the bridge. My motto has long been *don't step off the path*, but here I am starting to think that sometimes you have to get lost to find yourself. Like now.'

He leans in and dips his head to do a wonderful, terrible thing.

He kisses me.

How sweet it is, oh god, how utterly *wanted* his lips are. This is so different from the clinch with Steen, as different as light from dark. I could drink kisses like this for ever and still not have enough. I love it. I love him.

And every moment of the kiss adds to a private agony as I get a clearer, stronger vision of his death.

His breath quickens. His arms tighten. I'm trembling – no, shaking – no, *shattering* to pieces in my desperation to get away. I tear myself from him, feeling every rip in the intimacy as a physical pain.

'Rain . . . ? What's the matter? What did I do?'

I'm choked. Can't speak. Can't find the words to describe the horrific inner sight of a hand slicing a cold blade right across Reef's warm throat.

I'm already backed to the far end of the corridor when I hear Cousin Zoya asking Reef, 'Was that Pip? I need to speak to her. Where's she going?'

'Let me go,' I tell Reef. 'Leave me alone!'

That goes for Zoya too. Whatever she's got to say it'll have to wait. She's been hovering at my shoulder for a couple of days now, looking like she's about to speak, then saying, *'Nope, nothing's up.'*

Where to run to now? Where to hide? The canteen is buzzing with people, though it doesn't stink of herbs and Haze as usual. The hangar is full of tired techs patching up Storms. In the crew-room there's no peace either. Since no one wants to think about the upcoming Eclipse, it's all talk of the siege, of supplies running low, of what we'll do if the worst happens and the Crux break through.

'We'll keep fighting in the streets,' Lida is saying. 'We'll make them pay for every city block they steal from us. We'll *die* rather than surrender or convert to their yash religion.'

Dee says, 'I don't want to die.'

'Hey, Rain, what's up? Are you OK? You look a bit

sick . . .' Mossie waves at me as I hover in the doorway.

I *am* sick. Sick of bombs, of blood, of war – all of it. Why won't someone make it all *go away*? I want my mama. I want to go home.

I dodge out of the school, split across the edge of the sports field runway and start sprinting through Sea-Way's streets. I need no ac-reqs from Aura to find my route, even through road-blocks and refugees.

I'm vaguely aware of people around me. Some are lined up at ration centres to get their daily dose of food packets. Some are hurrying to work in shabby uniforms. Some are stringing up party lamps. These will be for the Festival of Light that's planned to cheer the final day – is it only one more day? – before the Eclipse begins. They'll keep shining all through the Long Night so no one has to be afraid of the dark . . . Or will Aura give orders for total blackout?

Slick-licked plant-life is being pulled from cracks in roads and walls, then loaded on to barrows to be burned in one of the many bonfires along the banks of River Seaward. There are other fires . . . for cremating bodies.

Here's the park, now a tent city for homeless foodlanders. Here's my street, complete with signs and arrows for the new underground bomb shelter. Here I am, at the entrance to People's Number 2032 Housing Block . . . at the top of ten flights of stairs, at the door to my apartment . . . standing in the doorway with eyes wide and mouth open.

Mama's home. She's not yet left for her shift at Glissom's. There she is, next to a plate of half-eaten breakfast. She's got her arms round a black-haired girl and both of them are crying.

28
FESTIVAL OF LIGHT

'Haze?' The name sticks in my throat. 'Mama?'

This is the scene I saw in the bath-house basin of water. This is Haze's fortune.

'Rain? I didn't know you'd be here . . .' Mama loosens her hold on Haze and rubs tears from her eyes. 'Don't look like that! Come in, shut the door, sit down, quick. It's a shock, I know.'

The lights are so bright! What is Haze doing in my home? What is she doing *anywhere* in my world? I wish I could slam her so hard against the wall it dents.

Haze moves so the table is between us. Her eyes are darting everywhere, looking for a way of escape. Stupid lump, she starts to cry again.

'Don't hurt me,' she gulps. 'It's not my fault. I just wanted to get away from the forest and find my mama. I just want everything that's mine.'

'I don't understand.'

Were three words ever so completely inadequate to sum up my confusion?

'Oh, Rain . . .' Mama looks sad for me, but she doesn't

come any closer to give me a hug. Then she frowns. 'Is that really your name?'

'It's *my* name,' Haze tells me, 'but I don't want it back; you can keep it. Keep your friends and your clothes and your flying. I just want my family. My life.'

I find my voice again. 'Whatever she's told you, it's lies, Mama. She's been making trouble for me ever since we met. She's mean, she's crazy.'

'And *she's* an impostor,' whines Haze.

Mama shakes her head. 'I never thought . . . I mean, we did *wonder*, your papi and I, but we never said anything. It was just a feeling, you know, when you sense something's wrong for no obvious reason. My baby was missing, and then you were found. Why wouldn't I think it was you?' She turns to Haze. 'I'm so, so sorry. I should've known there'd been a mistake. But she looked like my baby – how could she not be real?'

'I am real!' I shout. 'Mama, I'm standing right here in front of you! Look at me – it's *me*. Rain. Your daughter!'

'What's all the racket?' comes a familiar voice from the doorway. Right on cue, Pedla Rue, scuttling across the hallway to stick her nose in. She's got a can with a long spout that drips Slick, perfect for squirting into nooks where plant-life nestles. 'Well now, look who's home . . . Rain!'

'See – Pedla, *you* know me, don't you? Tell her! Tell Mama who I am.'

Pedla stops short. She squints at me, then Haze.

'All right, I give up. What's going on?'

'There was a storm,' Mama whispers. 'Last Long Night, all those years ago. We lost power and had to light candles. My baby wouldn't stop crying and crying. I was so cold, so tired . . . I only put her down for a moment, I swear. I went to the kitchen to make a hot drink. The candles blew out. I had to feel everything in the dark – it was horrible! When I got back to the bedroom the window was open and the cot was empty; there was just my baby's blanket inside, all crumpled up. I didn't know what to do! This was before Aura and connecting. I screamed for your papi and we ran out into the village.'

'Sorrowdale,' I say in a dull voice.

'That's right – how did you know that?'

I close my eyes and think back to that sombre morning walk in the ruins of Sorrowdale, now grown to town-size. Now destroyed by war. 'I remember bits.'

'You couldn't remember the storm, you were too young—'

'And it wasn't you,' interrupts Haze. '*I* was the baby that was stolen. People should've run to the god-house to ring bells as soon as the storm started. They should've known witches would come!'

Pedla hisses through her teeth. '*Witches* took you? I'm always telling people to watch out for witches! We just aren't protected any more. That's what comes of rooting up feybane bushes and taking down the god-house

249

bells. Why doesn't anyone ever listen to me?'

Haze nods. 'I learned the story from the old woman who slaved me. She said my mother ran to the god-house to ask where I was, but god was gone too, so my mother sat on the edge of god's garden where the dead are buried.'

'Then I found you again,' Mama sobs. 'There you were on a bed of feathers. I took you home, Rain.'

So those visions back at Sorrowdale, and in the wreckage of the Biopolis, they weren't just hallucinations. They were memories of the time I was found. The day baby Haze was stolen.

Mama says, 'I was so, so careful after that. I swore I'd never let anything else happen to my baby. I told you all the rules so you'd be good, so the witches wouldn't steal you again. Then Aura said none of the Old Nation stories were true, that there were no such things as witches. We came to Sea-Ways to start over. I honestly didn't know what had really happened that Long Night, until Haze came here today . . .' She breaks into full-blown weeping. 'We loved you, truly we did, sweeting. We didn't know you weren't normal. You looked like my baby, you cried like my baby, but . . .'

I've had enough. 'Shut up going on about it! It's all just insane! What if Scrutiners could hear you?'

Pedla sniffs the air as if suddenly smelling something rotten. 'All this time I've been warning folk about monsters, never guessing there'd be one living right on my doorstep, as sly as you please.'

'Oh, don't call her a monster!' cries Mama. 'She can't help what she is.'

'Don't call me anything!' I howl. 'I'm your *daughter*, Mama. You know I am. There's no such thing as witches!'

Pedla puts down her can of Slick and fumbles in the pocket of her shabby cardigan. 'You've always laughed at me for carrying these things around . . . Here, see how you like them ringing!'

I flinch as she thrusts a set of jangling bells in my face. 'Stop it!'

Pedla shouts over the sound of the bells. 'They don't grow children of their own, these witches. The stories all say they steal real babies and keep them as slaves, setting false things in their place.'

'That's what you are,' says Haze, pointing a shaky finger right at me. 'You're the abomination. The witch spawn. The changeling. It's *you*.'

Witch. A witch. A witch . . .

I can't get away quickly enough. The whispers follow me down all ten flights of stairs and into the street. The rumours grow, and a crowd grows too. Pedla must be messaging ahead to warn neighbours where I am. I walk, eyes down, thinking, *Don't look at me don't look at me don't see me i'm not here . . .*

Someone points.

'Is that her?'

'She's the one,' says another.

Fingers are busy on keypads. The word spreads.

251

I walk on, faster now, no idea where I'm going, no idea what to do, thinking, *Normal, normal — I'm normal!*

A man shouts. 'Hey you, stop!'

I don't look back. I start to jog, nipping through a shopping centre full of empty stores then down the middle of the street to where floats for the upcoming Festival parade are parked. Someone grabs at my arm. I dodge round a float with a cobbled-together tableau of soldier statues that will be illuminated as Umbra rises. I skid along an alley full of uncollected garbage. When I begin to run, men start chasing. My only clear route is across a main street to one of the Old Nation stone bridges that still span this section of River Seaward. Pedla Rue always said if witches were coming for you, ring your bells and get to the river — witches hate running water. Here's an unexpected twist on her words. I'm running away from the bells.

'There she is!'

The shout acts like a magnet to the crowd. Everyone swings round to look in my direction. Afraid of being crushed by the mass of people approaching in all directions I jump up on the bridge parapet. My stomach churns as much as the river below. I wrap my arms around a lamppost strung with Festival lights.

How can everything be unravelling so badly? Aura — tell me what to do! The only message I get when I connect is *welcome rain aranoza, location sea-ways city, grid ref 102:2929 — status update, please wait, please wait, please wait*

'Doesn't look like a monster,' says a woman with her

hair bound up in a turban. I'm sure she's one of the workers from Glissom's Gun Factory. She might even know my mama. Or the woman I thought was my mama.

'You can't tell just by looking,' says another, balancing a toddler on her hip. 'Poke her, see what she does.'

'Oh, leave her alone,' says the turban lady. 'She's in uniform and everything.'

They all babble at once.

'She's one of those plane pilots, the ones that go out in the dark.'

'The dark's not normal.'

'Aren't they the ones keeping the rail link to Corona free of Crux? I've seen one of their Storm planes. They're made of wood.'

'Wood's not normal.'

'*Night Witches*, the Crux call them, that's what I heard.'

Witch, a witch, a witch . . . there go the murmurs again, like a horrid torrent of running water, coming to sweep me away.

Pedla Rue shoves her way into the middle of the crowd, all elbows and eager spite.

She cries, 'Look at her, wild and wicked! Tricked us all, she has. Brought us all bad luck. Maybe brought the war on us . . .'

A wave of anger and fear spreads through the crowd. A few men and women start climbing on to the bridge parapet either side of me.

'Leave me alone!' I shout.

'Get down from there!' Pedla shouts back. 'We'll show you what we think of *monsters* like you!'

'Is she safe?' asks the woman with the toddler.

'Pedla, it's just *me*,' I yell desperately.

'That's what a witch would say!' answers Pedla triumphantly. 'And to think I ever thought she was nice and normal! She'll be gloating now the Eclipse is almost here. She'll be flying round your houses, stealing babies, you wait.'

The mother with a toddler squeezes him so tightly he squeals. The crowd reacts as if *I've* hurt the kid. I look down at the water, wondering whether it would be worse to jump in or be torn to pieces.

Pedla's thinking of helping me with that decision. 'Listen, everybody – witches hate running water. Let's push her in!'

'I'm not your enemy! It's the Crux you should be fighting!'

A tall man in the middle of the crowd cups his hands to yell, 'How do we know you're not a Crux? They can pass for normal too.'

Now the crowd really is turning into a tempest. I hear hundreds of voices clamouring . . . *Did you hear that? A spy! A Crux in the city . . . Come to kill us all, poison us, blow us to pieces . . .*

Pedla stamps her feet with exasperation. 'Forget the Crux! I'll *prove* she's a monster. Don't you know the old rules about witches? Cut some of her hair and give it to me. Cut her hair I say, and burn it!'

My perch on the bridge is completely surrounded. Why won't someone come and help me? *Be careful what you wish for . . .* As I scan the crowd I suddenly spot the white uniform of the first-yet-last person I want to see.

Reef Starzak.

He calls for silence. The crowd obey without a murmur. Now a Scrutiner is here they look shifty, like kids caught being bad.

'What's happening here?' he demands to know.

'It's her,' says Pedla Rue, but not so viciously now. 'Calls herself Rain Aranoza. She's not normal, and we've caught her. That's what's happening.' Reef's eyes narrow. Pedla swallows and starts to stammer, 'It's the eve of the Eclipse, when witches come out. They like the darkness. They steal babies . . .'

How stupid all that sounds when one of Aura's *Eyes in the Dark* is standing listening.

'Let me through to her,' he commands.

Just as he reaches the bridge Pedla's malice bubbles over. 'Scrutiners root out rottenness, don't they? Arrest her then! She's a monster!'

I wish I could fold myself as small as possible, like the pieces of paper from Old Nation days, or like the twists of prayers that hang on a Crux traption. I can't bear it that Reef will be the one to arrest me – another denunciation notch on his belt.

Reef jumps up on to the parapet, steadies himself, then edges towards me.

'Found you,' he says quietly.

'I . . .'

He puts his finger to his lips then turns to speak to the crowd.

'I'll tell you what this girl is. She's a member of an elite squadron of night-flyers – the very ones who've sacrificed their time, and in some cases their lives, to protect all you city people. Haven't you seen the Storms in the skies over Sea-Ways? Haven't you heard them fight to keep you free? Rain Aranoza is a pilot with Marina Furey's Storm squadron . . . the best of all the pilots, as it happens. In recognition of her immense skills and bravery Aura has seen fit to award her the highest accolade our Nation can give.'

What?

In front of all the people, in front of a flabbergasted Pedla Rue, Reef takes my hand – and there's no jolt now I already know how he'll die – and he lifts it up as a sign of victory.

'I came here to announce . . . Rain Aranoza is to be made a Hero of Rodina Nation!'

A few people cheer, as happy to celebrate as denunciate.

'Now, go and prepare for this evening's Festival,' Reef orders. 'Tomorrow the Long Night begins, and we'll need all the lights we can get until Umbra sinks again. Anyone who'd like to repeat accusations against this girl can come and speak to me directly.'

He has reinforcements.

A line of white-clad *Eyes in the Dark* have closed off both ends of the bridge. They have their ways of knowing who to single out for punishment. The loudest troublemakers are dragged away out of sight, Pedla Rue included. Gunshots echo in the dead-quiet side streets. Am I hearing right? Are these *executions*? Now the vision I once had of Pedla Rue's bullet-blasted death makes sense . . . as much as anything makes sense any more. If this is what they do to people who believe in the existence of witches, what about someone who's accused of actually being one?

Like water down a sink-hole, the rest of the crowd swirls and vanishes, leaving me alone with Reef.

Not quite alone. As we climb down from the bridge a truck comes belting round the corner. When it stops, the passenger door opens and there's Zoya's father, my very own Uncle Mentira.

'Hurry up, jump in,' he calls. 'No time to waste – the train to Corona won't wait.'

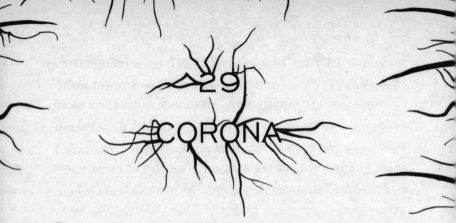

29
CORONA

I turn to Reef. 'Is Pedla *really* dead?'

He frowns. 'I haven't been updated about those civilians. You should go; this could be the last train out of Sea-Ways before the siege closes completely.'

'Go where?'

'To collect your medal, of course. You've got a guest of honour invitation to Corona City for their Festival parade and award ceremony.'

'Is this some kind of sick joke?'

'I wouldn't joke about something so important.'

'But . . . I was just at home. Haze was there, and Mama . . . and why are you being so nice to me . . . ?'

'Calm down, Rain, you're not making any sense.'

Briefly his palm touches my cheek. It's still a thrill to feel his skin, even if I'm also wondering, *Did he kiss his parents* goodbye-and-go-well *before they were arrested too?*

'I didn't mean to upset you back there in the classroom,' he says. 'I'd never do anything to hurt you, you know that, don't you?'

He's looking at me like he's seeing me, but how can he

know me if I don't know myself? What is there under my skin that's got Mama and Haze and Pedla so worked up?

'Hurry up, Rain!' calls Uncle Mentira.

I can't bear this feeling of being torn in half. 'Don't make me go,' I whisper to Reef. 'I'm scared. Please, tell him I should stay here with the Storms . . .'

'This is a huge honour, Rain. Think of it, you'll be a Hero of Rodina!'

'Reef – you don't understand. You heard those people . . . shouting accusations at me. They called me a witch!'

'And we all know there's no such thing as witches.'

'So how come your parents could get arrested for believing in them?'

'Bring her over here, Starzak,' shouts Uncle Mentira.

Reef steps away from me, eyes dazed. When I start walking towards the truck he doesn't try and stop me.

'Excellent!' says Uncle Mentira. 'Excellent indeed. I've messaged ahead for seats on the train and something more suitable for you both to wear.'

Both? Does he mean Reef? No, Reef has vanished. Ang is in the truck with us.

'Isn't this just amazing?' she beams. 'Not just me, but *two* of us from the squadron getting the award!'

'Oh dear,' says Uncle Mentira. His face furrows into a frown as he glances down at our boots. 'I forgot about shoes. They'll have something in Corona, I'm sure.'

'Are we really going to Corona? Can we tell everyone?

They'll be so proud. My family always said I'd do well flying.'

'Where else did you think they'd have such an important award ceremony?' Uncle Mentira beams. 'No – best not to message anyone yet, either of you. Keep it a surprise. Here, why don't I take your keypads and look after them; you wouldn't want to lose them in all the excitement.'

Once we're on the armoured train and speeding north to Corona – along the very same railway lines Storms have fought hard to keep free of Crux – Uncle Mentira explains what's expected of us during the procession that will precede the award ceremony. Ang rubs it in that I've never been to the capital, while she knows it like the back of her hand.

How well does anyone really know the back of their hand? I wonder, looking at mine as if it will suddenly burst into leaves and flowers, or go black and drop off. Aloud, I tentatively ask if we'd not be more use to the war effort back in Sea-Ways.

'Don't worry,' says Uncle Mentira. 'We know you're an invaluable asset. Ang, you can use the compartment next door to change. We're on a tight schedule and we'll need to go straight to the ceremony. Rain, you stay here with me.'

I shrink into the train seat and brace myself for an interrogation. Surely Mama will have messaged him? Surely Reef must be investigating things now? But Uncle Mentira just smiles and taps his fingers on his leg.

I can't stand the silence for long. 'I know Zoya told you

we were on the Storm squadron. The rest of us weren't allowed to tell our families.'

Uncle Mentira smiles. 'Yes, yes, Zoya's kept me up to date. It's very impressive. Impressive indeed. Fighting for your Nation. Saving lives. All very important, wouldn't you say? More than important – crucial.'

He's always had this way of speaking, as if everything has to be emphasised and jammed into your memory.

'She's a really good navigator,' I add, thinking he must be a bit mad that his own daughter's not nominated for an award too.

'Good enough.' He nods. 'Not better.'

Once Ang has changed – *'Don't I look amazing?'* she preens – it's my turn to go to the compartment next door. I peel off fusty flying gear and slip on a long, gold tunic-dress that has no sleeves and too many spangles. I'm glad I get to keep my boots on. They're familiar. Part of who I am and what I do. I feel vulnerable in a civilian dress – all thin, bare and breakable. Eye Bright looks out of my jacket pocket. I blink back tears. What's going to happen to my pet? What's going to happen to me?

Uncle Mentira knocks on the compartment door. 'Are you ready? Haven't you done yet? We'll be there soon. Very soon indeed.'

Once, before the war and the weird things started, I was looking forward to the Festival of Light. Once I was even afraid of the darkness the Eclipse would bring. Recently, like everyone, I've been counting down the days till Long Night begins. Others, in fear; me, in anticipation. I had the crazy idea I could hide in the dark.

How wrong can I be?

I'm blinded by how bright everything becomes. As we approach Corona there's a surge of power to the train and all the lights get stronger. In Corona there is no sky, only a continual arc of radiance. Roof-to-ground stream-screens beam out bold pictures of sunshine. Walls glow with inlaid lamps. People even wear light-casting clothes.

Ang is impressed. 'Don't they look awesome!' she says.

I think they look well fed, fearless and war-less.

I can't admire the massive buildings, the sculptures, or the illuminations. I can't take in the sight of the Festival parade, made up of the Nation's finest military machines and endless ranks of impeccable soldiers. I barely even register when Uncle Mentira hustles us over to a brand-new Storm with sun designs emblazoned on the wings.

Instead I'm seeing the faces of the crowds in Sea-Ways, uglified by their fear.

I don't start beating time to the great drum bands. I won't sing along with the patriotic crowds. I haven't got ears for the cheers as the Storm is wheeled along in the parade, with me and Ang inside, waving at the crowds.

Instead I'm hearing other voices. Mama crying, – 'She can't help what she is.' Haze accusing – 'Witch-spawn, changeling.' Reef soothing – 'Hush, Rain, you're not making any sense.'

Nothing is making any sense! Not the great white doors of the Capital Building opening to welcome me and Ang, not my boot-steps on the white carpet inside.

'Give me your jacket to hold,' orders Uncle Mentira.

'Watch where you're walking,' says Ang. 'You nearly tripped over my dress hem.'

I nearly trip over thin air I'm so dazed.

Ang claps a hand over her mouth. 'Look who's going to be giving us our medals! They'll be twice as special now . . .'

Marina Furey is there in full uniform, her own medal glinting. This has got to be a dream. No, I scratch my arm and it hurts.

'What a surprise!' Furey cries, shaking our hands vigorously when it's our turn to be presented in a blindingly bright hall. 'Well deserved, girls, well deserved!'

I just gawp. How can I look this amazing woman in the eye when I've just touched her skin and seen how she dies?

'What are you doing here?' I ask in a hoarse voice.

'All last-moment!' she grins. 'An ac-req from Aura, a rush for the train – spick and span uniform waiting for me to mess!' Under cover of hugging me she whispers in my ear, 'I can tell from your face you'd rather be back with the squadron too. Don't worry, we won't spend the rest of the war sitting here stuffing our faces. I'll see we get back to Sea-Ways.'

I know she will. I've foreseen it.

I blink away that vision and stare where Furey's pointing – a room-long banquet table loaded with more food than we see in a week at Sea-Ways. Zoya would be dribbling at the mere sight of such a feast, especially now rations on the squadron are tighter than ever.

Furey talks normally again.

'It's great to see you get all this praise, Rain. You've earned it, every last bit. I'm proud of you. The squadron are proud of you. Tilly says hello, by the way.'

Her face shadows. It must've been awful to leave Tilly behind. I wish she hadn't! I wish none of this was happening!

Ang lifts her Hero medal high, to be captured by cameras and spread to every screen in the Nation. I manage a couple of mechanical smiles, that's all. Big army soldiers are next in line for their awards.

Time seems to compress. I'm at the buffet. I'm holding a drink. I'm saying, *thank you, thank you, thank you* and hearing my name repeated. The room is too white. I need to get out of here!

Be careful what you wish for . . .

'Please, Uncle Mentira, can I just go somewhere and be quiet?'

'Exactly what I've been thinking all along,' he says, suddenly at my side. 'Come this way, through here, just along here, not that door, this one . . . Yes, it's part of the hub laboratory. Sit there and wait. No – I said, *wait*. The door's not yet locked but it could be. It will be. Not that it needs to be. You won't try to escape, will you? I know you'll be a good girl for me . . .'

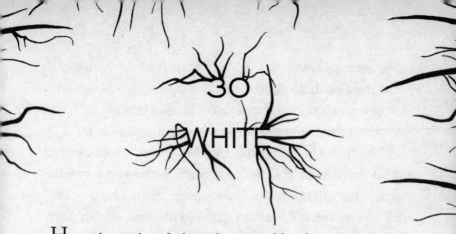

30
WHITE

How clever they feel, tricking me like this. How smug they are, in white uniforms, with black tattoos inked on their eyelids. How small I am, suddenly chained to a chair with bane-metal round my boots. Needles stab into my arms and legs. Pads press on to my head. I'm hooked to a humming machine.

White walls, white floor, white ceiling. Whites of eyes as they lean in to peer. White lights in my eyes as they probe. White ice in my veins as I shiver with fear.

It's some kind of laboratory, one of *the* laboratories in the hub where Aura is housed. I'd never have come here if I'd known. Was Furey in on the trick? Was Ang? Was Reef? I can't bear to believe it. If I sit very, very still and do as I'm told will they think I must be normal after all and let me go home – wherever home is now?

'Have a drink,' says Uncle Mentira.

'I'm not thirsty.'

'I didn't say you were. Drink anyway.'

'What is it?'

'Just drink, please. Down in one, or little sips. Do

you need a straw?'

I need all this to stop.

'She won't drink it,' announces Uncle Mentira.

'She'll drink it,' says one of the Scrutiners in the room.

They're all wearing stretchy fibre gloves the colour of dead flesh. They pull my head back. I clamp my mouth shut. They jab my jaw to prise it open. Some of the liquid trickles in. I sick it back up again, all over my gold dress.

'So sorry,' murmurs Uncle Mentira. 'It's necessary. Required. Essential. How are you feeling?'

'Cold.' That's the only word I can get out.

'Really? Here's your jacket.' He wraps it round my shoulders. 'No, leave all those pads and needles. We need to keep monitoring your vital signs. Just be good and everything will be all right. We don't want to hurt you.'

Be a good girl. Aren't I being good? Aren't I doing almost everything I'm told in the hope that if I don't sprout up I won't get yanked out? Except I know what people do to weeds. I look around for any sign of Slick.

Uncle Mentira smiles with his mouth, not his eyes. 'We won't keep you here any longer than we need to. It's the science, you see. Always, with me, the science, the chemistry. These blood samples shown here on the screen, they've been puzzling me for a long time, but now we've got you we'll be able to set up experiments to explain them.'

I shake my head. 'I don't know what those pictures are.'

'Of course you don't. I'll tell you. The image on the

266

left of the screen is your blood, greatly magnified. Pretty, isn't it?'

'Is there something wrong with it?'

'Oh no! It's perfectly normal.'

'Then why . . . ?'

'Look at the second image.'

'Is that one abnormal?'

'No! All nice and normal too.'

'Then . . . I don't understand. They both look the same.'

Uncle Mentira punches his fist in the air. 'Ha! You've got it. We'll make a scientist of you yet. They are both one hundred per cent exactly the same, which is why we're so intrigued because the sample on the right belongs to someone else. Not a twin, not a sister, not a blood relation of any kind. We took it from a girl named Haze – yes, you know her. Ah, before you ask, yes we did check there wasn't a mix-up in the blood-taking. Absolutely none at all.'

'I swear I never met Haze before I joined the squadron.'

Uncle Mentira nods kindly.

'It's all right. I know you're telling the truth. We had no records of her either. Why would we? She lived in the woods all her life, no better than a wild animal. Still, you must admit the physical resemblance is striking. She's thickset from hard work and tanned from sun exposure. Ignorant, of course, without the benefit of your education. Simple coincidence, a non-scientist might have thought. Then Aura flagged up the match in your blood samples.

Impossible for two people to be so exactly the same. We began to speculate. We wondered what would happen if we let the two of you interact. I studied the Scrutiny reports myself. Her behaviour can all be explained by superstitious irrationality on her part. You, my niece, were more puzzling. How very normal you seemed in every respect.'

'I *am* normal.'

'Oh, Rain, stop pretending.' Uncle Mentira puts his hands on his thighs and bends to look me directly in the face, like he's about to wish me Happy Birthday or offer some family-type advice. 'We know what you are. Suspected it, tested it, proved it. What we want to know now is . . . what are you capable of?'

What am I capable of?

Not polite speech. Not thoughts that make sense, that's for sure. I feel as if there are holes in my feet and all my blood is draining away. As if my bones are melting so only a shell remains, sitting in this white room looking like a person but completely hollow inside.

Somewhere outside the Festival is in full progress. Beyond these walls normal people are having normal lives in normal bodies.

Time neither flies nor drags, it ceases to exist. I can't think how to react or act.

'A kind of catatonia?' muses Uncle Mentira as needles jab into my skin and blood is sucked out. He pats me on the cheek. 'It'll pass.'

I can't focus any more. Instead of the white laboratory I see white snow in the forest.

Uncle Mentira gives my cheek a harder slap now.

'Don't drift too far. I've got a story for you. Your neighbour used to read you stories, didn't she? Stupid woman didn't know how wise she was. What do the tales tell us? Once there were witches. That's what they were called before Aura could study them and give their afflictions a proper name and category. The head witch, the most abnormally evolved, lived on a lake in the forest. She grew old, or ill, or mutated; we don't yet have evidence to judge. She needed to pass her witch-infection on. Am I making sense yet? Getting through to you? Talking your language?'

His words evoke images of the dead-grey lake where I crashed. I see a hut in the water, raised up on wooden legs, all gnarled and knobbled. I step across the still water and knock on the hut door. No one replies. I push open the door and smell what's inside – age, weakness, goat-milk and garlic.

Welcome, Rain . . . comes a voice as old as stone and dark as the Eclipse.

'Wake up, Rain!'

A circle of Scrutiners forms a copse around me. They're so tall when I look up, like silver-bark trees. If they spread their arms birds could land on them. A bird stirs – the corvil in my jacket.

'Ssh . . .' I warn it. 'Ssh,' I warn the Scrutiners, who are consulting keypads and screens.

'Ah, you're back.' Uncle Mentira breaks connection and waves the Scrutiners away. 'Sorry for the disorientation. We haven't yet figured out the correct dosage for keeping you docile but alert. Feybane hasn't attracted much scientific study until recently, so we're learning as we go.'

'I'm fine,' I croak. The words seem to come out one hour at a time. I'm about to add, 'I want to go home,' but then I remember I haven't got a home. They turned on me. Turned me out. Don't want me any more.

Uncle Mentira crouches down to look me in the eye as he speaks. 'We've been speculating about what it is you can do for us, Rain. Predictions are limited at the moment, with only Old Nation fey-tales as sources to go on, alongside reports of your behaviour since that initial crash in the Morass.'

I *knew* it wasn't paranoia. I *knew* I was being spied upon.

'Haze is full of stories. Full of lies.'

'Haze doesn't interest us very much,' says Uncle Mentira. 'She was just a skivvy, learning conjuring tricks and keeping goats. She's had nothing useful to say about the old woman who kept her working in the forest, apart from fanciful notions about controlling light and dark. Presuming they *are* fanciful . . . ?'

For the first time there's an edge of uncertainty in his voice – or is it fear? I don't care about his concerns. I'm wondering who's been making secret reports about me.

270

Was it Reef? It had to be him. First his parents, now me. And he said I could trust him!

I tell Uncle Mentira that I fly planes. That I want to go back to Sea-Ways.

'Leave military tactics to the experts, Rain. Aura predicts the future by statistical probability, not superstitious bowl-gazing in a bath-house. According to Aura Sea-Ways will fall. It's a lost cause. A Crux victory waiting to happen. Corona is far more important, more crucial. Corona is Aura's hub.'

'What about my friends?'

He shrugs. '*Friends* has become a rather inaccurate term for the people you once associated with under false pretences. Still, the reports did say you were loyal. Young Reef Starzak noted repeatedly – and admiringly – how you gave no thought for your own safety if others were in danger. That has been a most useful piece of information. Which is why I brought this . . .'

Without blinking he produces a People's Number Five Glissom pistol from a pocket in his white coat.

'I'm not afraid of you.'

'I know.' Uncle Mentira connects briefly then goes to the single door set smoothly in the white walls. I notice there's no handle on the inside. I can also see there's nothing made of bioweave in the room. No flowers will grow here.

The door opens, just a little way.

Zoya slips through the gap. I'm guessing she found the banquet all right, because there's a stain of something on

271

her tunic front and a crumb still lodged in the corner of her mouth. Funny to think I made this prediction back in the bath-house – *You get free run of a luxury banquet in Corona.* It seemed so silly and irrelevant at the time. Now everything I foretold is coming true.

Uncle Mentira says, 'Ah, here you are. Just in time. Come in.'

Zoya squints at all the lights. 'I'm missing the Festival. Everybody's out there.'

'Not everyone.' Uncle Mentira nods towards me.

Zoya's surprise is genuine. 'Pip! What . . . ?' Then she looks from me to her father. 'I didn't think . . .'

'Of course not,' he says soothingly. 'I don't expect you to. Your job is to do as you're told. Did you bring what I asked for?'

She nods, *yes*.

'Good. Safer to ask you to get it than risk taking some ourselves . . .'

My own Cousin Zoya.

'*Confide in me*,' she said. '*Trust me*,' she said. I should've known she'd have to betray me – who'd blame her? Anything not to be different, not to stand out, not to disobey Aura. It's just like the vision in the bath-house basin of water – one by one people I care about turn away from me in disgust. What's left?

Just me. Whoever – whatever – I am.

Little nodes connected to my wrists and scalp send

signals to a scanner which scratches out lines on a screen nearby – my blood pressure? Stress levels?

'Tense, isn't it?' says Uncle Mentira. He's got a curious gleam in his eye, rather like a corvil eyeing up a potential meal. 'Believe me, I wouldn't resort to such untidy emotional blackmail if we really didn't need some answers soon. Proper scientific research takes time we just don't have.'

A voice from the forest rustles in my mind. An old woman warns, *Rain . . . we haven't much time . . .*

'Leave Zoya out of this. It's got nothing to do with her.'

'That's not what my trigger finger says,' replies Uncle Mentira calmly. He holds the pistol to Zoya's temple. She flinches and gives a little whimper, like a wolf cub would, pinned down by its parent. 'I don't *want* to do this, Rain, do you understand that? My personal preferences do not include pointing a gun at my own daughter's head.'

'Can't you just let her go?'

'Can't you just give us a show? We need to know if you're worth all this attention.'

The scanner lines are getting longer and stronger. The air goes so still I think the posse of Scrutiners must be holding their collective breath.

'It's OK, Zoya,' I say, palms out as if to calm the whole room. 'He isn't going to shoot.'

I don't blame her for crying. I am too, inside. 'He's serious, Pip! Just do what he says!'

'Do what?'

273

'You *know*!' she screams in panic as her father presses the gun harder against her skull. 'Do that thing. The power. The black feathers. I had to tell him about it, *I had to*.'

Black feathers sprouting as I chased Steen Verdessica's plane out of the sky and into the Morass. Black feathers flying as I caught a Storm so Petra and Lida would be safe. A black feather circling as Haze leans over a bowl of water in the bath-house, chanting . . .

> *Black Night's daughter*
> *Bright White's kin*
> *Let the lights go out –*
> *Let the Witch come in!*

'You want a witch?' I growl at Uncle Mentira and all the stone-faced Scrutiners. 'All right. Fine. I'll show you a witch!'

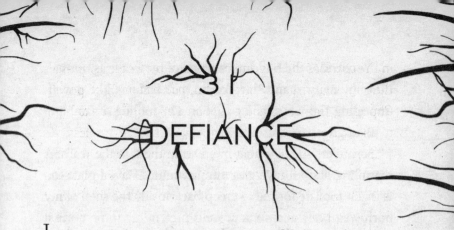

3
DEFIANCE

Lights explode. Darkness rushes in to fill the void. In my mind I'm a thousand klicks away, walking on a leaf-strewn path. My hands brush silver-bark branches and send up clouds of spores. In the real world I find I'm running my fingers along the white walls of the laboratory, looking for something I can gouge my nails into, anything alive I can tear or pull apart. Nothing. The walls and floor are opaque glass – burned sand that was once stone. My feet are heavy, trailing their bane-metal chains. It's a prison. I'm trapped.

The adults are useless in the dark. Even Zoya's night-vision won't help her in a room with no light at all. She's huddled up against her papi, blind eyes darting all around.

'Pip!'

Don't Pip me. I'm not that kid, not that tiddler.

Why's Zoya got her arm up? What's she pointing at? The door?

I sweep round the walls again and feel a sliver of free air. Zoya left the door open a crack! I seize it with both hands and pull it out of the wall, just as I did with Steen's prison door. This time I'm not breaking in, I'm breaking out. Out in the corridor the building is made of bioweave as normal. I dig my nails in and start to run, *pad pad pad* like a wolf, unpeeling the walls as I go. Soon I'm trailing a tumbling mass of grey.

Scrutiners spring out at me. I wrap them in the walls. A wormling of doubt wiggles into my mind. Have I gone too far? Is it too late for me to creep back inside the shell of my borrowed body and slink around pretending to be normal somehow? Don't know. This defiance is uncharted territory. Off the map. Off the path.

Don't step off the path.

Forget the path. What did Reef say? *Become lost.*

Lost? I'm losing everything I ever cared about with every moment that passes – family, friends, Reef . . . If I let the monster out will I lose myself or become myself?

The corvil struggles from my jacket pocket and climbs to my shoulder. It sounds a single *caa* that seems to echo for ever. I spread my arms like wings. My fingers seem to stretch along the bioweave up to the roof and down to the foundations, stopping only where they find cold glass. When I flex, the walls shred, exposing a giant hub of labs and computing rooms, floor after floor of cubicles and corridors, filled with scientists and secretaries fumbling for emergency lights. There is no heart to this place, only thousands of nerve centres creating the brain that is Aura. It's not alive. It's not interested in life . . . and yet it wants to survive. It wants me to protect it. It wants me to be a good girl by going bad.

A little sound catches my consciousness in the middle of all other noises jostling for my attention. It's the fainter-than-faint sound of hair strands brushing against each other. There's a click. A lighter-box sparks. A flame jumps out.

Uncle Mentira is behind me in the corridor. In his right hand he holds a lighter-box, flicking the catch so it clicks and ignites again. His left hand is closed around something secret. He opens his palm. The breeze from the torn walls wafts over a set of fine black hairs.

My hair.

I know who brought him that. My navigator. My cousin. My friend.

'*Your hair's a complete mess . . . Hand your hairbrush over,*' Zoya said.

Click.

Uncle Mentira lights the flame and holds it towards one single strand of hair.

Agony

One word – five letters – an infinity of kliks beyond the actual sensation of pain I feel as the fire touches the strand of hair.

I burn!

Not for real – not with normal flames that can be doused by water or smothered in sand. This fire is like having melted sun poured into my soul. If I scream it's not with any normal voice but from somewhere deep and primitive.

A well of rage finds expression in this scream. I cannot move. Cannot bear the pain. Cannot live a moment longer with such torture.

Snuff.

The fire goes out. The burned hair curls. The smell is vile. I collapse on the corridor floor. My lungs find air. My mouth finds words.

'Make – it – stop!'

'It will stop as soon as you see reason and follow orders.'

'Going – to – Sea-Ways . . .'

Click. The lighter-box burns again. Uncle Mentira holds the hair strand close. I see the flame reach up greedily – see every hue of orange, white and blue. Again – the pain! Again I scream for help. Again he blows the fire out. I try to rise.

My lips are cracked. I can only manage to mouth, 'Sea-Ways . . .'

Click.

No no no not again can't bear the pain can't stand the flames make it stop make it stop make it . . .

. . . stop.

On my shoulder Eye Bright has spread its feathers and launched into the air. It flies for the first time, straight at Uncle Mentira, beak stabbing and wings thrashing. Its claws grab the hair and the lighter-box. At the same time Zoya hurls herself through the darkness into her father, pushing him over.

'Run, Pip, run!'

In these chains? I lumber over to the ripped wall and look down. Why run when I can fly, or jump at least, grasping bioweave so the walls unravel as I fall. I feel beautiful black feathers float around me, so soft I could lie in them for ever. When I look up, a line of Scrutiners are peering down, blind eyes roving. Zoya's there too, with the corvil circling round her head.

'I didn't know . . .' she calls down.

I flounder out of the feathers and start tugging at the chains. It's killing me to wear them.

'Didn't know *what*? That bane-metal would bind me? That burning witch hair is a weapon?'

'I didn't know it would hurt so much. I didn't want to spy on you. I got ac-reqs. I had to do what Aura says, everybody does.'

I don't want to hear any more reasons or excuses. 'I'm going.'

'Where?'

'Where do you think? Back to the squadron.'

'What will everyone say?'

'Will you *listen* to yourself? Do you think you can spend your entire life worrying about what other people will think or say? Forget Aura, forget your father, do what *you* think is right!'

To Zoya's credit she only hesitates a moment then she says, 'I'm going to jump. Catch me!'

She leaps and screams simultaneously. Without thinking I spread a bed of feathers and let her land in it. She struggles

279

to her feet and tries to pick feathers from her hair. I'm already limping away. My ankles are burning where the bane-metal rubs. Zoya stumbles after me.

The city all around is almost completely lightless – did I do that? The darkness at the far end of the avenue we're standing on starts to vibrate. Something is moving down the street.

'How are we going to get back to Sea-Ways?' Zoya pants. 'They'll never let us on the train, even if it's still working, then there's the Crux blockade.'

A little smile twists the corner of my mouth and my heart starts to dance. 'I thought we could fly.'

Zoya gawps. 'Can you really do that?'

My smile widens. 'I can in one of those . . .'

I hear the sweet, sweet sound of propellers turning. There it comes, rounding the corner of the avenue, a fine sight. 'A fine sight, indeed,' Uncle Mentira might say, if he wasn't too busy floundering around in darkness.

Marina Furey jumps down from the cockpit of the Storm in her usual state of rumpled energy. She's got lo-glo sticks poking out of every pocket and even one round her neck. Her eyes are flashing. It's too dark for her to see the damaged laboratory hub behind me but she catches sight of the chains round my legs and the corvil now climbing clawfully up my sleeve.

'If I thought you had answers you'd have a *ton* of explaining to do, Rain Aranoza. As for you, Zoya Mentira, I got your bizarre *paper* note saying Rain might need wings in a hurry. Na! Did I ever tell you how much I *hate* being out in the dark?'

Now Zoya has her chance to look smug. 'I had to do what Uncle Mentira told me to but nobody said anything about not asking for help and I thought paper was safer than messaging through Aura.'

I stare at her. 'So you have got a rebellious streak after all?'

Zoya frowns. 'Don't tell everyone.'

'Do you know what's been happening?' I ask Furey nervously. I've no idea if I even look like myself or like the monster everyone says I am.

'Haven't a clue!' she replies. 'However, I do know things are bad in Sea-Ways and we need every Storm crew we can get if we're going to keep the Crux out of the city during the Long Night. The siege is now full circle. The blockade is complete. We've not got long before dawn, and then very little time before the Eclipse begins, so move yourself! I suggest you use this street as your runway and take off before the city's power is restored and an army of Scrutiners comes chasing us.'

'Us?'

'You didn't think I'd let you fly one of these wooden toys unescorted, did you? Give me time to get to the airbase here and we'll be right behind you in a People's Number Forty-eight Fighter Plane . . .'

'We?' asks Zoya. 'I don't know how to navigate one of those.'

'Neither do I, but I'm a fast learner,' comes a new voice. And here is *Ang*, climbing out of the Storm. She's got her Hero of Rodina medal pinned nicely to the front of her dress.

I turn to Furey. 'Don't do it. Please, I mean it. You don't have to.'

She looks down at me and shakes her head. 'Yes I do.'

'But you could get hurt . . .' *You could get killed.*

'My daughter's trapped in the siege, Aranoza. Do you think I wouldn't sacrifice anything to make Tilly safe, whatever Aura's ac-reqs or your feelings?'

'She'll be safe,' I say, thinking of my vision of Tilly that showed her living to old age. 'But—'

'Butt out, Aranoza. Go! Fly!'

Furey boosts me into the Storm, not wasting words asking what the chains are all about. Like a white flood, Scrutiners come running down the street. They needn't bother shooting, I'm not stopping. It takes all my strength to pull the Storm's control stick back, especially since this seat is too low for me. We only lift off the ground at the very last moment. The plane rises like my spirits.

The last I hear from Furey is a faint cry of 'Safe skies and combat glory!'

Ahead, a pale light softens Corona's suburban silhouettes. It's the last dawn before the Eclipse.

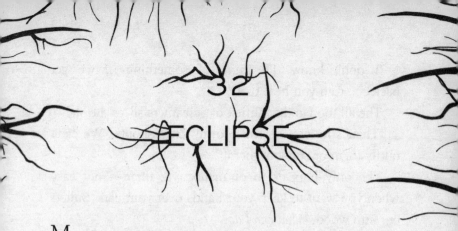

32
ECLIPSE

Mouth open I drink the cold air in. Eyes wide I watch the Nation rush past.

It's a painfully beautiful morning. Everything is stained with the pink and orange of sunrise, as well as the red of un-set Umbra. Flying towards it I feel tiny, just a speck on a vast planet turning in space. I'm bursting to be bigger. If I peel my skin off could I leap high enough to break the roof of the sky? Could I soar through comets and cosmic dust, past Umbra's russet-red rings? Could I plummet right into the searing heat of the sun and still live to tell the tale?

That's just it. I don't know. What *can* I do? See in the dark. See how people die. See futures swirl in still water. What use is that?

The Storm is slow, slow, *slow*. I can't count the klicks off fast enough. We follow the Transnation train tracks south to Sea-Ways. The sun pours out as much light as it can, as if it knows how close the Eclipse is. Soon there won't be days and nights, just many-days-long darkness.

'What are you going to say to everyone when we get back?' Zoya calls from behind me.

'I don't know. I'll think of something. *If* we get back . . . Can you hear that?'

The all too familiar shriek of Screamers slices the sky.

'There's no gun on this Storm!' Zoya shouts. 'We can't outfly them or shoot at them!'

The only hope is to outmanoeuvre them – not easy when you want to keep your hands over your ears. Bullets cut into wood. *What can I do?*

I spread my arms and take a deep breath, drawing a great gulp of energy in. I become wind in the leaves. Leaves on the trees. I scatter like spores yet still stay solid. It's the most amazing feeling. The dive-bombers turn for a second dive, hunting in pairs as usual. They scream at me. I scream back. The sky darkens. This is not the slow creep of Umbra's curve across the sun's white disc, this is a storm of black feathers – I am the storm!

I send the Screamers down to furrow the ground in smoke and flames. I'd yell with joy if I didn't suddenly feel utterly drained. My chains are so heavy! The Storm dips, losing altitude, then the nose rises again.

'I have control!' shouts Zoya, working the dual equipment as I rest.

No, the Crux have control – I see Sea-Ways ahead, completely surrounded now by hostile armies. Bomb-slingers send death into the city. Two more Screamers rise up to keep us from breaching the siege. Zoya has us twisting and turning while I somehow raise another furious cloud of unnatural black. One Screamer is silenced. Where's the other? Can hear it, can't see it . . . We're turning every way at once in a maelstrom of feathers and fear, screams getting closer, the Storm pulling apart, time stretching, control slipping, world spinning . . .

An explosion! Shrapnel jags the Storm's wood and wings. Fire flashes, smoke blinds – a new plane has joined the fight. A People's Number Forty-eight Fighter!

'It's Furey! She's found us! She's saved us!' Zoya whoops.

The fighter is so much faster than our little Storm. Furey has to make a wide arc before flying past again with a cheeky waggle of her wings. We wave to her and Ang, then they're gone. Not for long. When the next pair of Screamers screeches into view Furey is straight at them, guns blazing.

Around Sea-Ways army-issue lamps speckle the ranks of the besiegers. They're tiny compared to the sun they'll have to replace. Perhaps the Crux will pray to their god to bring the light back again. In the meanwhile, they'll have to deal with me and my darkness.

Except I'm tired. Na! Even the plane is sluggish. The fuel needle starts to tremble over the red section on the dial. Almost empty.

To the Crux on watch-duty we must be a smudge of a silhouette against the sun's last-ditch dazzle. It's all they can do to set their weapon sights on us.

Umbra touches the sun and takes a bite of the brightness.

'Furey can't fly in the dark!' shouts Zoya. 'And her plane's not wood like ours. The bioweave could start unravelling, doesn't she realise that?'

I think of Furey's steady grey gaze back at Corona. 'She knows.'

Three times Furey brings her fighter round to fire at the Crux anti-aircraft guns. Twice she swoops free, unscathed. That will please Ang Two-Times no end. On the third run she lets a last volley of bullets fly.

Umbra slides further across the sun. One fragile crescent of sunshine remains.

Furey's fighter trails threads of bioweave as it begins to lose height. She swoops past me and for a moment I have a clear view of her in the pilot seat, with Ang behind. Then the fighter tilts towards Crux gun-placements. Suddenly I know why I foretold Ang would win *two* Hero of Rodina Nation awards. Both of them will be well deserved. Furey is going to take out the Crux siege guns to give us clear passage to Sea-Ways. One last mission. One final sacrifice.

I can't bear that! I strain all my thoughts, all my power, to reach the fighter in time. They're too far ahead. I'm not strong enough.

Birds sing their last song. The air chills and stills.

An explosion.

They die.

The day dies.

The sun is swallowed. It is a perfect disc of black. Night reigns.

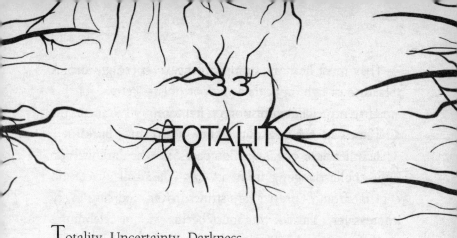

33
TOTALITY

Totality. Uncertainty. Darkness.

The black sun cannot warm us. The Nation shivers. The Storm staggers through this new night. Long before we spot the landing field the fuel indicator needle clunks to empty. The propellers stutter, the engine chokes and dies. We glide.

It's strangely peaceful to slide over Sea-Ways, lower, lower, ground-bound – down. In a peacetime Eclipse the streets would be dazzling with lights. Now blackout rules and power-rationing leave the city dim. At a bombed warehouse, flames are the only illumination, alongside the lamps of fire-fighting teams. No other trucks are out on the streets. We see no people scuttling down the pavements.

I open up the Storm's landing gear and take a deep breath. Time to face the squadron . . . and rejection. Time to discover the true price of stepping off the path. I gaze at my hands. They look normal. I touch my face. It feels normal. The black feather I pick out of my hair is definitely not normal. The fronds are so soft. I stick it behind one ear. My corvil croaks in approval.

287

They must hear the bump of wheels on the ground. A rectangle of light appears as a door opens. Petra's got this amazing *expectant* expression on her face.

'I knew it!' she calls out. 'I knew you'd come back!'

Another door opens. Fenlon peers into the dark with an unlit choke dangling from his lips – a small affectation copied from Furey. He strides over, cursing very impressively. I think this must be his way of celebrating our safe return. It's less painful than the usual back-slaps he gives.

'First you're off to Corona without stopping to say *good-bye-and-go-well*, next we hear the siege is complete and no one can break *out* of the city, let alone *into* it . . . and here you are, large as life and twice as miserable. Don't tell me you're going to mope all the way through the Long Night. I've had enough of gloomy reports – ration riots in the city centre, a spate of suicides already, and some hysteria about spies or something supernatural . . .'

Zoya pulls herself up from the cockpit. 'Someone should tell him,' she murmurs.

Fenlon's not done. 'Before connection went scatty there was an update about a People's Number Forty-eight Fighter stolen from its hangar in Corona. Nothing to do with you two by any chance?'

I swallow. 'Furey . . .'

'Might've known it! That woman was born to trouble as sure as the sun rises and sets, or in this case, gets blocked out by a great big gas giant of a planet. Sent you back without her, did she? Staying in Corona to live the high life in luxury, is she?'

'I'm really sorry. She was in the stolen fighter. Her and Ang escorted us to Sea-Ways. They didn't make it.'

Now, when time changes it's nothing to do with me, it's all about the way a man ages in mere moments. His shoulders slump, his spine curves, his skin goes grey.

'Ridiculous. A woman like Marina Furey doesn't die.' He fumbles for the choke, finds it, sniffs it for a moment then drops it to the runway and grinds it under his boot heel.

Petra sags too, as do the others who've gathered round.

Dee grabs Zoya as she climbs from the Storm.

'Ang's gone as well? Are you sure? She didn't look like she was going to die, and she didn't want to either. She always said my company would kill her off twice as fast as the Crux ever could.'

Zoya winces. 'There was nothing we could do. I'm so sorry.'

'Come on,' says Lida. 'We should go inside; the temperature's dropping.'

I blush. 'Can you help me out, please?'

Petra's shocked when she sees the pool of bane-metal chain-links in the cockpit.

'Yeldon, you'll have something to cut these, won't you?'

He leaps up and looks in. 'What the . . . ? Zoya, what's going on?'

Zoya is as grey as death. 'There's something a bit . . . abnormal . . . going on,' she begins.

It's at that point my strength seeps right away and I collapse.

34
LONG NIGHT

The hiss of steam. The bubble of boiling water. The clatter
of a spoon in a mug. These are the noises I wake up to. I
open my eyes to a sweet-smelling cloud.

'Drink this . . .'

I scrabble to get out of the reach of Haze and whatever
she's offering me.

'What . . . ?'

'Don't worry,' Haze says. 'It's not poisoned. They say
you're more useful alive than dead.'

'What are you doing here? Where are the others? Where
am I?'

'Never mind, drink this.'

'How long have I been sleeping?'

Haze shakes her head. 'Hard to say when this night goes
on for ever.'

'How long – tell me!'

'Four days' worth of night.'

Four days! The Long Night will soon be over and here I
am, lying around like one big lump of uselessness! I throw
off the covers. And nearly faint again. When I look down at

291

my arms, my skin is so fine I can see right through it to a pattern of veins like black lace.

The room shakes. Haze hardly flinches. 'It's just the Crux. They've been throwing bombs at us for ever. My papi . . .' She has the grace to blush. 'He says the Crux will come into the city the moment the Eclipse ends.'

'And my . . . your mother?'

'Still at the factory – the bit that hasn't been bombed. I was helping there till Zoya came and told me you were sick.' Haze frowns. 'She was mean to me. She said I had to get you better or she'd tell your corvil to peck my eyes out. So this is medicine I used to make for the old mother in the forest in winter when she felt weak, until she got so bad she couldn't stop me running away.'

'You left her when she was sick?'

'She stole me from my family and made me a slave! Why would I stay?'

Trust. Mistrust. Loyalty. Who knows what's what any more? I take the mug and gulp the hot liquid down. It seems fine. The warmth that spreads through my body is certainly welcome.

'Is Reef here?'

Haze shrugs. Doesn't know, doesn't care. 'Lida wants to see you.'

We muster in the privacy of Furey's office – the former headteacher's room. They practically have to drag me there by my arms because my legs are still numb, even this long after the chains have been cut off. At least my skin's not so laced with black. I may even look normal again.

It's bitterly cold after four days without sun. Frost crusts the leaves of plants pushing between the window-frames. Slick supplies must have run out during the siege.

I keep my eyes low, focusing on big boots, knotted laces, dirty trouser hems . . .

They're all here, the people I knew as friends. Dee, Petra, Mossie, Yeldon, Zoya, Lida . . . Others too, civilians from the city and, most shockingly, my papi. I'd know his cracked brown boots anywhere; I've tripped over them in the doorway often enough. What should I call him now I know he's not my father any more? You never think of your parents having names like normal people.

Little Tilly is here too, sitting in Mossie's lap. Tilly opens and closes her hand to me in a solemn wave. Someone must've broken the news of her mother's death. How can she even understand what *dead* means? I don't. I keep expecting Furey to burst into the office blowing a squall.

While the others shuffle uncomfortably about the edges of the room, Lida fumbles for a packet of chokes and taps one out. The mere sight of a lighter-box is enough to make me tremble with fear.

'So, here we all are,' she begins.

'All of who?' asks Dee.

'Dee, for once just *shut up*. All of whoever's going to be here right now, OK? All of whoever there is left. Plus our odd little Pipsqueak. Have you brought the chains just in case, Yeldon?'

Yeldon shakes a cascade of bane-metal. I grip my stomach.

Lida ignores me. 'Fact is, Sea-Ways is on the brink of being over run by Crux. Fact is, normal communications are down. Fact is, brutal and simple, we're screwed. You got something to add to that, sir?'

Papi has opened his mouth. He closes it again and looks, unhappily, at me.

Lida continues. 'Long Night is not going well, that's the point we're starting from here.' People nod. 'It's like the whole city's disconnected, literally and mentally. Four days we've been sitting here with Crux bomb-slingers smashing missiles down.'

Even as she says this another distant thud makes the air shake.

She drags smoke from the choke, coughs violently, then stubs it out and points to me.

'You predicted this, you know, at that fortune-telling thing we did. You said I'd get charge of my own squadron.'

'I didn't mean for it to happen like this. Because of Furey . . .'

' . . . dying. Right. Sorry, Tilly. Look, should the kid even be here?'

Mossie wraps her arms around Tilly. 'The bomb shelters are full.'

'And they stink,' adds Petra.

Lida snorts. 'She might be safer there than in here, if all the rumours about Pip are true.'

I keep my eyes down and mumble, 'I'm not going to hurt you.'

Lida's brow goes up. 'So what Zoya says isn't a fey-tale. You really are . . . ?'

Papi sucks in air through his teeth.

I just sigh. 'A witch? Yes. I think so.'

That makes Lida laugh, and not in a merry way. 'You *think* so? What am I supposed to do now? We've had no updates from Aura since the Eclipse started. Is that your fault?'

'I think . . . I mean, yes, probably, but only by accident.'

'She doesn't look like a witch . . .' says Dee cautiously. 'I've never actually seen her eating babies or drinking blood.'

My lip curls. 'That's disgusting.'

'So are *monsters*,' says Yeldon, crunching his arms so his muscles flex.

Lida turns to Fenlon. 'Does she look normal to you?'

Fenlon pulls a face. 'I never thought any of you kids were normal, buzzing about at night when you should be safe at home doing schoolwork and watching bad shows on the stream-screens—'

'I wanted Rain to stay safe at home,' Papi interrupts.

Lida rolls her eyes at him. Clearly parents cramp her style.

'Rain can't be a witch,' Dee decides definitively.

'Otherwise she would have something to stop Ang being dead.' She puts her hands over her face and cries without making a sound.

Papi looks massively uncomfortable. 'What happens now? I came here because that Scrutiner said I should.'

That makes me pay attention. 'Reef Starzak?'

'That's the one. Came to the house in person. Said I was to report to the squadron and speak to Marina Furey. Sorry, sweeting . . .' He nods towards Tilly. 'There's been all sorts of talk about . . . *witches* and the like, and this girl Haze has been telling me my daughter's some sort of changeling child! Are you saying it's all true then?' He's looking directly at me. I turn away, unable to bear his narrow eyes and the pain in his voice.

Mossie sniffs. 'I don't think Zoya's lying . . .' she says carefully.

'I'm not,' says Zoya.

'Fine,' says Papi, suddenly impatient. 'So let's say Rain *is* a witch, what—'

Yeldon erupts. 'Oh, we'll just say that, shall we? We'll just sit in the room and speak superstitions? I was brought up not to believe all that Old Nation stuff. Are you telling me she's a monster? She looks like a little *runt* to me. Small enough to feel my muscles if she wants a fight . . .'

His fingers curl to fists and his feet slide to a boxing stance.

Zoya tries to pull his arms down again. 'Don't fight . . .'

'It's all right,' he growls. 'I won't rough her up too much, just enough to make her think twice about trying any monster mojo on us.'

'It's not her I'm worried about,' Zoya says quietly.

Lida looks me straight in the eyes. 'I don't know anything about witch stuff, Pip—'

'My name's Rain,' I interrupt suddenly. 'I'm not a pipsqueak . . . or a runt.'

'Fair enough. Rain it is, then. You seem normal to me, so I'm putting these superstitious delusions down to battle fatigue, or maybe the excitement of getting a Hero of Rodina medal has scrambled your brain. Whatever. The important question is, what now? Our last ac-reqs were to lie low and keep the lights on till Long Night's over. We're to eke out fuel blocks and food as long as we can. Meanwhile, Mossie's got us knitting to keep us warm now temperatures are teasing the freezing mark.'

'That's crazy!' I burst out.

'Because witches don't like knitted knots?' asks Mossie, half offended.

'Because you could be doing something! You could run blockades, bomb the Crux, keep up morale – show them we're down but not out!'

Lida shakes her head. '*You've* been out for four days. You've no idea what's happening in the city. It's like this attack of mass hysteria just because the sky's gone dark. People are literally going mad without Aura and without daylight.'

Fenlon nods. 'They say a Scrutiner was attacked on the

street when he tried to stop people breaking into the People's Number Ninety-four Museum to liberate old god-house bells.'

'Not Reef?'

Lida explodes with frustration. 'We have absolutely no idea who it was, or where Reef Starzak is. That's my whole point – there's no one to connect to and ask. At least we're used to being out at night without lights and going without Aura for hours at a time. Everyone else is out of their heads.'

'So take advantage of this experience. Do something to save the city!' I persist.

'Do *what*?'

'Whatever you can. What about spreading word that we don't just have to sit and wait for defeat? We can rise up and fight, with bare fists like Yeldon if there's nothing else. Forget Aura! This is Rodina we're fighting for – our loved ones, our way of life, our homeland. Fenlon, how many Storms are currently operational?'

Fenlon folds his arms. 'Define *operational*. If you mean ready to fly, get shot at and crash, then I can have nine, maybe ten, ready in an hour.'

'Only nine?' I can't believe it. 'Did we lose so many while I was out of it?'

'What's with all this *we* and *our* stuff?' snarls Yeldon. 'Whose side are you on anyway, weird girl? What's *your* plan of action?'

I rub my eyes, which are still heavy and sore. 'Can you spare a Storm for me? I need to get to the Morass.'

Lida laughs at that, a harsh sound. 'Hadn't you noticed? The Morass has come to us!'

She's right. The school has become a garden. The bioweave walls are bulging with vine stems. Leaves are bursting beneath the ceiling lights, turning everything faintly green.

Mossie says, 'It started a few days ago and keeps getting worse. People tried burning it and the fires just got too out of control. The only good news is, it must be attacking the Crux as much as us.'

'Who says it's attacking?' I ask. 'They're just plants, growing where you don't want them.'

When Papi speaks his voice is gruff. 'Last Long Night it was the same. Trees sporing everywhere and these flowers sprouting. Back then we just yanked the weeds out and got on with it. That was before we knew there really were . . . witches . . . walking around like normal people.'

'But they're *not* normal,' Yeldon insists.

Zoya wants to know, 'What are you going to do when you get back to the Morass, Pip?'

'Anything's got to be better than sitting around here waiting for the Crux to stop praying for the light to shine again. I thought I might try to defeat the enemy army, save the city and end the war – something like that.'

Now they all look at me as if I'm disconnected as well as deviant, which, since Uncle Mentira took my keypad, is pretty much the literal truth.

299

'You want to defeat the Crux army?' mocks Lida. 'Are you really that powerful?'

'I've no idea. There's only one way to find out . . .'

I turn to go . . .

'Not so fast,' Lida says. She pulls her lighter-box from a pocket and deliberately flips it open in front of me. 'One message did come through from Aura. We've had the highest-priority instructions to contain you here if you should happen to appear, using whatever force necessary.'

Yeldon smiles with satisfaction. 'Apparently witches do have some vulnerable points . . .'

I nearly crumple to the grass-growing floor. All it will take is one strand of my hair from my pillow, my hairbrush, cut from my head, then . . . unbelievable agony.

The crew move closer. They move as one. They are, after all, loyal citizens of Rodina. Bred to obey. To belong.

Click, click, click, Lida flips the lighter-box lid. Then she smiles.

'As I've said, the orders are to use force, but how can I help it if you turn violent and overpower me with some abnormal witch power?'

'Violent? I haven't touched you!'

Lida steps aside and hands me the lighter-box. 'Having made me your first victim of brutality, I hope you don't somehow manage to force Fenlon to let you steal a Storm.'

Fenlon grins. 'There's one already fuelled and armed.'

I stare at them all.

Fenlon coughs. 'Er, any time soon would be good for

the breakout, Aranoza. I can't stand round here being a hostage all day. I have got other things to do, you know.'

Mossie is suddenly at my side, taking off her coat and slinging it round my shoulders. 'How dare you wrestle these warm clothes from me, you monster?'

Petra joins her. 'I'm appalled you knocked me to the ground and made me give you this good-luck hug.'

Yeldon shakes his head in disbelief. 'You're all letting her go? You're acting like she can be trusted, when we've no proof she won't destroy us all too? Fine! Take a Storm if you have to, but don't expect the rest of us to break faith with Aura by helping you after that. We're loyal citizens of Rodina Nation. You're a deviant *creature* of some kind. Go back to the Morass where you belong!'

35
THE MORASS

Where I belong . . .

That has a nice sound to it.

I go west. Light frost dusts my wings. Gunfire flashes as I break the blockade. The Crux are distracted by attacks from Sea-Ways civilians, who are braving the dark and their own indecision to fight. The people I thought of as my parents are somewhere down there, creating a diversion so I can fly free.

I don't fly alone. Eye Bright the corvil perches on my shoulder. Zoya scrunches in the nav seat behind me, wearing everything she owns and still shivering.

'You didn't have to come,' I tell her.

'I really did,' she insists.

'You could've stayed with everybody else, arguing about whether to do nothing, or next to nothing.'

'I know.' She sighs. I bet she wishes she had.

As soon as we near the murky green-black of the Morass edge I tell her she has control.

She squawks, 'What do you mean, I have control? What are you going to do?'

I turn round in the cockpit and smile at her. 'I'm going to see just how fun flying can be.'

I've already unlaced my boots. My feet will be cold but I don't care. When I land I want to feel the ground beneath my bare skin.

'Where are we going to land?' Zoya asks.

I climb out of the pilot's seat and on to a wing. The corvil grips my shoulder. 'Go back and stay safe with everyone!' I shout as I drop, as I fall . . . as I soar!

Not for me now the confines of wood and wingspan. Down I dive, trailing a cloak of darkness. I love it – love this freedom! I'm not buoyed up by air, I *am* the air. I'm the sky, the night, the wind teasing the treetops. I could fly like this for ever; I could circle the planet, breaking Marina Furey's round-the-world record . . .

Furey.

Her name is a jolt. Others follow – Ang, Henke, Rill . . . Mama, Papi, Reef . . .

Pain. Loss. Grief. Betrayal.

They're too heavy. I fall. I crash. I break through branches, shred nests and scatter leaves. The ground catches me. It's hard. As soon as I touch earth my senses spread. I reach through roots, round rocks and under still water. This is the forest again.

Home.

I run. The frost-cold forest runs with me. Wolves pace between the trees, corvils skim above them, a croaking wave of black. Eye Bright flies too, smaller than the rest.

We follow no path. The path follows me. I blaze my own trail over hill and under night. I come to the lake.

Here we stop, the forest and I. Here we pause. The water is as grey and flat as ever. There are lights in the darkness. *'Don't look at the lights,'* everyone said. They dance for me now, bobbing in a tired breeze. I start wading. Blind fish swim away from me. The lights get closer. They're made from fragile little bird skulls, filled with wax and lit with wavering flames. They mark stepping stones set just under the water's surface. Soon I make out a shape in the mist – a wooden house on wooden legs, with a foot-smoothed wooden ladder.

Welcome, Rain . . .

The door is open. I push it wider and breathe in the smell of ancient life and imminent death. There are lifeless rachnids curled in cobwebbed corners, chairs and cups furred with dust, and a bed covered in clumps of dry moss. Under a quilt pieced from all shades of grey an old mother waits.

I take a breath, tasting a torrent of questions.

The old woman raises one bone-thin arm above the quilt. *Just in time*, she whispers. *I sent the forest to find you and bring you home again. Now you've learned how the other world works you'll know what to do with it.* She grips my hand in a final, fierce clasp . . . and lets her last breath out. I'm too late. She's gone.

On the shores of the lake wolves begin to howl. My corvil flies up to an onion-hung roof beam. I wipe my eyes on my sleeve and pick two thorn-vine flowers from a bush blooming in the hut's stove. I put one orange flower on each of the old mother's eyes and bow my head in a wordless prayer.

The lake water seems colder when I start out over the stepping stones again. Where should I go? What should I do? I was hoping for answers . . . or powers. How can I face one Crux, let alone an army, when I'm just this bare-footed loner?

Back on the rounded pebbles of the lake shore I think back to the last time I was here, when I saw Reef for the first time. I wonder where he is now. Stuck in Sea-Ways with a crowd of hysterical citizens? Resisting the siege with soldiers? I've been trying not to think about the vision I had of his knife-sharp death. Wherever he is, he'll be night-blind until the Eclipse ends. Should I have stayed to find him?

No. I came here to do something about the Crux.

I smell them first, a reek of wrong overlaid with a stink of self-righteousness. They're camped not far from the lake in a vast clearing ringed by torn trees. There are hundreds and hundreds of men, machines, weapons and lamps. As I approach, eyes, lights and gunsights all turn towards me. I brace myself for the shock of shells and spitting bullets.

One by one the Crux soldiers bend. One by one they kneel. As one they lower their heads and spread their arms. They bow. They submit. To me.

The ground trembles with their devotion.

36
GOD-HOUSE

There's a huge building dominating this living carpet of worship. Its thick stones are spread with green-weave camouflage nets. As I stand there, stunned, the nets are dragged off and a god-house is revealed. It takes my breath away. The stones shine white and the windows are a cascade of colours. One I partly recognise from when I first came to the Morass – the picture window I saw wreathed in snow at the edge of the tree-eaten rift. It must have been removed and carried here to be part of this great monument. It shows a young woman stepping out from a black sun. Her hair is a brilliant gold corona.

The walls of the god-house are still jagged with scaffolding and the roof is unfinished. The doors are open. I pick my way around bomb-slingers, soldiers and silent traptions. I step inside.

The few god-houses still standing in Rodina when I was little were dreary places, dark with neglect and overrun with rablets. In those dark relics, the walls were hung with paintings of brown-stained, sad-eyed saynts. This place is surprisingly peaceful, with clean walls and not a rablet-dropping in sight, or even a rachnid web. The floor flows with rippled silk. It feels delicious under my bare feet. The painted glass windows are lit by Old Nation oil lamps. Perfume cones make the air taste rich. I see one chair only – a marvellous, wide, golden thing set high on a platform with cloud-soft cushions.

'Go ahead,' says a familiar voice. 'Be comfortable. It's yours, all of this. A god-house needs a god, after all.'

I turn slowly. Everything about this place is unrushed and unreal.

Steen Verdessica stands in the doorway with his army still bent low to the ground outside. He stares at me like I really am a god, not a girl with dirty feet and creased combat clothes.

'I hoped, I *dreamed* you would come,' he whispers. 'I knew your culture could never accept you. Can you imagine how I felt when I guessed your true nature?'

'That I'm a monster?'

'That you're a God. *The* God. The Light Bringer.' He laughs and stretches with pleasure. 'When I said I could worship you, it was the truth. What I failed to mention was that the entire Crux nation will worship you too, starting here in the Morass. Since the last Long Night we've been planning to conquer this land and offer it back to you.'

'You invaded Rodina just to come here?'

'Just to find you. What do you think has fired us on to fight so victoriously?' Steen gazes at me with sun in his eyes. 'It's been worth every sacrifice. We hoped to have your god-house finished by Long Night, but the war took more resources than we thought. When you come to the Crux homeland we'll worship you in God-houses that beggar the grandest palaces. Any one of them – all of them – will be yours. Everything we have, everything we are, all of us, all of me – *yours*.'

With utter grace he sinks to the floor and spreads himself at my feet. That's quite a sight.

Good god – to *be* a god! To loll on those cushions with men at my feet. To be anything, to do anything, with the worship of millions. Rodina would have to bend their knees and worship me too. Uncle Mentira would grovel like a wormling if I was a god. Everyone would be sorry they ever said anything bad about me, or betrayed me or called me a monster. My real friends would think I was amazing, fantastic, the best ever! Reef would find me astonishingly beautiful, beyond any other girl in the entire world . . .

Reef.

Be careful what you wish for . . .

Crux soldiers are carrying a limp body into the god-house, bound with bright bane-metal bands. I have to clench my hands so Steen can't see they're shaking.

'We found your favourite Scrutiner wandering blind in the forest,' Steen gloats, unsheathing an impossibly bright knife. 'It will be an honour for him to serve as a sacrifice . . . and a pleasure for me to kill him.'

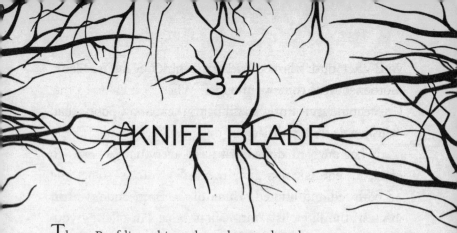

37

KNIFE BLADE

There Reef lies, skin pale and eyes closed.

Why did he return to the forest? Surely not looking for me? He must have heard what people in Sea-Ways were saying about me. He must have known why Uncle Mentira was taking me to Corona. I'm one of the witches he once came to the Morass to hunt. If he were to die now he'd never see me revealed as a monster. My vision would be fulfilled and I could glory in godfulness without him. Steen is here, pulsing with admiration – what more do I want?

Steen holds out the knife blade. I take it. Reef's throat is bare. I could kiss or cut it. The air begins to tremble. God or monster, what am I?

'Choose whose side you're on!' cries Steen, suddenly impatient.

I take a deep breath in. The god-house starts to shake. Roots writhe beneath the floor. Outside, corvils hurtle round the clearing. One crashes into the picture window. Blood smears the face on the coloured glass. My face. *Wham!* Another corvil collides with the glass. Another feathered body falls, a dead red-black lump on the ground.

Bird after bird follows. The glass cracks. Shatters. Black-feathered birds come pouring in.

Steen staggers upright and fights them away. Bane-metal bells jangle on his wrists.

'What are you doing, Rain? To us you're a God. To everyone else you're a thing they call a witch – something to be hated and hunted. Think of the connection we had back in the Biopolis. Think about what I'm offering you. Power! Worship! Adoration!'

This should be a grand moment where I embrace god-head or spurn it magnificently. To my utter embarrassment I find myself crying.

'I don't want your adoration! I don't want to be your god. I'm *me*, just me, why can't anyone understand that?'

It's no good. I cannot keep myself within this skin any longer.

Lamps spill. Silk catches fire. It burns with a blue-green flame. In the clearing outside soldiers leap up and arm themselves. Traption turrets swivel, seeking an enemy. Silver-sleek wolves leap out at them. Thorn-vines twine round guns, limbs, necks – *snap!* Further out in the forest mirror-leaves blink into eyes. Awake now, the trees slowly feast, beginning with ground.

Power flows out of me. I can't control it. Can't keep myself *me*. My body's breaking up. Skin's splitting. Life's pouring out, spreading in great waves of utter, unending dark. Fear makes me shake. I'm disintegrating, disappearing, lost . . .

Not lost.

Found you, says a voice, as if whispered underground a thousand klicks away. A hand grips my hand. *Hold tight.*

At this touch, dark turns to light, massive light, all the light imaginable, shooting up like a spear then spreading out under the clouds. It's not day, it's not darkness, it's a wave of impossibility – a second sun. This is dark light from the heart of the forest. My heart. My forest. It spreads and stretches until it beams over every branch, under every leaf, into every dark corner. The world turns white.

Battle explodes in the light of this fake day. All the invading forces are scrambled. Instead of stars, the sky is a constellation of Crux planes. Soldiers swarm like insects. At the centre of the war it's just me. Me against the whole Crux army. Eyes closed, I can still see. Body motionless, I can still move. I spread invisible hands across the lake and the water stretches out, flooding the shore. From the unseen lake-bed I dredge up every skeleton, every plane, every boat that's ever been buried there. Up they come, dripping grey weeds and water. These I fling at the Crux Air Force, and when Crux planes and pilots come tumbling down, trees are only too ready to greet and eat them.

The whole world shakes. The very sky cracks. I can't keep this up for much longer! There are bombs and bullets, corvils and missiles. I'm here, I'm there, I'm everywhere. I'm spread too thinly, I'm stretched too far . . . I can't do this alone! There's only one of me!

311

Then I hear a new sound – I know this noise! It's the gritty rumble of Storm engines.

'Witches!' call all the Crux still left alive. 'The Night Witches are coming!'

Here they fly, nine tiny Storms, each with faithful friends. They're here, they've come, they're on my side! First Lida's plane, the *Revenge*. Next Dee with Zoya . . . Dee in her lucky hat. The other Storms follow, chasing whatever Crux I can't catch. I'd cheer if I still had a voice. I offer up one last utter, bursting, supernova . . .

Then silence.

Just silence.

Simple. Quiet.

I gasp – my first breath since the storm began. Flames lick the gutted god-house. Reef is lying at my feet, not to worship me but to keep me connected through all the catastrophe. It's his hand that's been stretched out to seize mine. He held fast and kept me from disappearing. Now he's not moving.

I sink to the floor. Smoke thickens.

'Reef?'

I'm too weak to break the bane-metal chains wrapped around his body. Still gripping my hand, he opens his eyes and looks straight at me. An arm's length away, I look back.

His voice is weak. 'Are you OK?'

I want to laugh but can't find the energy. 'I think I stepped off the path.'

'I think you blasted the path to oblivion.' His eyes close briefly. The black ink on his lids stares at me.

I tell him, 'You can let go, you know. I understand. I mean, you've seen what I am now. It's a bit late to be reporting me to Aura but I know you'll probably hate me.'

'Report you? Why would I do that?'

'Isn't that why you've come to the Morass, to hunt me?'

'Oh yes,' he says. 'I've been hunting witches for years.'

'And now you've found one.'

'So I have.' Still he doesn't release my hand.

'Are you supposed to capture me and send me back to Corona?'

'Are you stupid?' he murmurs tenderly. 'I'm not letting you go now.'

'But . . . you hate me?'

'Do I? Doesn't feel like it.'

There's a long pause where I think of all the things I could say, but none of my words seem to be in the right order. I end up with, 'So when you were hunting witches, it was to find out if they existed or not?'

'I had to know – were my parents arrested wrongly? Were they superstitious criminals . . . or was Aura simply clamping down on anything that statistics and science couldn't explain?'

'How crazy – you were with one all along and you never knew it. I didn't know either. I wish I'd trusted you.'

He says, 'Didn't I keep saying you could share your secrets with me?'

'I thought that was just a trick, to get me to show myself. I thought you'd throw me in prison too, or worse.'

He shakes his head gently. 'Now that Aura can't possibly deny that witches exist, the only business I have with prisons will be to get my parents released with a full pardon.'

I grin. 'I can help with prison breaks if that doesn't happen!'

I wish wish wish I could shake off this exhaustion to reach further and hold him. Some deity I am – sprawled on the floor like a bird without wings! Eye Bright lands on my shoulder and bites my ear – affectionately, I think.

I have to ask. 'Weren't you afraid I'd take up the offer of being worshipped as a god?'

'The thought may have crossed my mind, but only about a million times or so. Mostly I was afraid you'd be hurt when you finally used your powers to the full. That you, the girl I love, would be swallowed up and disappear.'

Love love love! He said *love*. Dare I believe him? Is it possible to be happy, after all the doubt and destruction? *Love* is just a word people say, after all. I look in his eyes, his beautiful, clear bright eyes. They say *love* too, no need for words.

I have to take a breath. 'And you don't just want to put me in a laboratory like Uncle Mentira and use me as a weapon of war?'

He smiles. 'Not top of the list of plans I have for you, Rain.'

I smile back, wondering if there's even any war left to fight. The forest is calmer, I know that much. No machines, bombs, guns or god-followers left. Let the Crux worship their idea of a Light Bringer without forcing others to have their faith! Let Rodina march to the beat of science and common sense, without Slick spraying everything that grows outside the realm of normal rules! Let the Morass be safe as a place of *possibilities*!

As roots reach down to soil, and shoots sprout up, I feel my senses stretching to the edge of the forest and beyond . . . to the night-frosted fields of the foodlands, the dark, blossoming buildings of the city, and further still . . . stopping only at sea-waves and running rivers.

I feel a great peace spreading.

I ask Reef, 'Can you hear the birdsong?'

He nods. 'Corvils sound like that when they've had a good feast.'

Oh.

'Reef?'

I think he must've fallen asleep. He opens his eyes slowly. 'Yes?'

'When exactly did you know I was different?'

'Right from the first moment. But not different – special. As for the witch thing . . . that took longer to figure out.'

'I can't believe you still knew.'

'It's my job to notice things, remember?'

What he doesn't notice, what *I* don't notice till far, far

too late, is the dusty shape of Steen Verdessica rising from a mound of rubble, with fire as his backdrop. I see the knife, but it's stuck in a splinter of broken time. Such a bright blade – such a fast slash. One moment Reef's throat is whole, next a red line is drawn along the skin. Blood drains out and Reef's life flows with it.

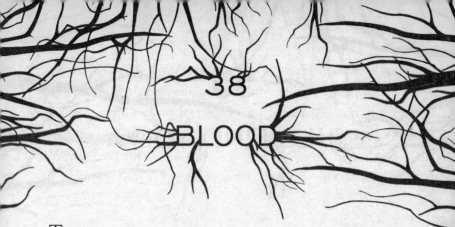

38
BLOOD

Time slows. The blade seems suspended in the smoky air. Bright beads of blood hang beneath it. I move without thinking. I have Steen's neck. I have him by the throat with his feet dangling. I need no knife. My hands reach inside, past his skin and muscles, deep, deep inside to where his spirit cowers. I wrench it out. His life.

I am death!

Reef is choking, spraying red drops and making the pool of blood around him swell.

Wolves howl louder, or maybe it's me. I let go of Steen and drop him to the floor. It's Reef I want, beautiful, black-haired Reef. I slip in his blood. Stuff my jacket against his wound to staunch the flow. Set my mouth to his mouth so he can breathe however many breaths are left to him in this life. I pour what's left of me into him.

The pool of Reef's blood spreads. The fire spits, sizzles and dwindles to sulky smoke. My light vanishes. The false day darkens. Night rushes back. I'm done.

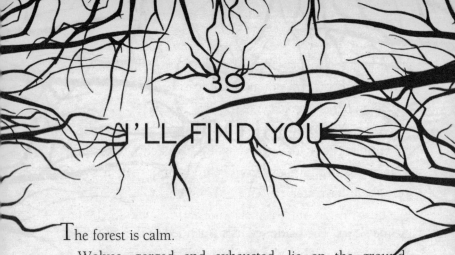

39

I'LL FIND YOU

The forest is calm.

Wolves, gorged and exhausted, lie on the ground, panting. Corvils fly back to their nests to preen with blood-stained beaks. Thorn-vines creep over mangled machinery.

Flutters of movement catch my attention. Out of the trees thousands of lace-wings are flying. They're so beautiful with their pale-green colouring and delicate feathered antennae. They fill the clearing, landing on whatever corpses the ground hasn't swallowed. They feed.

Life is life.

I hold Reef without moving, without crying, without knowing anything other than the fact he's gone. He looks so peaceful. I bend to kiss him one last time. His lips are still so warm and soft. How could I ever have thought he'd betray me when all along he wanted my trust?

I can't stand. I'm too tired and Reef's body is too heavy. Eye Bright swoops up to the top of the ruined god-house, scattering lace-wings with its black feathers. Am I alone now? Is the war really over? Overhead there are specks of green and red in the sullen gloom of the Eclipse – wing-lights on Storms. I'm not alone, at least.

'Down here,' I croak. 'We're here!'

As the Storms curve over the clearing I see the sky is lightening. The shadows are passing. The Eclipse is ending. A sliver of sun shines out from behind Umbra's disc. I wish Reef could have seen the end of Long Night.

I bury my face into his neck, not caring about the blood. Except there is no blood. Reef's skin is smooth and unbroken. His throat is warm. His pulse is throbbing. I start to kiss where the wound should be. This is impossible! Wonderful!

I am life!

He stirs. I find his lips again. Still drowsy, he returns my kisses, soft at first then harder and deeper. He reaches his hands up and tangles them in my hair, then cups my face until the kiss becomes sweet and slow. Finally he opens his eyes. When he finishes gazing at me he blinks to see the new sunlight.

'Did I miss something?'

I try to comb my hair with my fingers, to look as close as I can to normal. 'Not really. Nothing I couldn't handle.'

He sweeps strands of black from my eyes, which must be full of smiles. We sit together, perhaps for moments, perhaps for hours. The sun grows warmer.

Rain . . .

A cool, fresh breeze brings my name, and with it the smell of home.

319

'The forest is beautiful in summer,' I murmur, watching the trees toss their branches . . . along with bits of half-eaten armour.

Rain . . .

The forest calls again. What else is waiting for me in the shade of the silver-bark trees? Maybe one day I'll leave to find out. I'll wander where paths don't exist, to discover if I'm alone, or if I'm *One of Many*. Perhaps, when I do go, I won't just disappear. Reef will kiss me on the brow and whisper, '*I'll find you . . .*'

For now I'm content to be still. To be me, with him, in this place.

The sun leaps out from Umbra's lingering shade, a perfect circle of gold.

The Long Night is over.

For now.

AFTERWORD

No, it's not the huts that are burning –
It's my youth, in the fire
Iulia Drunina

'Where do you get ideas from?' This is a question authors are often asked. For *Night Witches* the answer is from Russia. From World War Two. From the stories of the first-ever women to fly combat missions.

I knew from the moment I first got into the plane that
I was born in the air, and it became my main purpose
in life – to fly.
Captain Mariya Dolina – pilot and heroine of
the Soviet Union

The 1941 German invasion of the Soviet Union began with catastrophic strikes on the Russian Air Force, followed by fast, brutal land advances. The Russians were quick to respond. Among the Russian infantry, tank crews and air

323

squadrons there were an estimated 800,000 women in combat.

The Air Force boasted fighter aces such as the legendary Lily Litviak, a young woman with twelve 'kills' to her credit. Lily was famous for her bleached blonde hair and fearless flights over the besieged city of Stalingrad.

As well as daring fighters there were the day and night bomber crews. The most famous all-female regiment began life as the 588th Night Bomber Aviation Regiment, formed in 1942. The Regiment was so impressive it soon earned a promotion to 'Guards' status, becoming the 46th Taman Guards regiment. These night-bombers flew more than 24,000 combat missions. They clocked up a phenomenal tally of medals, including twenty-four awards of the highest accolade – Heroine of the Soviet Union. They flew in many major combat zones, from Stalingrad, to Sevastopol and Warsaw. By 1945 they had helped chase the invaders right back to the heart of the German capital. On the Reichstag – the German parliament building – one young bomber girl scrawled this in graffiti: 'Hurrah! The 46th Women's Guard Regiment flew as far as Berlin. Long live Victory!'

> *Today these women have avenged the heavy centuries*
> *of the oppression of women.*
> Josef Stalin

The female regiments were the creation of a remarkable woman called Marina Raskova. She was the first woman to qualify as an Air Force navigator and the first female instructor at the great Zhukovski Air Academy. In 1938 she joined an attempt to set a long-distance flight record across Russia in a plane called *Rodina*, which means Motherland. After the German invasion thousands of girls and women clamoured to be allowed to fight in defence of their motherland. Raskova appealed for girls in the Air Force. She was swamped with new recruits – air crew and mechanics – who underwent harsh training programmes to get them ready for battle. Raskova was hero-worshipped by the regiments because of her skills, her compassion and her commitment. Sadly she didn't live long enough to see the end of the war. Her plane was lost in a snow storm.

You knew your friend was going to fly it in combat,
and you did everything, even beyond your physical might
and strength, to have it in perfect condition and to save
the life of your aircrew.
Senior Sergeant Matryona Yurodjeva-Samsonova –
airplane mechanic

The young women of the 46th Taman Guards flew old wooden biplanes called Po-2s. These had been designed just as training planes, without cockpit covers, radios or sophisticated instruments. They were fitted with four small bomb racks, but didn't get parachutes or self-defence machine guns until near the end of the war. Air crews flew in scorching summer weather and in the bone-bitter cold of Russian winters, when mechanics struggled to keep the fuel from freezing . . . and their own fingers from rotting with frostbite.

The Po-2s were nicknamed 'flying sewing machines' and 'flying coffins'. On the ground the women were sometimes mocked by men who couldn't believe mere girls were capable of such stamina and bravery. As for the Germans, they came up with the most evocative name for the air crews that buzzed and bombed them every night. They called them *nacht hexen* – night witches – saying the whooshing noise of the planes sounded like witches on broomsticks passing over.

My spirit has always been emancipated, unconquered
and proud. I was spell-bound by the mystery of flight.
I thought of it as my integration with the universe.
Snr Lt Yevgeniya Zhiguelnko

Superstitions about witches and magic were driven underground by communism in the Soviet Union, along with most religious beliefs. They did not disappear completely. Spring still revived old rituals of offerings to Mother Earth, and tales were still told of the most powerful witch of all – Baba Yaga.

Witches were said to summon their power from the earth, where the dead are buried, never from demonic sources. I first came across Baba Yaga as a child, reading the eerie story of clever Vassilisa, a girl who survives her

326

visit to the witch's lair and is rewarded with supernatural help.

In stories, Baba Yaga is often portrayed as an ogress with stone teeth who devours children in her house raised up on chicken legs and surrounded by a bone fence. More impressively, the mythology also hints that she holds power over night and day, and that she guards the fountain of the water of life. She flies not on a broomstick, but in a mixing bowl called a mortar, speeding her way through the skies with a pestle.

Despite their communist upbringing, some Russian night-bomber girls tried fortune-telling in the magical darkness of New Year's Eve. They followed dream messages, and trusted in a mystical power to keep them and their comrades safe. After the war, a statue of Baba Yaga was sculptured showing her as an Air Force mascot complete with modern flying goggles!

They converted the whole great country into a big concentration camp of life-term inmates. They would turn people into programmed robots stuffed with slogans and cheers for the great Stalin.
Senior Sergeant Anna Popova – flight radio operator

Witches were not the worst thing to fear in Soviet Russia. Josef Stalin's communist rule brought tremendous change and upheaval as the vast country was forced to abandon old ways and dedicate itself to a new kind of society where all were supposed to be equal, and work for the common good. Under Stalin a mass surge of industrial advances gave Russia the strength and equipment to beat back the superior technology of German forces. Modernisation came at a terrible price. Stalin demanded total obedience. Secret police and networks of neighbourhood spies meant it wasn't safe to say, or do, or even dare *think* anything individual. There was an atmosphere of fear and mistrust. Arrests were common. Those arrested were rarely seen or heard of again.

> *Friendship, mutual support, and love of our motherland*
> *helped us to endure and to await the victory.*
> Senior Lieutenant Serfima Amosova-Taranenko

This nightmare of paranoia and betrayal was matched by the fierce love and loyalty of the women in Marina Raskova's regiments. The young women fought to defend a beloved country, regardless of how oppressive the regime. Many fought and died. Ageing Night Witch survivors still meet in Moscow once a year, to laugh, to drink and to remember darker days and fallen comrades.

Researching all this history had me enthralled and appalled. At times I felt I was flying with the real night witches on some starlit night, or through thick sea-mists. In fact, my only flying experience has been in sleek modern gliders and rather stinky training planes. My only meetings with witches have been on the pages of fairy-tale books.

My story *Night Witches* is a fantasy tale set on a fictional world, with invented characters and cultures, but it draws on the bravery, loyalty, fear and betrayal experienced by Soviet women during the war. I've also explored universal questions – How does it feel not to belong? How do you find the strength to do what you secretly feel is right? Who can you really trust in a world where loyalty is supposed to be blind? Most importantly – where can you find the power to be yourself?

In *Night Witches* science, religion and imagination battle together for dominance. Life wins.

I want to say we experienced many feelings and emotions – fear, joy, love, sorrow – as we faced very hard experiences. Sometimes when we successfully completed a mission we even sang and danced there at the airfield because life is life, and we were young.
Snr Lt Zoya Parfyonova – pilot and heroine of the Soviet Union